HIGH TRAIL TO UTAH

ALSO BY REG QUIST

HIGH TRAIL TO UTAH

THE SETTLERS
BOOK SIX

REG QUIST

Hight Trail to Utah
Paperback Edition
Copyright © 2023 Reg Quist

CKN Christian Publishing
An Imprint of Wolfpack Publishing
9850 S. Maryland Parkway, Suite A-5 #323
Las Vegas, Nevada 89183

cknchristianpublishing.com

Paperback ISBN 978-1-63977-461-6
eBook ISBN 978-1-63977-460-9
LCCN 2023947625

HIGH TRAIL TO UTAH

PROLOGUE

IN THE HIGH-UP MOUNTAINS, WINDING WHEREVER MAN and horse could make way, there was a trail. The little-known path rose into the mountains that separated Colorado from Utah, collectively known as the Rockies. But the Rockies, defying all the efforts of man to name and conquer them, were too big, too grand, too varied to be enclosed in a single word. Or a single description. And so, in this mysterious land, where few had traveled, the trail remained a mystery.

The Rockies were much more than peaks and valleys, ice caps, and wind-twisted trees. There were many unknown and unnamed areas that made up the name Rockies. Valleys and lush summer meadows, beaver streams, and a myriad of wild game. Forests and brush-lands. Steep granite hillsides, unclimbable and forlorn in their glacier-capped isolation.

It was a rugged, high-country land. Fit only for the brave. Or the foolish. Or perhaps, the desperate.

The tracker knew only one name, that of the Red

Feather Lakes. All else was a mystery. He had left the lakes behind a week ago. For the second time.

He wasn't the first to come this way. Nor were the ones he followed. The ones he was determined to find and arrest. Criminals, all.

The trail they followed was ancient. Few knew about it, and even fewer had ventured onto it. No one knew of its origin. Perhaps a man with a burrow or a mule, loaded with beaver traps and great hopes, as he wandered the streams connecting the many lakes that had first blazed the route. Perhaps. But it was more likely such a man would be following a track left by Indians. Feasibly ancient Indians, the forerunners of the known people. For the Indians were always moving, exploring, and trading with others who were arriving, in their appointed time, to take their place and claim the land.

But the blazes on the trees and the rocks cleared from the path spoke of white men. The followers of those ancient wanderers.

Disappearing into the long grass in the valleys, skirting lakes and streams, and then appearing again as a weathered notch in a tree, or as rocks rolled away to clear the path, or the rotted stumps of downed trees— now overgrown by aspens that had sprouted where the pine had been felled—the trail led the wanderer westward. But it was a difficult trail. Many who had begun had given up, the trail lost to them, beyond finding. To those who were lost and never again found, even their names and their stories had faded away with time.

That some had succeeded in their western travels was shown by the fact that the pathway continued on, enticing the traveler to watch for the next notch in a tree and sometimes, again, where boulders had been rolled out of the way, lying uneasily in an unnatural row. A row that spoke of the hand of man.

At one place, deep into the higher point of the trail, higher than any wise man would attempt to winter, were the ruins of a small log cabin, measuring no more than four feet at the ridge pole, providing only room enough to crawl in for shelter. Rotting and turning back to the earth, its roof long ago giving up the struggle, the cabin, the work of a hopeful man, would soon be gone, leaving no trace in the harsh stillness of the mountain. It was said that bones had once been found in the now doorless cabin, bones of a man, gnawed and scattered, showing the tooth marks of a predator.

Only a man intent on escape, or perhaps freedom unknown to him in past times, would push all the way to the end of the trail.

And such were the men Ivan was following.

The lawman was, in fact, following other followers. Men who rode in desperation, seeking the way. The lawman had the easier part, with the many horses and mules of the ones he sought, tramping down the grass and pushing the trail growth aside, leaving a long but easily followed trail. Still, it was a dangerous path he followed. One where the lawman had to ride with care, watching every blind spot, every trail side bush, every boulder big enough to hide a man. For surely there would be a man watching the back-trail, someone whose goal was to prevent a man such as he from gaining an advantage.

DEPUTY SHERIFF IVAN IVANOV

HUNKERED DOWN ON HIS BELLY, HIS RIFLE LYING BESIDE him, alone in the vastness and beauty of the rocks, lakes, and hills, he waited. The cover was good on the hillside where he lay. There was little chance of being seen. His horse was staked out far enough back into the lightly treed clearing that it was unlikely the other horses would sense it. And just below, well within rifle range, although he had no intention of shooting, lay the trail. He had seen the opening in the forest ahead on the evening before as the sun was laying its last light on the scene.

He had been following the slowly fading tracks. For two weeks he had followed, after being forced to return to a remote homestead seeking help for Cap, who had broken his leg. But his query was again within sight, gone to camp for the night, unaware of their follower.

Immediately turning back, he had skirted the trail by a half mile, paralleling the route the thieves had taken. Looking for an opening into the higher country.

In his following, he'd had no need to study the country around or look for blazed trees. The movements of four men with their four horses, two heavily loaded pack mules, and the wagon team that was also now burdened with the heavy wooden boxes—since the wagon had been abandoned—were impossible to hide. He had only to stay far enough back to avoid detection and watch for any rearguard who had staked himself out in the bush that skirted the way. He would await his opportunity, allow the larger group to seek out the trail.

When he was at a comfortable height and well ahead of them, he settled in for the night. Both he and the faithful gelding were beyond tired. But a cold bite from his camp supplies for Ivan, and a belly full of the abundant grass for the gelding, would put both man and horse in good condition for the day ahead.

Until darkness wrote an end to the long day, he would study his prey with the glasses purchased some months before. Knowing he faced four men in difficult terrain, and hopelessly distant from any help, caution was called for.

DEPUTY SHERIFF IVAN IVANOV

As it was, so often in the early years, where the telegraph had yet to arrive in some small villages, the news was either carried by the stage in the form of a letter that would be dropped in a mail sack carrying many other written missives, and a few packages, on the boardwalk by the stage whip. Or, if the news was exciting enough, shouted for all to hear from that same whip as he pulled his team to a halt.

As Tate leaned his slight weight back on the lines, the four hard-run geldings slowed and then stopped. As always, Tate had called his team to a halt in front of the mercantile at the Fort, across the road from the marshal's office—the small office and jail that the sheriff shared. Marshal Wiley Hamstead had been murdered not long before, and a new man, Junior Wardle, brother to Key Wardle, marshal at Stevensville, a slow three-hour ride to the south, or two hours for a man in a hurry, had been named in Wiley's place.

The long-time county sheriff, Rory Jamison, had been called out a few days before on a cattle range war threat, which was, in reality, more of a threat from two stubborn men, neither of whom would give an inch.

In eastern Colorado, there was no shortage of grass-lands. Or river-frontage either, for that matter. At the location in question, in any case. Ranchers had settled the better lands before pushing the newcomers onto the bunchgrass ranges now being fought over. When the call came for the sheriff, Rory was tempted to let the two fools fight it out themselves. But knowing it might lead to bloodshed, he saddled up and took to the trail. There was no telling when he would return.

Tate started shouting for the sheriff before his stage quit rocking, settling into a dust-covered rest. "Sheriff. Sheriff. Rory. You anywhere hereabouts?"

The shout could be heard up and down the street. People came from the stores and stood on the board-walk, anxious to know what was happening. In small towns all across the west, life was quiet. Little was expected from any day that would be different from the day before. Any excitement would bring on the lookers.

Deputy Sheriff Ivan Ivanov eased from the marshal's office door. Everyone knew Tate's voice. As one of the more reliable carriers of news, Tate held a certain respect up and down the stage route.

Raising his voice even as he was walking toward the stage, Ivan hollered, "Rory's away, Tate. I'm here filling in. What have you got?"

"Murder. That's what I got. Two murders if yer want'n the details."

"Care to tell me where that happened, Tate, and anything else you know about it?"

"If'n you'll come close enough so's I don't have ta be shout'n across half the town, it'd make it easier."

"Tate, I've never heard you do anything but shout.

Didn't know you had another gear in your voice. But now that I'm standing close enough to whisper and be heard, perhaps you'd give me the details of what you saw."

"What I saw, young fella, and what I've been try'n ta tell you, happen to be you was listen'n, was that two men were murdered up the line a ways."

"Up the line where, Tate, and how did the news come to you?"

"News come from the stage stop. That one that was burnt out last year, where the station man and his wife were murdered. First stop south of the state line. Tough couple 'a men there now. Ain't likely ta be on the receiv'n end of no gunplay unless one 'a them was ta find himself on the wrong end of an ambush, an' thet ain't hardly likely since there's neither tree nor rock big enough to hide behind, anywhere close by."

"Any idea who the men were, Tate?"

"Stage-stop-man, Grueller by name. Says he fed them. Them and two, three, others running a wagon north. Heavily loaded wagon. Wooden boxes in the back. Grueller figured they was pack'n out gold from the mines to the rails at Laramie. All the time allow'n thet ain't no way the normal route. The two dead men were guards. Or so said Grueller. Says those two stood with the wagon when the other two came in to eat. Grueller, he took a plate out to each of the murdered men. Grueller, he ain't much fer cook'n, got a fella there with him ain't much better, but at least it relieves Grueller of the responsibility.

"Wasn't fer the bullet holes in them two and the blood, I'd be inclined to think it was what was on thet plate what done fer them. Weren't more than a couple hours after they took to the road again that a traveler called in with the news of the deaths. It was him that talked about bullet holes and blood. No sign of the wagon. Just the two bodies ly'n in the sun. Thet was yest'day."

With the sheriff away and with a green, newly taken-on deputy at Stevensville, where Ivan normally held the position, Ivan was reluctant to ride out, but had little choice. He had noticed that wagon as it plodded through the Fort a couple of days before. Noticed, and taken note. He thought then that it looked like a guarded wagon. The teamsters and the guards had all looked like tough men, men who would sign on for a dangerous job, confident in their own abilities. To think of two of them being dead set Ivan's mind a bit sideways. It was hard to think of such things.

The thoughts brought back the memory of rico-cheting lead, more lead tunking into tree trunks he was hiding behind, knowing the sound was similar to what it would be if it had hit his body. Memories of crawling on his belly, hoping to dig out a desperate fugitive without he, himself becoming the target. The memories of loading dead men across their saddles. The recollection of digging through dead men's saddle bags and bedrolls, and worst of all, their pockets, looking for evidence or identification. In his years carrying the badge, although he carried it in his pocket, never on display, he had experienced all of that. And more.

There was also a price to pay for riding with the badge. When he could simply ride back to the ranch and settle in with his family, he sometimes wondered what kept him at the job.

There was a price to pay for riding guard too, some-times a heavy price.

Thinking those thoughts was not going to bring him

any closer to solving a couple of murders though, so he forced mind in another direction. He knew he had no choice, so he might just as well get at it.

IVAN WAS JUST TYING his bedroll behind his saddle, a habit he had picked up from Rory—never go unprepared. One or two cold, hungry nights would teach a man to pick up supplies when they were available and keep a bedroll handy. He was making the last check of the cinch when he heard the clopping of hooves behind him in the livery. As was normal, the rider had dismounted outside and was walking the animal to his stall.

Ivan didn't bother turning around. Recognizing the slightly off-timed step of the gelding, he simply said, "Back, are ya Cap? Thought you might be away longer. I'm told that's a fine-looking widow lady running that ranch out there. Kind of wondered if you hadn't run off that bunch of her cows yourself just so you could be the hero bringing them back."

"Never bothered much looking at the widow. Just pushed that little bunch into the corral and turned for home."

"Cap, when I grow up, I want to be just like you. Competent and self-controlled is what I mean to say. Now, you take me. I ain't never been one to chase the skirts nor set much mind on the matter, but that don't mean I can't sort out the ones a man might like to come home to from the rest."

The silence told Ivan that the conversation had worked its way to a conclusion. He finished with the cinch and then, once more, checked the saddlebags and the bedroll. He lifted the 44-40 from the scabbard and checked that the magazine was full. He did the same for his belted .44 before untying the horse and easing him out of the stall.

Cap was curious, as always. A man who had seen more than his share of grief and who lived with loneliness, the deputy had little that interested him except his badged duties.

"You headed back down to Stevensville?"

"No. Wish I was. Very pleasant young lady there who doesn't run away when she sees me coming. Of course, you would have no interest in any such thing, so I'll say no more.

"No, Tate came through town a short while ago, raising dust and his voice all at the same time. Tells me there's been a double killing up north, close to the Wyoming border. Wish it was just a bit further north. Then I could leave it to the Laramie boys. But I'm fix'n to ride up. Never know. You just never know. Might lead to something. Might not."

"Son, a double killing is most assuredly going to lead to something. It can't be no other way. Wait till this gelding has time to chew down a feed of oats and I get some lunch myself. I'll ride with you."

NEARING THE NORTHERN STAGE STATION, Ivan began feeling a bit unsettled. The weather was hot. The murders were near enough two days ago. Dealing with the bodies would be unpleasant, to say it mildly.

Cap noticed the hesitation when they swung off the road onto the stage company property. The place looked deserted, but the lazy coil of smoke from the chimney told them it wasn't.

"Cautious. Almighty cautious, Ivan."

"I saw a shadow move across the window of what I'm guessing would be the kitchen, judging by the stove pipe above it and all. We'll just move carefully, with our hands in sight, and dismount at the hitch rail. We'll be careful not to show any threat. There's been unpleasantness enough at this station, going back I don't know how long, but certainly back to that stagehouse keeper and his wife being murdered. That's a bit less than a year ago, I'd say by memory. I'd be a bit jumpy too."

The two lawmen stepped to the ground at the tie rail. Ivan led his mount under the broad overhang and into the shade. Seeing what he had done, Cap followed suit.

The door eased open. The man standing there with a shotgun resting in the crook of his elbow looked as if he could handle about anything that came along. The second man who stepped out, this one with an apron wrapped around his broad middle, looked as if trouble had become a part of his life too, somewhere in the past.

"Don't know as how I like having your animals that close to the house. Or the kitchen window neither, for that matter. Don't want no mess in there."

"I'm Deputy County Sheriff Ivan Ivanov, and this is my friend, Deputy Cap Graham. We've got miles to go, I'm figuring, unless you can tell us something that will cause us to think otherwise. These animals will benefit from the cool of the shade. I promise to clean up anything they leave behind that doesn't fit with the décor of the place, you know, fruit trees, finely trimmed grass lawns, flower gardens, and such,"

Without thinking, completely missing the sarcasm wrapped in Ivan's words, the other three men all raised their eyes and turned to the yard. There was nothing growing within a hundred yards. Various shades of red rock, blown sand, and a misplaced tumbleweed were all that met their eyes.

With a half-grin, the stage man replied, "I've got to admit it lacks a little in green growth and genteel refinement. Nearest shade might be in Montana for all we can see from here. But none of that means we want your animal's leavings stinking up the place."

"Well. We've dealt with that. Now, if you could offer a cup of drinkable coffee and a soft, padded chair, we might have a question or two for you."

"Depends on what you call drinkable. Our water is half gyp, and the cook hasn't washed his hands in recent days."

Ivan moved toward the door, grinning. "Sounds just about right."

The two deputies entered the door just in time to see the apron-clad man stowing his carbine behind the kitchen worktable. With a tilt of his head in the direction of the pot simmering on the stove, he invited Ivan and Cap to 'help yerselves to the pot'.

Ivan took a seat at the long table. There was a bench on each side that would hold six. Eight, if there were that many on the stage that decided to chance the food. Cap sat sideways on the bench, swinging one leg over, then the other. Gesturing at the bench on the other side, Ivan said, "Have a seat and tell us a story."

"You want a 'once upon a time story'? Or maybe something about pirates, or cowboys and Indians, which we haven't seen any of around here."

Becoming frustrated, Ivan said, "What I want is for the nonsense to stop and for you to tell us the story about two dead men that were found recently. Now get to it."

The stage man laid his shotgun on the table with the mechanism close to his hand. The cook lifted his carbine again and set it on the counter he continued to stand behind.

With his eyes boring holes in the man at the table, Cap lifted his Colt .45 and laid it on the table. Ivan waited just a moment before saying, "Men, you're fools. I told you who we are and why we're here. Now, unless you have something to hide, I expect the foolishness can be drawn to a halt, and you'll get on with the story."

Then, turning his hand over so that his thumb was pointing at the shotgun, he said, "Forget it. You'd lose ten times out of ten."

Before the reluctant man could say anything, Cap turned to the cook, who still held down his position behind the counter.

"Mr., unless you want to be thought of as unwelcoming, you make your way over here and take a seat beside your friend."

Cap waved his arm as if showing where the fellow was to sit. But somehow, magically, he managed to dip his hand down. When it came back up, it was holding the shotgun, which soon disappeared behind the bench, leaning against the wall. Taking the move as a warning, the cook left his carbine where it was and crossed the floor to join his partner. The caution shown in the eyes of the two workers was replaced by fear.

Ivan turned his eyes from one to another, trying to read them, trying to know what their next move might be. Seeing nothing particular, he let out a big breath and said, "Now, let's start again. I'm Deputy County Sheriff Ivan Ivanov from down to Stevensville. My partner is Cap Graham, deputy county sheriff normally hanging his hat at the Fort. We work with Sheriff Rory Jamison.

"We're here to try to get to the bottom of a reported double murder. Tate, the stage whip—and a good friend of mine—says you knew of the bodies, and you might know something about the wagon. Start with where you saw the bodies and where they are now. And lay some names before us."

The shotgun man said, "We can't be too careful up here. We're alone, and neither of us gets paid enough to die for."

Ivan chuckled a bit before saying, "That's how a lawman lives every day, fellas, so don't try looking to Cap or me for sympathy. You could always quit. Return to Laramie and sit in a chair outside the saloon, which I suspect is where the stage manager found you. Now get to the point of the telling."

"Fella rid'n alone come in here yesterday afternoon. Says he rode down from up Laramie way. Head'n to the gold diggings. Or so he said. Says his horse shied and come near to sett'n him on the ground. He got the beast under control and spurred him until he left the trail. Come within sight of two bodies. Says he didn't step down nor go any nearer to the dead men. Talked of blood and bullet holes. Says it wasn't no way a pretty sight, so he turned back and come on this way. We passed the news on to Tate when he come through here this morning."

Cap had listened intently and had a question. "Tate say anything about his team acting up?"

"Said he was runn'n them pretty good at that point. Was going fast enough that they would have been past before any odor hit the horse's nostrils. Sounded reasonable to me, knowing how Tate likes to keep them moving."

Ivan took over the questioning. "Tate says you fed them boys."

"Understand, we didn't neither of us ride up there. That travel'n rider, he outlined their looks pretty well. Shirts, hats, an' such. We's judg'n which they were by that description.

"Wagon guards. Stayed with the wagon while the driver and swamper come in to eat. Watered and cared for their animals alright though, their own saddlers and the team. Gave them what rest they could and a feed of oats we sell a bit of from time to time. Good men, I'm thinking, going by sight. I liked their manner and their care of the horses. Else, I wouldn't have bothered taking their dinners out to them. They squatted right there in the shade of the wagon and ate. Thanked me and left their empty plates on the flat of a rock you'll see out to the side of the cabin.

"Heavy man, heavy for a rider, anyway, he appeared to be boss. Big. Rough sort of fella. All brushy hair and beard to where it was hiding his looks. Boots all run over. Pants and shirt looking like they were held together by luck and filth. He did what little talking was done. Paid us and got back on the trail. We ain't seen him or them since. Don't want to neither."

THERE WAS nothing for Ivan to clean up from the horses, and they were soon back riding. Cap, who spoke seldom, and carefully, said, "More to them fellas than just keeping the stage station."

"You're right again, Cap. Got any ideas?"

"No. No, I don't. Might think on it a little though."

Ivan grinned and responded, "Myself, I'd rather think on that pretty lady down to Stevensville, but you're right. I'd best keep my mind on business. Unpleasant business. But then, ours often is."

3

DEPUTY SHERIFF CAP GRAHAM

THE ODOR FROM THE TWO BODIES WAS NOT PLEASANT, BUT neither was it overwhelming. The two deputies dismounted close by, then led their horses a bit further away and upwind. To have the nervous animals break free would help no one.

The bodies lay about six feet apart, one on his face and the other in a semi-fetal position with his face to the sun. There were signs of small night creatures nibbling on fingers and faces, anywhere not protected by boots or clothing.

Cap, with more experience leading him to judgment, said, "Dry. Dry country. Hot. But not as hot as it's going to be in another month. Might be coyotes around, but they'll be holding to the water courses and the bit of greenery, if such exists. Don't see much right at this location. Anyway, those bodies are in better shape than I was prepared for. That's no-way saying it's a pleasant sight. What I'm saying is that I've seen worse. Stuff I hope to never see again."

Ivan didn't have any comment, so he did what they

had come to do. He bent to the first man and turned him onto his back. The fleshy part of his ear had been eaten off, and there were signs of tiny creatures feeding on his cheeks and nose. But the face was still recognizable. Ivan was able to say, "Never seen this one before."

He then reached into the shirt pockets. The normal small gathering of tobacco, papers, and a couple of matches filled one pocket. The other held some papers and a folded envelope with a name on it. He would look at the name later. It had long been his habit to complete his search before sorting things out. That would normally include saddle bags, but there were no horses and no saddle bags.

An experienced lawman could almost predict what he would find in the pants pockets—a folding knife to supplement the belt knife. Both were near enough ubiquitous on the frontier. A stub of a pencil, a broken comb, a waterproof tube of matches. The shell belt and holstered .45 were still in place. That it hadn't been taken meant it was not needed by the others or that something was happening to force them to move quickly.

If the men had jackets with them, they must have been folded over their bedrolls.

Cap had found about the same material on the second body.

THEIR FIRST CHORE COMPLETED, the deputies moved a few feet away and eased down onto a couple of flat rocks. Cap chose one that would face Ivan and give him clear viewing of anything to the north and east. Ivan could take in the sights in the opposite directions. It was unlikely that anyone was around to watch, but neither man was familiar with taking unnecessary risks.

Ivan hesitated, but was still the first to speak.

"No horses nor saddles. Bedrolls gone. Rifles gone, but Colts left behind. Nothing important but a few coins in their pockets. No signs of badges or anything saying they were lawmen or professional guards. Wagons gone. We needn't wonder where to. The tracks are an inch deep. They'll be there until the next three heavy rains wash the sand flat again. My earliest guess is that the two on the wagon planned the heist with the two others. The two that pulled down on these ones, the hired guards. When these two refused to go along with the theft, they named their own doom. This was planned a long time ago."

Cap nodded in agreement before saying, "That leaves us wondering who the two new riders and shooters were and why they rode onto the wagon way up here."

A man could take three long breaths before Cap continued, pointing over his shoulder with his thumb, saying, "West. There'll be no fixed trail to follow. Not after those first few miles anyway. Making their own way once they're in the hills. Tough country for a wagon, judging from what we can see from here."

Again, Ivan was silent for a bit before saying, "Now, Cap, I'm thinking your eyes have seen the story pretty much as it really happened, but we have no solid proof. But we're seeing more tracks where the wagon was sitting than just the team and two saddle animals. And that's without even walking around for a close look. How do you see it?"

Cap raised his arm and pointed toward the north. The two-track road held an abundance of hoof marks, as well as the wagon wheels from the stage and several other conveyances. In this almost rainless country, tracks could last for weeks.

"Leading off the trail right up there, down that bit of a dip where dirt has been dug out to build up the road, there's tracks. Tracks of two horses. They lead right to where the wagon was sitting. See that jumble of hoof marks. And the boots of riding men."

Cap had picked up on something Ivan had so far overlooked.

"No boot marks approaching these bodies. Looks as if they were shot from a distance away. Possible by the riders of the animals that left their marks coming off the road. You see those second bullet holes in those bodies? No need for either. Those men were dead when they fell off their horses. But the others, they stood back by the wagon and did for each of these just to be sure. That's why their belt guns are still in place. No one wanted to leave their footprints by the bodies.

"Nasty business. Murder. Nothing but murder, this here that we're looking at. Can't be anything else."

"You're a good one to figure, Ivan. Kinda sort things out. How do you figure this? After the killings, is what I mean."

Ivan looked long at Cap, trying to read his thoughts, then looked again at the jumble of marks around where the wagon had sat. He knew the wagon was sitting still by the fact the horse droppings were in one place. Had they been moving, that would not have been possible.

"I hate my thoughts, Cap. When Rory dragged me into this lawing business, all I knew was what I'd lived. On the ranch, I mean. Seldom got to town. Ranch life and the few times my father or mother talked about the continuing fighting and warring in the old country. Would-be strong men and make-believe warlords making life a misery for the folks that just wanted to work their land and live their lives.

"But as to personal knowledge, I was green as the grass on the newly leafing hillside trees of spring up on our I-5 Ranch. But I've ridden some miles since then. Seen some things. Seen a lot of meanness. And if you won't think too small of me, I'll say I've wept over some awful sights where the innocent were made to pay.

"Now here I'm figuring that wagon was carrying gold in the wooden boxes the stagemen told us about. Gold or at least something just as valuable. Most gold from up in the hills is wagoned down to Denver. That this single wagon came this way is a mystery to itself. And with only the four men. Most wagons run in trains with adequate guards.

"I'm figuring these men before us as guards. Honest men, most likely. Men who wouldn't go along with what the others had planned.

"I'm thinking the newcomers, coming in from the north, judging by how their tracks leave the road, simply drew down on the guards and shot them out of their saddles. All planned and carried out to steal the gold. That leaves more than just the one unanswered question.

"But no matter what they planned, they couldn't just arrive at the rails with a wagon loaded with gold and pretend all was well. Too much money involved. If it was a legitimate and proper thing, the miners would have someone at the railyard to check the boxes over and see to their loading. No, they have to take that gold somewhere else. Might even hold it in the far-off country or up in the hills for some time to let the matter cool a little."

Ivan sank into silence again, as he often did, before

waving his arm west, past Cap, and saying, "You've traveled more than me, Cap. What's over that way?"

Cap grinned and shook his head. "Well, partner, what do you see?"

"Rocks. Hills. Bigger hills. Forest. Mountain peaks. Snow and ice. Distance."

"When you've said that, Ivan, you've answered your own question."

"Do you know of a trail that a wagon could follow?"

"No. No, I don't. That don't mean there isn't one though. But perhaps you've missed something. Among that mess of tracks, there's the clear tracks of mules. My guess is that the wagon was abandoned further along, and the boxes moved to the team and the pack mules. Four strong animals can carry a sight of weight. And they can go where no wagon can go."

Ivan nodded slowly, as if thinking it all through. The question that came out of his thinking was, "What's our responsibility here, Cap? There's a lot of gold and other minerals being shipped here and there. Is the county sheriff responsible for the safety of those shipments? It's an awful big country, and you can count the entire county force on one hand."

"You're correct in your thinking so far, Ivan. But we have to take the thinking just a bit further."

"You mean we're not responsible for the movement of the gold, but we are responsible for upholding the law. Murder has been done. That puts it in our pockets."

Cap settled his thoughts with, "You ready to ride, or do you want to top up your trail provisions first?"

"Just as soon as we roll enough rocks over these bodies, I'm ready."

4

DEPUTY SHERIFF CAP GRAHAM

THE TWO LAWMEN TOOK THE TRAIL AT AN EASY CANTER. There was no possibility of losing their way. The wagon wheels, the team, and four saddle horses, plus the mules, left a trail a blind man could follow. But as Ivan looked at the hills ahead and the forested slopes, he knew there was more challenge to come. But where they were, the riding was easy. The hills were like big haystacks, grassed and sloped. Steep in places but rideable if a man was to ease the climb by taking a slanted approach.

They had gone a little more than ten miles when they saw sign of activity leading into a grassed and treed hollow. Ahead, they could see the tracks continuing on and were tempted to keep going. But Ivan's curiosity drove him to turn in at the hollow. Scuff marks marred the otherwise untouched sod. The sign showed the prancing of restless animals. Other marks showed where the team, with their big shod hooves, had been led to the side before moving on, as if they had been released from harness and wagon. A bruised dent in the grass indicated that the wagon drawbar had been unhooked and dropped to the ground. The two men read more signs and speculated on what wasn't obvious.

"They swung the boxes onto packsaddles Cap."

"There's no doubt you're correct. At least one of them knows something of the trail ahead, as if the wagon would soon become a problem. Packing is all that's left to them. Wagons gone. Can't rightly sort that out, but still, might just as well move on ourselves."

They followed the much shallower wagon tracks for a mile before the tracks turned off to the south, up an easy slope that showed signs of previous travel. The horse and mule tracks held a steady westward position.

Ivan grinned at Cap, nodded at the wagon trail, and said, "I'm somewhat curious, Cap."

Cap led the way, turning where the wagon had turned. Always cautious, Cap lifted his carbine and held it across his saddle. Ivan did the same. The trail continued, winding across the slope, to a humped top in the haystack hill, and then leveled out, heading directly to a shack with a corral and a small barn beside it. The two men spread out and studied the place as they proceeded. Confirming that they had been seen, a man took one step clear of the barn door, holding his rifle down along his leg. The shading from the rifleman's hat hid all but his chin whiskers.

Ignoring the man, Ivan swung to the left of the corral, directly to a wagon that had been pulled up beside the pole-built, horse enclosure. He rode a circle around the wagon and then dismounted. He leaned into the box after lowering the tailgate and studied the wooden bottom and the fixing that had recently been attached there.

The wagon box had been drilled. Bolts had been inserted and tightened. Bolts with iron rings welded to the tops. The rings still had short pieces of sturdy rope hanging from them. The rope showed the newer gleam of recent cuts, as if whoever had loosed the boxes hadn't bothered untying the rope, holding instead to the use of his knife.

Cap looked on from his seat in the saddle. Ivan looked up and gestured with the end of one piece of rope. Cap nodded as if he understood the story the rings and the ropes told.

"Here, you men, get away from my wagon. Get away, I say before I drills a hole through the each of you. Get away and be gone."

Cap grinned and turned his head to the man.

"Lige Bannister, As I live and breath. Fancy finding you hiding your miserable self away up here. You never in all your days had the wherewithal to buy a wagon like this, and you ain't never had the courage to steal one or to pull the trigger on a long gun. Not when there was someone close by to shoot back. Put the gun down before you hurt yourself. Put it down and tell me how it is that you found yourself up here. Long way from Prescott."

"Cap? That you, Cap?"

"Sure enough. Wish I could say I come with a warrant to tag onto your worthless self, but I ain't. So perhaps Ivan and me, we'll toss a coin to see which of us shoots you to rid the world of another vexing problem."

"Cap, you ain't' going to do no such a thing. Didn't I make you welcome? Wasn't I just going to pump water for your animals? Well, wasn't I? Wasn't I just going to invite you in for coffee? If you have any coffee with you, is what I mean.

"What you doing way up here anyway, Cap? Heard

27

you'd given up the badge. Ain't no gold to dig for up this way. No reason, far as I can see, for you to even be here."

Ivan was becoming impatient with the whining and weaseling of the man.

"Put a cork in it, old man. I'll tell you when I want you to speak. And put the gun down."

Bannister carefully leaned the rifle against the corral rail and took a step back.

"No, don't run away. I want to know who you are and what you're doing up here."

Still not taking his eyes off the cowering man, Ivan asked, "Who is this man, Cap? How is it come that you know him?"

"Why, this here is Lige Bannister, Ivan. Ol Lige here, he's got run out of more places than a man could count. Lying. Cheating. Stealing. Can't seem to help it. Steal a chicken. Cheat at a bunkhouse game of checkers. Ain't nothing too small for Ol Lige to make smaller. Last I saw of him, he was leaving Prescott. Walking. Walking fast, you understand. The boys downtown, they were building a fire with the intent of heating up some tar. Others were gathering up feathers for the ritual. Lige figured anywhere else would be a healthier climate."

Ivan turned back to the man. "Alright, you can talk now, but only to tell me where you got this wagon and when."

"The wagon's mine. Brought it up from down south. New Mexico—"

Ivan stopped him from saying more. He lifted his carbine to hip height and pointed it at the man.

"Now, let's start again. And no more lies. We know where the wagon came from and we know when, so there's no need to lie. What we need to know is if you saw the men who had the wagon. How many were there?

Did any take to a different trail, or did they all move out together? Anything else you might have seen. And you can keep the wagon. Those men won't be back. Only thing is, this is a stolen wagon that was carrying a shipment of gold in the boxes that were tied down with these ropes. Cap and I, we'll leave you alone, but if anyone else comes looking for the gold, they might be almighty interested in how it is that you've got their wagon."

"Didn't I just say that I was going to get shed of the wagon? Maybe take it down to town and turn it in for evidence."

Cap said, "And how would you do that with no team? And for that matter, how did you get it up here with no team? Did the thieves pull it up here for you? Thieves and murderers, I might add."

"They done no such a thing, Cap. I pulled it up myself. Just me and my one gelding. And a hard pull it was too, what with that hill and all. But I'll take it back down. I don't want nothing to do with no thieves or no murderers."

Ivan stepped back into the saddle and led the way out of the little yard. Behind them Lige Bannister was hollering, "You men got any coffee to spare an old man?"

"Ignore him," Cap suggested, "He's been on the take as long as I've known him."

Ivan grinned and said, "You've got another story to tell under the dark of the moon some night, Cap. A story about an old man who was scared half to death just to have you in his yard. That, and the story of where you know him from. Aw, so many stories. Keeps a man stirred up inside just to think of it. Anticipating, you might say."

5

DEPUTY SHERIFF CAP GRAHAM

THE LAWMEN FOLLOWED THE TRAIL CAUTIOUSLY. THESE men had stolen a valuable shipment of gold and couldn't expect to escape without pursuit. By this time, their expected arrival in Laramie was well past. The stage drivers going north would have carried the news of the guards' deaths, just as Tate had on the south route.

It had occurred to Ivan that they had no assurance that the shipment was gold, but with the activity in the mountains, there was every possibility of their guess being correct. In any case, what was stolen no longer mattered. Murder had been done. Justice demanded the law continue with the pursuit.

Six horses, two of them heavy animals, plus two mules, left a plain trail in the grass. The deputies stepped their horses onto that trail and headed out.

THREE SLOW, plodding days later, Ivan and Cap pulled off to the side and slipped behind some low-growing brush.

The crew they were following, not wishing to be seen, had skirted around the single ranch that was establishing a presence at Red Feather Lakes. With the area being more or less open, the time was not yet ripe to approach the murderers. As clearly as Ivan and Cap could see, they knew the murderers would also be able to see their approach.

Now, with the riding becoming rougher, the trail much steeper in places, and the surrounding hills and forest closing in after the runners had swung to the southwest, the time was close.

"Cap, as tempting as it is, I'm figuring we can't just stake ourselves a position in the rocks and bush and shoot these fellas down as they ride near. But danged if I can think of a better approach. I'm reasonably sure they're not about to hold their hands high and surrender just on our say-so."

"Got an idea, Ivan. I figure they're going to start leaving a lookout behind. If we can spot him before he spots us, we might pick them off one by one. Arrest them instead of shooting them. It's chancy, I know. But a shootout with five tough men is no picnic either."

"Let's push on ahead, Cap. They won't start putting a man out until there's good cover for him. If this route they're following gets any tighter, that could all happen soon."

As itchy as Ivan was in the saddle, longing for action that would bring the chase to an end, nothing happened for another three days. Then, it didn't happen at all as they had imagined and planned for.

The route was rough. Many trees overhung the trail. There was some danger of overtaking the murderers without being aware themselves. Ivan was on the point of forcing the issue, but the steadying hand of his older riding partner held him back.

Riding day after day at nine to ten thousand feet, when men and horses were accustomed to a much lower elevation, was dragging the stamina out of man and beast alike. The animals up ahead, especially those carrying the heavy boxes, must be feeling the same drag. In any case, the forward movement had slowed to an agonizing pace.

Cap was in the lead. The clop of his horse's steel-shod hooves was loud on the rocks of the trail, but it couldn't be helped. Cap was holding an aspen branch away from his face when his horse's front feet started down a steep incline. He could easily see where some of the horses they were following had left scratch marks on the rocks as they scrambled for footholds. His gelding was doing the same. The distance to the narrow valley below was no more than fifty feet, but it must have looked like the Grand Canyon to the horse. Shying nervously, the animal hunched its back, tucking its hind feet under, and spreading its front feet as wide as the trail would allow, in an attempt to gain a firmer grip. It was in that awkward position, with the entire slope ahead of it, when the startling sound of the shot racketed through the air. Where the bullet went was anyone's guess. The gelding was tipping forward, and gravity was doing the rest. The startling sound of the shot drove additional fear into the horse's simple mind. Just a small lift of its hind legs was enough to send it head over heels down the slope. Its front legs collapsed. Gravity took over. There was no stopping it.

Even as Ivan shrunk back at the sound of the shot, as well as the sight of his friend's horse losing its battle with the rocky hillside, he could see that Cap was trying to gain release from the animal. He couldn't roll off side-ways. Between the rocks and the forest, there was no room to either side. Cap kicked his feet free of the stirrups and was pushing on the horn in an attempt to lift free of the saddle. His only hope was to drop off the rear of the animal. But there was so little time. He didn't make it. The first forward tumble put an end to that effort. Everything else happened so quickly that all Cap could do was ride it out.

The attacker, perhaps to admire his ugly work, not knowing his shot had missed its fast-moving target, stepped onto the trail as if mesmerized by the sight. Ivan had carried his 44-40 across his saddle since they had first begun the chase. It was now a simple matter of lifting it, taking aim, and firing. Before Cap's horse had rolled to a stop, Ivan had shot the killer. As the man fell, holding his upper arm while blood flowed, he let loose of his horse's reins. The frightened animal turned to the trail and was gone from sight in just a moment. Rising from the ground more quickly than Ivan thought he could, the shooter, in a stumbling run, followed the horse.

Ivan tied his gelding off at the top of the slope and made his way to where Cap lay in a heap. He immediately saw that his friend's leg was broken, lying at a miserable angle, and there was blood on his scalp. What may be hurt or broken internally, he had no idea. The man was unconscious, but not dead.

The horse had broken its neck in the fall. There was no helping the animal.

Only after he had examined Cap did Ivan climb back up for his own horse. Getting the gelding down the slope was not easy, but it was soon done. Fearing the return of the others, he knew there was no time to treat Cap gently or be concerned about what else he was hurting. With a great effort, he hoisted his unconscious friend face down across the saddle. He tied him well enough for a temporary fix and then urged his horse back up the slope. He wrapped the reins around a shrub and returned to the dead animal. He managed, with some difficulty, to release the cinch. He lifted the saddle free and entered into a tug of war with the saddle cinch and the weight of the dead horse. Cap was going to need the saddle and bedroll. And Ivan, who would be going on alone, was going to need the provisions in the saddlebags.

It wasn't easy, but Ivan finally had the saddle loose. He stashed it as high as he could in the branches of a tree and brought the saddlebags and bedroll back to his own animal.

Ivan started walking, leading his own horse. He moved back to the east at least two miles, listening all the while for pursuit, before he turned into a grassy glen surrounded by pine and aspen. There, he lifted Cap down and laid him out on the grass.

Tucking a gather of dry twigs and small branches under a mountain evergreen tree of some kind—Ivan wasn't sure which, nor did he care—taking a chance on the bit of fire smoke being seen, he made coffee. Cap had stirred a bit and, a couple of times, had allowed a slight groan to escape his lips. When Ivan glanced up from the fire, Cap's eyes were open.

"Don't know just what it's going to take to kill you, Cap. I thought your horse was doing a fair country try at it, but there you lie, all rested up from a nice sleep and ready for the Saturday night dance down to the town hall."

"If that's all you've got to say, I'm going back to sleep. Hurts too much to be awake anyway."

"Well, you've got you a broken leg. That much is sure.

34

Just what else you managed to do to yourself, I don't know. But if you thought I could move you to where you could lean against that tree, I'd get a cup of coffee for you."

"Go ahead."

"It's going to hurt some."

"Get 'er done."

AFTER TWO CUPS and a half-hour rest, Cap was showing a little more life. But there was a long way to travel to reach any real help.

"Cap, I've whittled out a couple of splints here. Going to have to wrap your leg tight to the wood. I'll do it as she stands now, bent and awkward, or I'll try to pull it straight. Your choice."

"Best give 'er a pull. Can't hurt any more than listening to your yapping."

Ivan sat on the grass facing Cap. He took a firm grip on the off-angle leg, with one hand on the ankle and another a bit higher, on the shin, just below the break. He had his foot braced against Cap's groin and butt. Cap had his arms over his head, wrapped around the aspen to try to hold his position.

"You do realize I've never done this before."

"Do it."

Struggling through their collective ignorance of medical matters, and cowering at the scream from Cap, Ivan did what had to be done. He slowly let go of the leg and pronounced it straight.

"Don't move, or we'll have to do that all again."

Cap, with the sweat of pain trickling down his face, had no response.

A few minutes later, the leg was splinted and tied.

The only rope either man had was their saddle ropes, sized more for cattle work than doctor work. But it was the best they could do.

"Now, Cap, what else hurts. Anything that will hold you back from riding?"

"Everything hurts. I'm starting to gain sympathy for old Boon Wardle, from where Rory shot him out of the saddle. Poor fella hurt for weeks. Anyway, we only got the one horse. Going to be awful slow if I have to walk on the one leg. What's your plan?"

"Get you on the horse and head for that settler back to the Lakes."

With that agreed on, Ivan walked for four long, wearying days, leading the gelding, and took uneasy rest for three miserable nights before they spotted the cabin. Cap had wavered between consciousness and rambling incoherence the entire time. But the deputy was still alive, and there didn't seem to be infection in any of the many cuts and scrapes he bore. As poor as the situation was, Ivan counted it as a successful trip.

"HELLO THE CABIN."

"I see ya. Bring that man up ta the door. See, can you do it without touching any guns. I'd hate to be forced into bringing an end ta what someone else started."

With the last of his strength, Ivan allowed Cap to slide off the saddle and into his arms. With the settler's help, he got him inside and laid out on the only cot in the cabin.

Ivan leaned back to relieve the pain in his spine after Cap was comfortable on the cot. He looked at the settler and said, "Thanks, friend. Thanks for the help. I'm Deputy Sheriff Ivan Ivanov. This is Deputy Sheriff Cap Graham. We normally hang our hats in Stevensville and down at the Fort. What you see on Cap is the result of an ambush by one of the thieves and murderers we were hoping to bring in. Would appreciate if you could get Cap down to the Fort for doctoring."

"And what about you? You can't get him down ta where there's help?"

"I'm going back. There's still four men left to bring in."

"As you like. Might just as well follow up one dang fool thing with another. Odds er good I'll find yer bones someday after the wolves and cats have taken the best of you. But have it your way."

"I admit you're probably right, but I've got it to do. Those boys went and made me mad. Angry. Plus, I don't like to lose. I see a wagon out there. I'm hoping you have a team."

"I have. And I've got work thet needs doi'n too. But it's time I went ta town anyway. Low on flour 'n bacon. Some other things. I'll take your man down."

Ivan thanked the settler and then asked, "You got a name?"

"Riley Billows."

"Well, Riley, I'll thank you in advance for what you're agreeing to do. I'll help you get Cap into the wagon, and then I'll be on my way."

"You'll do no sech a thing. What you'll do is go 'n fork a heap a cut hay inta the back a thet wagon ta cushion yer friend. Then we'll bring the rig up ta the door 'n together we'll get him in 'n comfortable. You'll put your animal in the shade under thet lean-to out there that I try to tell myself is a barn. I'll see ta his feed'n, and you'll stretch out on that bunk and get a night's sleep. Those men will still be there tomorrow or whenever you catch up to them. You go in yer present condition, you're apt to fall asleep in the saddle and wake up dead. Now you hear me. And no arguin'.

6

DEPUTY SHERIFF IVAN IVANOV

IVAN KNEW THE FUGITIVES WOULD HAVE MADE GOOD TIME while he was walking his horse to Riley Billows' small holding. That didn't especially worry him. The trail was long, and time was on his side.

He felt strong and refreshed after the rest and the good meal he prepared in the morning using Riley Billows' provisions. He took to the trail, reversing his walk. At a steady trot, he was a good, long way from the Billows shack when he bedded down the first night. He did not totally trust the route ahead, suspicious that the fugitives may have staked out another shooter. Caution was called for. The four-day walk to the Billows place had been recovered in a day and a half of riding. He would soon be closing in on the gang.

As he approached near to where Cap had been injured, he could pick up just the weakest scent of Cap's dead and decaying horse. It was becoming ripe.

Pulling up to consider, he figured he had nothing to keep him there. He eased off the trail and into the forest. Holding the gelding to a slow, measured walk, avoiding rocky ground, he pushed on past the area and its steep hillside as quickly as the winding openings through the trees allowed. He then swung back south, searching for the broken trail left by the fugitives. When he found it, he would attempt to follow by paralleling the route. To ride the trail after the shooting, days before, would be to invite another shooting. He couldn't be sure the others had given up the surveillance of their back trail. Caution was called for. Extreme caution where the trail was sheltered by rock or trees, limiting visibility.

The men he was following held to some route that he knew nothing about. Riley had told him the rumors of a blazed trail from long ago, although the man had never followed it himself.

Steady movement at over seven thousand feet, and often over nine thousand, was wearing on man and beast. Ivan couldn't imagine living at the altitude, or with the winters. And yet there were the beginning signs of exploration and, here and there, a corral or a small lean-to as if some adventurous soul was going to tempt the climate and the loneliness to get possession of the abundant grass that grew among the high mountain forest and the occasional natural clearing.

Even as late in spring as it was, there was still ample evidence of winter. Snow lay deep on the shade side of hills or in the deep forests. The streams ran bank-full with snowmelt runoff. But where the snow had already melted, the grass grew green and abundant.

The main indicator of Ivan's proximity to his prey was the camps. They were easy to find and not difficult to figure out. He could see where the firepit had been dug out. He could see empty cans and partially eaten food dumped on the grass, indicating that none of them excelled at camp cooking. He could easily see where the wooden boxes had been stacked overnight and where the pack saddles had rested. These men were not trying to hide their presence.

After moving beyond the spot of the ambush, he had seen a bloody rag a time or two in a campsite. A sure sign there was at least one wounded man that needed the help of the others. It could be the one Ivan had shot, or it was possible something else had happened.

The crumbling of the edges of sunken hoof marks or the condition of the remains of the fires were his best indication of time.

On the fourth day out, he felt a slight warmth in the campfire remains. He had come upon the spot in the early afternoon. The fire must have been from that morning. Estimating the distance the group would be able to cover since breaking camp, he rode swiftly for two hours and then dismounted. From there, he would go forward on foot, leading the horse. Fearing discovery or another ambush, he moved slowly, looking for soft places to lead the horse through. The sound of an iron shoe against a rock would ring through the distance, arousing the camp. Assuming the group had gone to camp.

The sound of a breaking branch brought Ivan to a halt. He slipped into the brush after tying the gelding around a bend in the trail where it wouldn't be visible from the camp. There, he waited. He was rewarded with a steady rhythm of breaking branches and the sounds of an axe splitting wood. The fugitives were settling into camp, for sure. It was time for the deputy to seek shelter.

USING MORE caution than he had ever been forced into before, he followed for three more days. In that time, he was studying his query. These men were careless campers, leaving messages in the grass around and in the firepit itself. Messages that could be read, telling of how their supplies were holding out and if they were posting a rear guard.

The first week of trailing and searching camps had shown Ivan an abundance of emptied cans and a surprising amount of bacon rind that would indicate the quantity being fried up. Logic and experience told him the men had to be nearing the end of their easy camping. He knew that hardtack and jerky would be the diet if they didn't start being more cautious with their provisions.

As for coffee, the primary staple for trailing, there was no way to know how their supply of ground beans was holding up. It was common for the camp cook to re-boil the grounds for several days, calling the black mass 'the mother', and adding just enough new grounds to brighten the taste to where it could be tolerated. To run out of coffee was to risk rebellion, and Ivan had clearly seen small heaps of once-used grounds beside the cooking fires.

It all reminded him to care for his own fixings lest he found himself on the trail with nothing to drink but snow melt.

He wondered how the wounded man was holding up, but he saw nothing that would tell him.

Ivan knew little about moon cycles or cloud formations, but he could well see that the night was darker than usual, with any weak moon that may be roaming the night sky being hidden by storm clouds. He had lived through a couple of high-up thunder and lightning storms before and didn't relish another, but even his simple telling of the weather warned that the night was going to be wet and loud.

Not knowing how the horse would respond to lightning and thunder, he pulled the stake the animal was tethered to, preferring to trust the well-rooted aspens as a holding post. He would have to check often. The close-growing trees were perfect for the horse to get himself tangled in, but that was less of a problem than having the animal frightened into pulling the stake and running when the lightning began.

He made a shelter of sorts for himself under the branches of a large spruce that grew nearby. The bottom branches sagged almost to the ground, and the multitude of overlapping branches above should hold off most of whatever rain fell. He cut branches from a close-by tree and laid them out on the ground under the spruce. They might soften his sitting or sleeping area, if he was there long enough to get some sleep. He put the thoughts of fire and a warm dinner out of his mind and sheltered in for a few hours. He had a plan. It might even be a foolish plan, but he couldn't just keep trailing these criminals, day after day. And he had no desire at all to go to Utah. He had to somehow bring the chase to a close.

He took careful note of where the horses were staked, and planned out a safe route from his camp to that area. He watched until deep dusk made more watching pointless. In that time, the careless campers had not posted a guard. Nor had they built shelters. The term 'lowlanders' crossed his mind. But they would learn. Lightning and thunderstorm on the lowlands was an event of some proportion, but in the high country, it was an entirely new thing. If Ivan's predictions for the night proved true, yes, they would learn. And unless those tether stakes were firmly driven into the sod, there would be fewer horses available for packing in the morning than there were when darkness fell. Of course, making sure of that was a large part of his plan.

THE FIRST EXPLOSION of lightning came at around midnight. Or so Ivan guessed. The follow-up thunder literally shook the mountaintops. The massive sound was so startling that when it finally rolled off to the east, the absence of sound seemed to be total. But, of course, the silence couldn't hold. Within seconds, the sky was full of lightning strikes, some coming so near they caused fear in man and beast. Others were distant. The thunder was a continuous roll of sound. Squatting at the single opening into his makeshift shelter, where a couple of branches grew slightly apart, Ivan watched as a pine exploded not too far away. Fire and chunks of wood and branches seemed to fly off in every direction. The sap that had dripped over the years, clinging in great gobs to the bark, was doing its best to hold the fire alive, but the downpour of rain that followed the wind-driven clouds soon caused the flames to sputter to nothingness.

He had been sleeping, but he could sleep no more. Awake with the first crash of thunder, he knew his night's rest had come to an end. He had work to do. And the dark of night, storm or no storm, was the time in which to move. He had donned his slicker before dropping off to sleep. Now, he tied down his hat, went to the horse, and tightened the cinch. He took a moment to settle the frightened animal before swinging toward the downhill trail he had staked out in his mind before the sun went down. Knowing the grass would be slippery, he walked slowly and carefully.

At the bottom of the short slope, he paused. Studying the area with the light of the lightning strikes, he saw much rustling and pulling on tether ropes from the horses. But he saw no action at the camp.

He took a long chance based on what he could see and the fact he had seen no guard sent out before darkness fell. He tied his own gelding to a small but sturdy-looking shrub and cautiously stepped forward. He was looking for the team. Either the team or the mules. They were the animals with the most carrying ability and the steadiest on the trail. Closing in, he waited for the next lightning. He didn't have to wait long. The flash was sharp, bright, and short. And it lit up the team just fine.

Running now, all caution pushed aside, he closed on the big geldings. They were the strongest and the steadiest and the most likely to welcome a stranger's smell and touch. There was no point in talking to settle the horses. He would have to shout over the thunder to be heard. He simply pulled the slip knot that held the tethers to the night halters on the big brutes. Now set loose, he was able to turn the first animal's head and point him away from camp. Being a team, the second gelding turned and followed. Ivan didn't try to rush them, although his every thought pleaded for them to hurry. He walked ahead, and the team followed, appearing to be unscathed by the storm.

With a simple step to the side, Ivan was able to release his own horse while the big team continued in the direction he had been leading them in. He stepped into the saddle and again took his place at the front of the team. As if it was all planned and normal, the obedient team plodded along. To rush was to make noise. And even under the thundering dome of the storm, it might be possible to hear hoof beats.

Ivan followed the well-marked trail, now slightly visible with the bit of available light glistening off the chewed-up grass. He followed until he came to a clearing heading south and a bit downhill. He swung into the new opening, and the team followed. He had no idea where the trail led, but he didn't really care. Away. That was all he wanted. To reduce the ability of the gang to load out the boxes was the goal. Removing the team from their reach was the start.

Ivan continued southward for what he guessed might be five miles. When the trail widened into a small clearing with heavy forest on one side and a steep mountainside on the other, he stopped. There was an overhang large enough for himself and his saddle horse. The team could run loose. They were well able to fend for themselves.

Ivan put in the remainder of the night under the partial shelter of the rock, waiting for morning and searching his mind for a new idea. Morning came before any workable idea materialized.

7

DEPUTY SHERIFF IVAN IVANOV

THE STORM WAS A ONE-NIGHT WONDER. THE CRASHING OF thunder following the sharp spikes of lightning left the odor of freshness mingled with ozone. The bright morning sun seemed to take special pleasure in accentuating the many shades of green in the spring grasses and leaves.

Stepping out of his rock shelter, Ivan stretched and yawned. It was a glorious morning, full of brightness and promise. A man could get used to mornings like that. But there was his mission to remember, the purpose of his being where he was. He dropped his arms to his sides and looked all around the campsite. There was nothing to see that wasn't natural. It was as if he and the horses didn't exist. He found the thought troubling. But he had settled in the night before without more than a chew of jerky, and he wasn't about to face a long day without more to go on. Looking around, he saw no sign of the team. Or of any other movement.

The wind, over time, had blown enough twigs and small branches into the rock overhang to support a coffee fire. He lit the fire and put a half-filled coffee pot on to heat. While he was doing that, he searched through Cap's saddlebags for provisions. Cap had kept his bedroll but had insisted on Ivan taking the provision along as backup to what he already had.

Three strips of bacon packed into a couple of cold biscuits, several days old, and two cups of coffee set Ivan up for whatever was to come. He cleared away the evidence of his camp, scattering the charcoal-tipped branches through an adjacent aspen grove. Aspen seemed to grow everywhere he looked on this chain of hillsides and small valleys.

Staying alert to be sure the team wasn't following, Ivan reversed his route from the night before, watching every minute for men searching for the team. He saw no one, and when he got to the camp from the night before, it was deserted. Moving just a bit to the west on the path the fugitives had taken, he could see by the boot marks that two men were walking. Undoubtedly, the saddle horses were packing the wooden boxes, a role the animals would not be familiar with or appreciate.

8

SHERIFF RORY JAMISON

THE LONG, WEARYING MILES IN THE HAY-FILLED WAGON box were better for Cap than sitting a saddle with his poorly splinted leg jutting out at an angle. But that didn't mean it was good. Or easy. Finally, though, Riley Billows leaned back on the reins, pulling his team down from their easy jog.

"Whoa up there, fellas. We'll walk 'er from here."

The team came to a rest in front of the doctor's small house and clinic. Riley sagged on the hard wooden seat and leaned forward to tie off the reins.

"Are we there?"

"We're there, Cap. You jest set easy. I'll gather up some help and git ya ta where the doc kin put ye back together."

The news of the injured deputy reached the gossip center of the Fort in under five minutes. It took another five to arrive at the cabin on the outskirts of town where Sheriff Rory Jamison lived with his often alone and lonely wife. But in this case, Julia, Mrs. Jamison, was working at the saddlery and gun shop. She had started the job there when she first moved to town, well before the wedding. In fact, she had moved to town specifically to make sure there would be a wedding. Her chosen, Sheriff Rory, was a bit footloose and familiar mostly with doing what he wished, when he wished. She took it as a serious, personal matter to corral him and work that wanderlust out of his makeup. She took the job with Mr. Sales only to earn her keep. There was no long-term plan involved in the work.

Pleading with her sometimes-grumpy employer had never gotten the results she was looking for. But flattery and a charming smile had worked every time. With a few kind words about the quality of the leather stitching on the saddle Mr. Sales was putting the finishing touches on, Julia had received the sought-after permission to go to the cabin to inform Rory about Cap's arrival and his injury. She kept her horse at the livery, only a few steps away from the saddle shop. She could ride bareback as well as she did in the saddle. She removed the halter from her gelding, slipped on the bridle, and with a grip on the bay's mane, swung aboard. From there, it was only a matter of seconds to make the run home.

She found Rory sitting on the porch where he had been mending a tear in his canvas jacket. But he had fallen asleep. Her laughing call woke him. He sat up with a jerk, feeling foolish to have been found sleeping. She would tease him about it later, but at the moment, the news was more important.

"You'd best saddle up, Rory. Cap's just been hauled to the doctors. I wasn't there myself. But the news is all over town. Cap will be wanting to see you."

Rory stood, belted on the .44 Colts that he had lying on the table before him as he worked on the jacket, and reached for his hat.

Still shaking off sleep, he and his recent bride rode side by side back into town. They parted at the livery stable.

Rory, who had sought one doctor or another's help more times than he cared to think about, either for a fugitive shot while attempting escape or, on occasion, for himself, opened the clinic door and walked into the small waiting area. Tapping on the treatment room door, he hollered, "Doc. You in there? You got Cap with you?"

"Come in, Sheriff."

Rory walked in to find the deputy asleep, under the influence of ether, which was a blessing to both patient and doctor, but that could also cause considerable illness when the patient woke up. Nausea, headache, and horribly upset stomach were common effects of submitting to the medication. But it did allow for a pain-free resetting of Cap's leg and the treatment of his many cuts and scratches.

"What happened to him, Doc?"

"You know as much as me. Fella just dropped him off and drove his wagon away. There's no bullet holes, I can tell you that much. It's possible you could take that as good news."

"Who brought him in?"

"Fella called himself Riley Billows. Says Cap was brought to his place up at Red Feather Lakes. I'm not sure where that is. You might want to get down to the mercantile before he leaves town. Seemed to be in a bit of a rush. Said he needed supplies and had to get back quick."

Rory figured he might have a deeper understanding of wilderness settlers than the doc. He'd have bet money the man was at the dining room having himself a rare, seldom enjoyed, woman-cooked meal.

Proving his hunch to be true, he first located the wagon behind the mercantile and then, being told by Grady Stiles that Riley had left his wagon and team there while he went for dinner, Rory walked that way and entered the café.

Only one man could be Riley Billows. The four others sitting at tables were two ladies taking afternoon tea and two ranchers swapping tales of horses, each claiming to have had the best in the country until hard times befell either themselves or the animals. Rory didn't have to listen to know the tales. He had heard them all before. He walked over to the third occupied table and said, "Riley Billows?"

"That would be me."

"Sheriff Rory Jamison, sir. May I join you?"

"Set yerself down."

"I need to thank you, sir. You went out of your way to bring my friend and deputy down off the mountain. Good of you."

"Might could be I'll need help myself someday, Sheriff. Ya jest never know. Anyway, I needed supplies. Trade with Stiles fer firewood which he sells to town folk fer a good price."

"It's still worth my thanks. And I know that if Cap was awake, he'd be thanking you too. Doc says the leg was broken pretty bad and only half pulled back into place, but he figures he got it fixed and it should be alright. Couple of stove-in ribs will heal. Although they'll hurt some until they do. Was Cap alone, or was Ivan with him?"

"Fella called himself Ivan walked him in, Cap rid'n one-legged on the horse. Says he walked four days. Tough kid, that."

"You're correct, Mr. Billows. Ivan is a tough kid. Did he say where he was going after he left you?"

"Back. Back to get the ones they were chasing. Said they'd made him mad what with all the runn'n they was doin' after the murders and the theft. Don't know as how I'd want thet young fella on my trail."

"When was that, Mr. Billows? How long were you in getting down here?"

"Two days and one night from my holdings at the Lake ta town. A horseback, and with the determination that Ivan had, I suspect he'd be about caught up ta those runners before this time."

"Well, thanks again. I don't expect those thieves will double back, but you watch yourself on the return trip. And if there's ever anything you need, you somehow get word down to town. I'll sure come a runn'n."

Riley nodded his acceptance of that statement and dug his fork into the gravy-smothered mashed potatoes again.

RORY AND JULIA were sitting on the porch enjoying a pleasant evening following a hasty dinner. Julia took Rory's hand in hers and said, "I know you're going after Ivan. There's just nothing else you can do. When do you figure to leave?"

"Morning. I've got to have a talk with Cap, and he's still sleeping. Doc says he'll be pretty groggy and could be sick when he wakes up, so it's best to give him that time. I picked up some trail supplies this afternoon and I'm ready. I know this is all hard on you. It's what we talked about before we married. You're being good about your time alone, but I still wish I could shorten that time."

Julia squeezed his hand a bit harder and said, "I need to do up those dishes, and then we'll see if you can get a good night's sleep. Leave refreshed in the morning."

"I'll wash. You dry and put away."

She stood with a grin, and together they went to clean up the kitchen.

9

SHERIFF RORY JAMISON

RORY SHOOK CAP'S HAND WHEN THEY MET IN THE morning. The deputy had struggled through a rough night. The leg was alright, but his ribs hurt. Every time the nausea from the ether hit him, he threw up into the bucket the doc had provided. And with each heave, he seemed to hurt his ribs even more. With some of the open cuts and scrapes a long way from healed, he had to be careful how he moved. It had been a long, painful, troubling night. But he was wide awake and thankful for all that had happened since the horse fell.

"Wish I could have thanked Riley again. You sure he's left town?"

"I watched him start out of town last evening. He was determined to get home. But I thanked him for you. Now tell me everything."

It didn't take long to reduce the chase to just a short tale, sticking to only the important points. The most important was the trail to follow to where he was most apt to find Ivan. The Billows place at the Lakes was out of the way. Rory could save a day or more of riding by following the more direct route, winding through the lowland.

Cap had a gift for describing country. He ended with, "Riley said he had heard of a blazed trail up that way. Old. Mostly grown over. Or so he'd heard. Ivan and me, we didn't have to look for it. We just followed the men we were chasing. But I expect they were trying to follow the blazes and any other sign of travel. Big country up there. And rough. High. Peaks and canyons. Could find yourself trapped, facing the need to double back and start again. Some meadows here and there. Man could get lost on a cloudy day, were he not able to set himself by the sun. Can lose track of north and south after turning around rocks and winding through forest all day. But Ivan, he'll be following tracks. Grass tore up pretty bad by all those heavy pack animals."

"I follow what you're saying, Cap. And I remember just a bit about the area. I've met Lige Bannister. I'd know how to get to his place. I found him in my census search, added his name to the voters' list. Now you take care, my friend. Don't try to rush that leg back to health.

"Junior Wardle needs a place to hang his hat while he's serving as town marshal. If you were to invite him to join you in the cabin, he might be a help to you till you mend up a bit.

"Now, I'll be on my way. I'll hope to be back soon. Me and Ivan both."

When Rory stood to leave, Cap thought of something else.

"Riley said something interesting. Worth thinking about. He said no one really knows that area at the top of the state very well. Few folks here and there is all. No clear routes through the hills and no reason to cut one out. If someone was heading to Salt Lake or thereabouts, he would most likely take the rails. Packing a heavy load through an unknown country makes no sense. Worth thinking about. Where might those fellas be heading to? And could it be that one of them knows the way?"

Rory snugged his hat down and listened. When Cap had spoken his piece, Rory nodded and answered, "Riley makes sense on that. Worth thinking about for sure. But I don't have an answer to the question."

He was just reaching for the doorknob when Cap again stopped him.

"Here I've gone and just talked about myself like some self-centered kid. But it comes to me now that you were heading out east where you'd heard about two ranchers fighting over free land. How did that come out?"

"Easy and simple. I explained that there was no end of land out there and enough water to do for everyone, so long as they didn't stray too far from the river. I told them to go ahead and choose the land they wanted as long as it wasn't already claimed. I warned them that if they got into a foolish fight and one was hurt or killed, I'd come out and arrest the other one and make their life very unpleasant. Seemed as if they took me seriously."

"Might have something to do with your reputation."

"Might."

THE SHERIFF RODE LATE that evening, arriving at Lige Bannister's shack after the sun had disappeared behind the western mountains, leaving just a shading of red rim that seemed to be fading even as Rory watched. As he rode near, he had seen movement near the corral, but no light showed from the barn or cabin.

He called out, "Lige Bannister, Sheriff Jamison here. Show yourself. We need to talk for just a bit. Then I'll leave you to yourself again."

From the direction of the crudely built barn came the muffled reply, as if the talker was answering from around the corner. "That really you, Sheriff? I've got me a twelve gauge here if it's someone intent on pulling a fast one on ol' Lige. Don't you be mak'n no mistake now."

"It's me alright, Lige. You show yourself, or I'll ride back to town and take your name off the voters' list. I put it on, and I can take it off. Won't leave you this coffee I brought for you either."

"I didn't no way vote and ain't likely to, which you most probably already know. So do your worst. But ride on up. Wasn't I just going to invite you in for coffee? Well, wasn't I?"

"Lige, you never in your life invited anyone in for coffee. Now show yourself. All I want is a bit of information."

Lige sidestepped into partial view, keeping to the darker shadows thrown out by the barn. He squinted at the man sitting horseback in his yard. He didn't like the looks of the carbine pointed in his direction, but he could see enough to know it was the sheriff, one of the few people he knew in the area. And one he partially trusted, although trust did not come easily to Lige Bannister.

"What information you want'n, Sheriff?"

"Only this. Did any of those thieves ride back this way? Have you seen anyone since the two deputies left you a few days ago?"

"Nary a soul. Seen Riley Billows pushing his wagon almighty hard toward town. Couple a days ago, that was.

I can see for many a mile from up here on my hill. Seen him coming back up today, early. Must'a slept out along the way. He didn't come close enough to visit. Never does, for that matter. This is an alone place I got here. Suits me."

"Alright, I'll be riding. I put a bag of beans on the corral post here. I wouldn't want you running out of coffee. But if I find you've been lying, you'll wish you were back in New Mexico."

The hermit said nothing as he watched the sheriff disappear into the darkness. But he knew the words spoken held truth. And a threat. He would have to watch his every move. And he would have to get rid of that incriminating wagon.

10

MY WAY AND DANCER

Ivan wondered as the trail left by the fugitives took a southwest turn, avoiding the heavy forest to the west. It was a move only an experienced and knowledgeable guide would make. Behind that forest, they would have seen peaks that were higher than the ones they had been skirting. Peaks and high valleys filled with snow on the shady side. And lower down, unseen until a rider was right upon them, crevasses that would be bad news to anyone coming upon them in the dark. Formed by earthquakes and massive subterranean upheavals over the eons, it was country to avoid. Ivan had no knowledge of what lay to the west either, but the change of direction told him someone with more wisdom than he had seen previously was now guiding the group.

What didn't make sense to Ivan, as he studied out the trail, was the plodding slowness of the fugitives. The last two camps were barely ten miles apart. The loss of the team would be a blow to their plans, but even walking men could make more than ten miles. There were enough mysteries in connection to the gang to keep Ivan awake at night, sorting it all out. If he let it, that is. Most nights, weariness overtook him, and he slept soundly.

The next mystery he couldn't solve was the constant changing in direction. The overall route was still southwest, but the winding and twisting through the rough country seemed extreme. Beyond the necessary. Almost as if the one picking the trail was wandering aimlessly through the country instead of holding to a destination. Considering the original thoughts of what he was thinking of as a new guide, it was all a mystery.

Ivan followed an easier path, cutting off many corners, and had no trouble keeping in touch with the group's trail. The questions kept coming until Ivan, studying the situation from a safe distance, with the aid of the glasses he was in the habit of carrying with him, saw something new—an Indian, walking well ahead, was leading the group. The Indian was dressed in white man clothing except for the tanned buckskin breeches, the moccasins, and the feather that rose triumphantly from his much-abused hat. Above, hanging over the breeches, was a four-point Hudson Bay blanket coat, badly worn, and showing the passage of time.

Ivan studied the man, watching his movements as he pushed low growth aside, stepping through the gap in a way that Ivan knew would be close to soundless. Indian for sure. But how had he come to be there? And who was it? And where had the coat come from?

THE BAY HAD TRADED for the past couple of centuries, down into Montana and Idaho and further south, establishing a rapport with the natives. The Blackfoot had hunted and trapped, trading with the company for the many years since 'The Governor and Company of Adventurers of England trading into Hudson Bay' had opened their fur trading forts all across what was to be known as Rupert's Land and into the southern reaches of the Rockies.

For a Blackfoot to be wearing a four-point blanket coat was not remarkable. Except that Ivan had never seen his friend My Way wearing one before. He thought this as his eyes told him the almost impossible. The Indian was, indeed, his friend and sometimes deputy, My Way.

And further back, walking beside her led horse, was an Indian woman. Ivan didn't know much about the Tribes, and almost nothing about their native clothing. He had no idea what Tribe this lady was from. He had never seen a Blackfoot woman, so there was no way for him to even guess.

The woman was dressed nothing like My Way. As far as Ivan could tell through the glasses, she was covered head to feet in tanned skins. Draped from her shoulders, she wore a loose-fitting, beaded and fringed over-shirt, hanging loosely to well below her waist. Beneath, was what could have passed for men's pants, but the fit and style said otherwise. Fringed down both legs and pulled tight at the ankles, the fit spoke of feminine. There was no disguising that fact.

The few Native women Ivan had ever seen had worn no hats. That this lady had a crushed and stained Stetson on her head, with two long, black braids hanging to the mid-point of her back, might have indicated a desire for protection against the sun, or it may have signaled her personal choice and independence. Any conclusion Ivan could come to would be purely guesswork.

Her horse was burdened with a wooden box, like all

the others. My Way's horse must have been one of the bunch being driven. There was no way to tell.

Now, where did the Indians come from? And when?

The most logical possibility was that the group had somehow met the Indians while Ivan was walking Cap to the cabin of Riley Billows. It was all possible, but Ivan had seen no other travelers in his days in the mountains, and he hadn't expected to. This was lonesome country. *High and lonesome*, he added to his internal thoughts. Were the Indians willing participants, or were they captured for their horses? Or were they traveling through to some destination of their own, and the gold thieves and murderers had just happened upon them? If any of those possibilities was true, it seemed surprising that they had not simply been shot and their horses taken. Perhaps the fact one of them was a woman had influenced the group, or it could be they had asked the Indian to guide them to wherever they were going. Or they had insisted on them being guides at the point of a rifle. So much speculation. So few facts.

Ivan was at a disadvantage from his present perch. He couldn't see the faces of the gang members. It was only that My Way had turned in response to being called that he had seen his friend's face. Even then, he caught only a blurred image.

The glasses were somewhat less than military grade, and he was at a range where he could expect no more from them. The view from above was good for seeing the whole layout, but being behind them a short way hid their faces from view, making the limitations of the glasses almost redundant. He would have to risk getting ahead of the group if he wanted to have a better chance of identifying anyone. Ahead and closer. But that could wait. There was little chance of losing contact with that many horses scuffing the grass and breaking the willows and other small shrubbery that banked both sides of the trail. He decided it might be well to see what else was in the surrounding area. He may need a place to run to or to seek shelter.

As he was slowly riding, working through that decision, the terrain changed. Now, off to his right was another gash in the land. This time, he was riding close to its termination point. Stopping and working his way through the brush, he looked at the opening. He saw that the gash was really quite small, but the bare, treeless uprise behind it was virtually impassable. Had one of the criminals known about that, or was it the Indian guide who rounded the obstruction? It was an idle question that didn't need an answer.

Ivan rode back to where he could see the horses moving below him and a distance to the west. There was a point of land rising above its surroundings, just a few miles to the west. He pointed his horse toward it. The rough riding slowed his forward motion considerably. But two hours later, he was atop the high, rocky mesa. He had left his mount below, where there was grass and water. Seating himself against the darkest background he could find, he settled down to watch. He had passed the group of horses and men and was now just a bit ahead of them. He dug the glasses out again and lay on his belly in the shade of a higher rock, adjusting the glasses so he could watch. The shadowing rock would prevent any reflection from the glasses.

He focused first on the Indian. The man's face was still not clear at the distance, but there was much that was familiar about his actions, his movements through the bush. There could be no doubt. It was his friend My

Way. The Indian woman was clearly a stranger to him. And somehow, he felt, a stranger to these men.

From where Ivan lay, he could see at least two easier paths the group might take. And yet, the guide led them into the densest forest and around every obstacle, almost as if he was searching out the most difficult way.

Ivan watched until an hour before sundown, when the group went into camp. He then slid down the side of the rock and went to his horse. He had an hour at least to look over the country before full darkness. From his high perch, he had seen a long, crooked row of greenery off a bit to the north. And higher by perhaps a few hundred feet. Almost as if there was a meandering watercourse marked out by trees and grass. So little up that way was truly green that the row stood out. Most of the land around was either grey rock or mature forest that showed a much more subdued green, almost a grey-green color, quite different from the freshness of well-watered spring growth.

A half-hour of riding led Ivan to the small stream and then, after crossing and riding uphill, took him to a plateau where he suspected the stream had its beginning. The plateau was, by guess, at least one thousand acres. But with the rolling land cut here and there by rocky intrusions, it was difficult to tell. He had no idea what was beyond any of those rocky dividers.

The grass was abundant, and the outline of trees extended further than Ivan had thought while looking at it from below. The stream didn't begin there as he had first believed, but trailed off to the west before it turned behind another mountain offshoot. The rim of trees copied the path.

Paying closer attention, Ivan noticed that the water was flowing to the west. But the downhill portion had clearly been heading east. That had to mean two things. First, he had misjudged the beginnings of the watercourse in the multitude of twists and turns in the mountains and forests, getting to that point, and second, he had somewhere up there crossed the great divide. The water on his home side flowed east. Where he now sat his horse, it flowed west. He had never made a study of such matters or even given it much thought, but he had heard some talk, and now, there it was, right before his eyes.

Also before his eyes, and much to his surprise, was a cabin. Studying it from the distance, he decided it was a well-built cabin, put together by someone who cared, and who hoped to be protected from the winter cold. The sight reminded him of Kiril and the fine workmanship in his cabin, the one Ivan now thought of as his own. How far was that from where he now rode? How many mountain peaks between here and there? Would he ever see the cabin or home again, or was the foolishness of chasing five murderers going to be his downfall?

He turned his horse toward the cabin and rode the half-mile, arriving within hollering distance with just a bit of light left.

"Hello the cabin."

"I've seen you. Step down and come to the porch. If you're intending on being friendly, that is. If you're not intending on being friendly, stop for a moment and say your prayers while you've got the chance."

"Deputy Sheriff Ivan Ivanov here, friend. I'm as friendly as those I meet. Reacting to the situation as it shows itself is what I mean."

He tied the gelding off to the nub of a branch that had half broken off a big spruce and walked to the cabin.

He left the .44-40 on the saddle, but he wore his Colt. He kept his hand well away so as not to be misunderstood.

The man on the porch stood, watching carefully. Ivan stopped and turned, looking all around. The plateau was beautiful. Green and lush. He could see snow banked under the rocks on the north sides of a couple of small mountain upthrusts. He then turned back to the cabin and continued to walk. Coming closer, he said, "Beautiful spot. But high. And lonesome. I'm fond of a bit of lonesome myself from time to time, but this might be taking it to extremes.

"Following a band of thieves. And killers. I know where they are, so you're in no danger up here. They're camped for the night down below. You seen anything up here that I should know about?"

"I've seen nothing out of the ordinary. And I miss very little of what happens within this plateau. I'm not sitting here because I'm concerned about who might be in the neighborhood. I'm sitting here watching the elk. They've been down below for months. Returning now for the summer. I enjoy having them around. Them and the other migrating animals. I'll have one hanging in the ice cave back in yonder bye and bye.

"Got a few that stay the winter too. Smaller breeds of animals mostly, hiding out in dens and such. Bears now, they've been quiet for months, living off the fat of last year's feeding. But they'll be showing themselves around pretty soon."

Ivan turned a complete circle again, taking in as much of the horizon-to-horizon magnificence as the twilight would allow. He turned back to the settler and enquired about his presence.

"I first came up here looking for grass and solitude. I found both. Went back down for the few head of cattle I owned and came back up. I found a grassed box canyon just behind here that was easily closed off. Grass holds the cattle happy and fat all summer. There's water just about everywhere up here, so the cattle do just fine. I cut hay down on the meadow you rode across, enough to hold us for the winter. Of course, when the herd grows, I'll have to reassess all that.

"I brought a load of tools and supplies up the first summer and got the cabin laid out and roofed. That first winter was a bit rough, but in the spring, I helped birth a dozen calves. The next trip down, I bought some cabin fixings and hired a team of Mormon packers to tote it all up for me. The stove was the biggest challenge, but those boys knew how to work, and they had the pack animals to do the job. Brought up enough supplies to hold some aside for selling too. My name's gotten around the hills as one to come to when short of coffee or flour and simple things, mostly canned or salted and smoked. Probably more folks tucked into these canyons than you flatlanders suspect. This ain't exactly a booming area, but there's steady growth. New folks every year. So, with all of that, now I'm a contented man."

Ivan grinned into the near darkness. "I didn't hear any mention of a woman in all of that."

"No. No, you didn't. Think about it though, time to time. Problem is, it's a far way to the Colorado side, and no promise if I should ride that far with courting in mind. All that's on the Utah side is Mormons. Seems as if you take on a Mormon lady, you take on her entire clan. That thought bought me up short. Held some concerns for me, so here I stay, alone and content."

Being shrouded with the declining light, Ivan was left to guess at the looks of his host. Judging by the high voice and the easy way of talking, he figured the man to be tall and thin. Perhaps even ungainly in his profile, making him wonder how a man of that description and makeup could do everything this man had done alone in a hostile environment. Well, it didn't matter to Ivan.

The two men sat quietly for a while, each lost in his own thoughts. Ivan wondered if his host was quite as content with his aloneness as he had first said. He seemed to be enjoying having another human person sitting on his deck, even if he didn't come right out and say so. And that reminded Ivan that he had not asked the man's name. Most men would automatically offer, but this fella hadn't.

"You didn't mention your name."

The man turned in the almost total darkness. As if he had to think about it for a moment, he paused before saying, "Tug Granger. Sorry. I'm alone so much, I don't give any weight or thought to names. Likely to forget my own someday."

Again, silence took over the little porch. Tug finally broke the stillness of the night by saying, "Tell me about these killers you say you're following."

Ivan told just enough for Tug to get the basic facts. He finished his telling with, "Strange thing is, I was watching from a hillside this afternoon, wondering at the crooked trail they were leaving behind them. Then I spotted their guide. Walking on foot, ahead of the rest. It was an Indian. A sure enough Indian. Then I seen, coming along with the rest, an Indian woman leading a packed and heavily burdened horse. Strange, that. There were no Indians with them when I last saw them."

Although Ivan couldn't see his face, Tug was grinning.

"That would be My Way and his woman. Dancer, he

calls her. I don't figure we could pronounce her Ute name, but Dancer filled the gap."

Ivan was grinning as widely as Tug Granger was, although neither could see the other.

"My Way. Yes. I know the man. I thought I could recognize his movements today, the way he pushes a branch aside while he's walking. The way he steps carefully, as if every foot fall might stir up a snake. Yes, it was certainly My Way. And, that changes everything for me.

"I'm going to make the assumption that he's a captive. The My Way I'm friends with wouldn't know how to steal lunch if he was at the point of starvation. He doesn't have enough interest in wealth to bother with a shipment of gold. He's not a murderer either. I've never met his wife or son, but he called her 'Dancer' when we rode together. Has to be the same one."

"Dancer. Yes. That's her name. They've been here several times. Apparently, they intend to go south. Into the Ute lands. But there doesn't seem to be any hurry about it. He's taken up the coffee habit. Dancer didn't know how to make good coffee. I showed her how, and now we're friends. Yes, if those two are with the fugitives, they're captives. Needed for their horses as much as for the guiding. And if Dancer's horse is being used to pack a load, someone is going to pay, sooner or later. Dancer surely loves that animal. But how is it that you know them?"

"I don't know Dancer. Just heard about her. And they have a son too."

"The son is mostly grown. He's living with his grandparents at their Blackfoot village somewhere to the north. But that still doesn't tell me how you come to know My Way."

Ivan told him the story of My Way arriving in Stevensville, riding with the Wardle clan.

"When Sheriff Rory needed a tracker to side me on a hunt, he approached My Way. From there, a strong three-way friendship was built. We rode much together, had more than one great adventure, until My Way decided it was time to go home. Home to his wife and son.

"And now here he is. He and his wife. Guiding a pack of thieves and murders, laying out the crookedest path through the wilderness a man could ever hope to see. My Way's presence explains a lot, but exactly what the Indian's delaying game is would be difficult to guess. But this much is for sure, My Way will have a plan, and he'll do it himself. It's never been in that Indian's thinking to wait for help."

Ivan was invited to spend the night on a cot Tug Granger kept at the ready on the veranda.

"I usually take my rest out here, but you take 'er for the one night. That way, you can fight off any grizzlies that come along before they get to me."

Ivan assumed Tug's grin was still in place when he said, "Seems fair. Mind you, if a griz really does come along, you may find me on the roof when the sun comes up."

The two men went to their bedrolls with no mention of dinner.

MORNING FOUND Tug building a fire in the rock ring at the side of the building. Ivan went to the creek for a morning wash. When he returned, Tug offered, "Only use the stove in the cold times. Kind of like the taste of

71

my coffee over an open fire anyway. Smoke does something to it. To the bacon too. Going to fetch me some chickens next trip down. I surely do miss the sounds of an egg or two sizzling in the pan, now and then."

In the clearness of the morning light, Ivan was silently embarrassed by his misjudgment of the man. He was tall, alright, and some thinner than most, but his shoulders and arms told a story of strength. His big, scarred, long-fingered hands supported that story, and perhaps told a story of their own too. He wouldn't be called a handsome man, but Ivan could read purpose and integrity in the weather-beaten face.

Since Tug talked as if he didn't really need an audience, and Ivan appreciated quiet in the mornings, he walked over to the high point of the plateau to study the lower ground. Sure enough, there was the smoke of a breakfast fire off to the southwest. Unless there were people up there that Ivan didn't know about, the fire had to belong to the thieves. It was time he got down there to see what he could do to bring matters to a close.

11

MY WAY AND DANCER

EASING CLOSER TO THE FUGITIVES THAN HE EVER HAD before, Ivan lay prone on the ground behind a low parapet of rock, surrounded by aspen. He had left his gelding a good quarter mile away. Having the horses sense one another, sending out their welcoming 'good morning' to the others, would not be a good thing. And facing the entire bunch of thieves by himself would not be wise. But he was beyond impatient. He had to do something or go home a failure.

He was ahead of the group, but he was reasonably certain of their direction. If My Way was following logic, they should pass close enough for him to see each man. And the woman. So, he waited.

A half hour later, the thud of horse hooves broke the silence. Then the scratching, as branches were pushed aside. Then, an unhappy, demanding voice.

"Indian. If you want to grow old, you'll quit your fooling around. Don't you be thinking I don't know what you're doing. Now you find us a way out of here. A short way. A fast way."

The woman's voice was heard next.

"My Way only speaks some English. All that talk will mean little to him. You let me go to him, and I will explain."

"You stay right where you are, woman. And don't be getting any ideas of running."

"Mister, when I leave out of here, I won't be running because of the likes of you. And it will be with my own horse. And preferably with your bones rotting in the grass behind me. But now look. My Way has something to show you."

With a single step that turned the gang leader toward My Way, he studied the Indian. Saying nothing but, perhaps, showing a small victory grin on his face, My Way simply held out his hand, his index finger resting on an old, much faded hatchet mark, a notch in an ancient pine, a blaze on the long trail to Utah.

The silence between the two men carried on for several seconds before the leader, gritting his teeth the whole time and sensing defeat on his demand for a faster route, turned and walked back to the group.

There was no more talk, but Ivan was left with a solid impression of the woman My Way had taken for his wife. She sounded as if she meant every word spoken. And My Way, as silent as he could often be, and understanding most of what was said, in spite of Dancer's claims about his command of English, was no slouch in a fight, gun or knife, either one, with you making the choice.

Ivan decided he had to let My Way know he was there. But the movers had gone on, leaving him behind, forcing Ivan to move forward to another watching post. He rose carefully and ran as quickly as he could, still holding to his more open, less obstructed path. He hoped to not have to go far. The horse would be alright where he was, but Ivan didn't care to get much further from the staked-out animal.

AS SLOWLY AS My Way was moving, Ivan was soon ahead again. He watched, and then, as he saw movement in the brush, he took a desperate chance. When My Way appeared through the brush, he stood. Hissing 'My Way', Ivan made himself visible to the Indian. My Way only glanced up and then turned away.

In a singsong voice, My Way started to chant quietly. Most of it was unintelligible to Ivan, but a couple of times, he heard his own name in the mix and then a few English words mixed in, along with arm and hand movements that might have indicated running or walking. The English words seemed to support the idea of running. Then he heard 'shoot', followed by 'come'. The arm movements changed to indicate a fist holding a Colt, then the voice clearly said, 'die'. He was telling Ivan to do some shooting. Perhaps to cover the Indians' escape. But the woman was twenty yards behind. How was Ivan to account for that dilemma?

Ivan trailed along, getting further and further from his own horse. The trail now was straighter and more predictable, although there were still a good many obstacles to work through.

AROUND MID-MORNING, the leader called a halt. "Hold up there, Indian. These horses need a break and a watering."

My Way walked back to the group. In what Ivan

assumed was the Blackfoot language, My Way spoke briefly to Dancer. With a nod, she passed the lead of her own horse to My Way. The Indian then took the lead to another gelding, one Ivan assumed was his own. Both were carrying heavy boxes.

Dancer stepped easily through the grass and into the brush. Grinning, one of the teamsters started to follow. The leader said, in a voice that would accept no argument, "Leave her be. I've told you before. Don't you be doing anything stupid until we're away from this rock pile. You hear me now? That goes for all of you."

My Way led his two horses to the stream close to where Ivan was hiding. Dancer was further away, but the way the woman had moved through the brush, Ivan knew she could soon make up the distance. He might never get a better opportunity.

Thankful he had dragged the .44-40 along with him, he rose to one knee, facing the group of men and horses. He had to act quickly. A couple of the men had started their animals toward the stream. If they got spread out to where they could fight back from different angles, he could be in trouble. Him, and his Indian friends too. Lifting the carbine to his shoulder he placed shot after shot into the ground under the horse's feet and around the gathered men. He had no heart for simply killing the men, although they surely deserved it.

The lead glanced off the hard ground, ricocheting in every direction and setting up a terror of whining noise. The screams of terrified horses and the angry, frightened shouts of men filled the morning air. Two of the big wooden boxes came loose and fell from the horse's backs to the ground. One burst open, but Ivan didn't have time to study its contents.

When, by count, he had squeezed the trigger twelve times, he quickly backed away. The cowering thieves, having ducked behind rocks and clumps of brush, would be a moment or two figuring out that they hadn't been shot before they could retaliate. That's all the time he, My Way, and Dancer would have.

Ivan swung around the stack of broken granite behind him and ran. The Indians were together by this time, with a knife Dancer had hidden away somewhere in the folds of her clothing, My Way was taking the time to cut the ropes that held the boxes to their saddles. With a push, he tipped them off the leather and swung on himself. With a single, strong, graceful leap, Dancer swung aboard her gelding. Ivan was putting every ounce of energy he had into running toward them. The two riders helped to narrow the distance. As they rode closer, what he witnessed amazed him.

Dancer, riding at a full gallop, swung her horse close to her husband's and, with a single, strong leap, was sitting behind My Way, one arm wrapped around his waist while she held the reins to her own mount out for Ivan to catch.

My Way pulled his horse to a slower gait, turned toward his running friend, and with a leap that came close to matching Dancers, Ivan was seated, and the horse was running full out again. One of the loose horses was running along with them.

Ivan heard a couple of shots far behind, but with all the rocks and trees between them, plus the distance, there was little chance of being hit. They ran far enough to be out of Colt range before Ivan directed their path back to where his own gelding was tied. Within less than five minutes, they were each seated on their own mounts and clear of any chase. It wasn't likely the thieves would leave their stolen cache to chase the Indians and their unknown accomplice into a strange land. Still, the fugitives needed that loose horse, so there was no real telling what they might decide to do.

MY WAY AND DANCER

AT A SAFE DISTANCE, THE THREE ESCAPEES CHOSE A GOOD camping spot, a place where they could build a coffee fire and be sure of secrecy. Without discussing it, they sat in such a way that they could, between them, watch in all directions.

My Way asked the first question.

"How you come to be here I-van?"

"I'm here because that gold is stolen, and those men are thieves and murderers. And I am still deputy sheriff. I'm just doing my job. But what are you doing here? This is a long way from Blackfoot country." Then, with a grin, he asked, "And who is this woman who rides with you?"

"This woman is my wife and the mother of our son. She is Dancer. She is Ute. Ute have strange names. Strange to my ears and to my tongue. I call her Dancer for many years. From the start."

Ivan turned his head, still grinning, and said, "Hello, Dancer. I'm Ivan. I am pleased to meet you. I don't know if you can dance, but I know you can run. Run and ride. Thanks for lending me your horse."

"And thank you for helping to get us away from those men. Those are not good men. I was thinking that when they believed themselves to be out of the mountains safely, bad things would happen to My Way and me. It is good to be away. And to have our own horses."

"You speak very good English, Dancer. If you are Ute, how did that happen, and how did you come to meet this Blackfoot man?"

"I learned the English growing up on the reservation. Many of our people speak the English. I met My Way many years ago. Our son is now nearly twenty years. He lives with his grandparents up north.

"When I refused to marry the son of one of the sub-chiefs, my Ute tribe walked me to the edge of the camp and told me to go. Not to come back. Refusing a husband chosen by the chiefs was not done by women at that time. Maybe not now either, I do not know. I went north to find the Sioux. I have family with the Sioux. I walked many miles, hiding when others were around. Eating what I could catch. Or kill with a rock.

"I was a few miles south of Laramie when this Black-foot Indian saw me and stopped. He could see that I was walking. That I had no horse. And he could see that I was tired and hungry, although he said nothing about that. He stopped and took his foot from the stirrup. He said only, "Come up here." I was happy he came my way, so that is what I called him. My Way. He also does things the way he wants to do them. My Way is a good name.

"He is still not very much good for staying home, but he is interesting to live with, and sometimes fun. Although he does not like to think of life as fun. Now we are going back to the Ute camps. I wish to see if any of my family still live."

Ivan thought that through. It was really none of his business, but he spoke out anyway.

"There are easier ways to get to the Ute lands than through these hills."

"Yes, but nowhere more alone. Or nowhere more beautiful."

"I'll have to concede that to you."

By that time, the coffee water was boiling. Ivan reached for the pot, but Dancer brushed his hand away. The fire and the food preparation were her work, and she wanted no help.

13

SHERIFF RORY JAMISON

SHERIFF RORY DIDN'T TAKE THE TIME TO RIDE UP TO THE Lakes to see Riley Billows again. There was little to gain from talking to the man—and with the much-damaged grass and the broken, low-hanging trees easy to follow— he hurried along. In his mind, the most important thing to do was to hurry to Ivan's aid. With the fugitives so far ahead, there had been no need for caution. He had made good time for the last two days.

The trail was looking fresher. The bent grass was still lying horizontal. The deep hoof marks in the few places where the ground was soft were clear and sharp. In another day or so, they would be collapsing around the edges, indicating the passage of time. He had found Cap's dead horse by following the stink. He veered off the trail far enough to avoid the worst of it and continued west, soon coming back to the path the others had taken.

Now, days further along the chase, he had been wondering about the crooked trail, seeing no purpose in it. He salted all the information away in the back of his mind and concentrated on forward movement. Fighting back impulses, he reminded himself that there was no call for carelessness. To gain a bit of distance at the cost of discovery would be futile. And to ride up on the group, or even a straggler from the group, would present a situation he would rather avoid.

The day before, he had found the escaped team. Believing it to be unlikely there would be another team running loose in the area, he dropped back and fell in behind them. He slowed to an easy walk, gently pushing the team over to the well-marked trail. Hoping the big horses would find the odor of the animals they had traveled many miles with and follow their trail, he pushed them at a walk for an hour and then dropped aside to see what they would do. When they continued to follow the trail, he resumed his position at the rear and encouraged the big, well-fed animals into an easy trot they could hold for hours.

If the thieves had used the team as pack animals, which was logical, there would be at least two boxes that no longer had transport. That was bound to slow down the group's westerly movement. There was no telling what was happening up ahead, and Rory was anxious to find out. He couldn't know for sure, but the loose team looked much like Ivan's handiwork.

DAYS LATER, with the advantage of the clear morning air and the view from the slightly elevated camp he and the team had taken their rest on, Rory, ever observant, had noticed the two breakfast smokes. The one of the plateau to the north didn't interest him much. That there were folks settling that high country didn't surprise him, and he could see no reason for the fugitives to climb that high if escape was their goal, and it almost certainly was. Whoever was up there would hold no interest for him. But the lower smoke was begging for attention. And caution.

The smoke from the hillside most likely meant a cabin and a settler. That made the sheriff wonder if he was still in the county that had voted him into office and now paid for his services. His wondering was little more than curiosity. He had often ventured outside his official capacity to solve a crime.

He was working his way slowly toward the lower smoke that had been reduced to almost nothing when he heard the shots. They were a long way to the west, but they told a story of their own. It was a story he wanted to know more about. At the very least, there was a confrontation of some sort.

Chancing discovery, Rory upped his pace. The sounds of firing were intense for a half minute, which is a long time in a gun fight, before dwindling to the occasional pistol shot. Then silence. He could hear the distant but still distinct sound of iron-shod hoofs clattering on rock, as if riders were attempting an escape from the gun fight. And he could hear faint, gruff shouting in the aftermath of the confrontation. It seemed like an unlikely time for grinning, but he was, nevertheless, grinning. He could picture the turmoil, as he had the loose team, as being the work of Ivan. My Way's name didn't enter his mind. But Ivan had been known for upsetting some carts from time to time. He had found it an effective way to gain a step or two on fugitives in the past when he was outnumbered or outgunned. Ivan's thinking would be, why not do it again?

Rory was reasonably certain that the clattering of the

hooves on rock would be Ivan. But there was more than one horse making the sounds. Again, it would be like Ivan to attempt to drive some horses away. Anyone wandering this high country on foot would have a job set out for him. And being on foot while trying to carry stolen gold would simply be impossible. He decided to leave Ivan to himself and go on to where the shouting and the pistol shots had sounded from. He slowed his pace to a steady walk and moved west, the ever-present team still holding to the trail.

A rifle or pistol shot can be heard for well over one mile, and an angry man's shout, almost as far. But a bullet can travel that far also, and further. It was time for extra caution. Building on the assumptions he had made, Rory knew it was time to reduce his forward movement to a cautious walk and return to extra vigilance.

The camp, if camp it was, would be in turmoil. Angry, fearful men would shoot at anything that moved. And, as they were almost certainly short of horses, they would also be desperate. A sensible thief would cut his losses and flee for freedom, hoping to live to steal again another time. But perhaps these weren't sensible thieves. It didn't matter who or what they were, the sheriff wanted them, but not at the price of carrying any of their lead himself.

THERE WAS a certain satisfaction in sitting on the spring grass with My Way and Dancer, drinking freshly boiled coffee. But Ivan knew it couldn't last. Rising to his feet, he said, "I'll be going back now. Catching that gang of murderers, and stopping the theft is still what brought me up here. Now I'm anxious to get it done and to ride home as soon as possible. Seeing you two so happy together reminds me of a certain young lady down in Stevensville."

Dancer smiled when she asked, "Would her name be Tempest Wardle?"

Somewhat shyly, Ivan said, "Yes, the lovely Miss Wardle."

"That would be the ranch girl that helped My Way when he tackled something that was too big even for him. He was a long time coming home that time. I was getting ready to look for a new man when he came riding home like he had only been gone one day."

My Way said nothing, but the look that passed between the two Indians said there would be no new man, not ever.

Not wishing to discuss that matter any further, Ivan said, "No reason you two can't be on your way. The Ute lands are still far to the south. Thanks for your help, but I have to get back to taking down those men."

Ivan could not help noticing that Dancer was still very attractive in middle age. With the living conditions in the mountains or on the reservations, a woman her age, after living through multiple births, was often showing the harsh effects of time, and the heavy work demanded in such a life. But Dancer had turned the eyes of the fugitives and, Ivan suspected, would turn a few eyes in town or city also.

Knowing Indians were not always respected, it was possible she wished to avoid mixing where she didn't have to. Riding home through the hills would normally have meant reaching their desired solitude. But Dancer, showing that the trip home could be delayed a bit, rose gracefully from the grass and went to her horse.

Looking at Ivan, she said, "My Way, he may be tired

now. He will need his rest. He is no longer young. I will ride with you."

Ivan was about to say something, but instead, he burst out in laughter. Wisely, he held back his words as he tightened the cinch on his horse. My Way, preserving his dignity and showing no reaction to his wife's teasing, stood and went to his own animal. What the two would say to each other when they were alone, Ivan had no idea. But for the moment, it was best to let the moment pass into history.

It was tempting for Ivan to object to having the Indians expose themselves to trouble again, but he knew they wouldn't listen. They would probably ignore him and his words. In their minds, the men who took their horses and forced them into serving the group were going to pay a price. Ivan and Dancer would decide what that price was to be.

SIDE BY SIDE, they rode back to the location of the outlaw's watering stop. The stray horse continued to graze, ignoring their movements for a half minute, and then picked up his head and followed along. The fugitives were no longer there, but they had left the wounded man behind, propped up against a large rock. He appeared to be asleep, but Ivan didn't trust appearances. He stopped a few feet from the man and said, "If you're still alive and awake, open your eyes and look at me."

Reluctantly, it seemed to Ivan, the man opened his eyes.

"Good. Now you can see this Colt narrowed on those

same eyes. Throw your pistol away. Far away. And then you keep your hands in sight."

The man did as he was told. It was only then that Ivan holstered his own weapon and stepped down from the saddle. He moved to the young man and bent to one knee.

"How badly are you hurt?"

"Arm and shoulder. Are you the one who done it to me?"

"That would be me. Sorry. I missed my shot. If I had shot truer, you wouldn't have had to suffer all this misery and then end up in jail or hung for all your trouble. Can you stand or ride?"

"Stand a bit, supposing I've got something to hang on to. Could ride, I'm thinking, if the trail's end weren't too far away."

Ivan took a deeper breath to confirm his suspicions before saying, "That wound is ripening. I suspect it's poisoned and enflamed. Not far from gangrene. Those boys do anything for you?"

"They let me live. Buff, he wasn't going to at first. Said I'd be more nuisance than I'd be worth."

"Buff. Is that the leader of the group?"

"Buff, that him. Short for buffalo. Used to hunt the poor beasts. World might be a better place if the buffalo had lived, and someone had shot that filthy old man instead."

"And what's your name?"

"Tag. Seems I was always tagging along when my brothers set out to do something. Called me Tag, and it stuck."

"Well, stand up here, Tag, and let's get a look at you."

14

DEPUTY SHERIFF IVAN IVANOV

IVAN CAREFULLY SEARCHED THE WOUNDED MAN FOR weapons and any identifying letters or other papers. When he lifted the man's jacket, he accidentally brushed against the wound. Tag gasped in pain and folded over, coming close to falling when he unconsciously let go of the tree branch he had been holding, to lift the pressure off his wounded arm. Ivan grabbed him by his good shoulder and held him upright.

The last thing Ivan removed was the man's shell belt and holster. The Colt was lying in the grass a few feet away.

Ivan called over his shoulder to My Way.

"I'd like if you'd bring that loose horse over here. Tag can ride him bareback. I'd also like if you and Dancer would take this fella up to Tug Granger's place. See if he'll heat up some water, clean out this wound, and let Tag rest up a bit. I'll pick him up on my way back. But don't trust this fella for even a moment. Keep in mind that Tag, here, is both a thief and a murderer. If he causes you trouble, shoot him."

All Tag had to say was, "I ain't no murderer. When them other two rode up and put the lead to our two guards, I near fainted off my saddle. No, Sir. I ain't no murderer.

"And there's no need to ride bareback. Buff, he threw my saddle into the brush over there," indicating direction with a jut of his jaw. "As to the other, I'll own up to being a thief, but I've killed no one. I tried to leave when they gunned down those two back there at the stage station, but Buff, he'd have none of it. He said every man was needed. Too bad he didn't decide that before those others were gunned down. I'll give you no trouble if you can get me some relief for this pain and maybe save the arm at the same time."

When My Way returned with the stray horse, he suggested that Dancer could take the wounded man up the hill. He would ride with Ivan. But Ivan was adamant.

"You go with her. And be ready for trouble. If you want to come back down after, that'll be up to you and Dancer. And Tug Granger. Suppos'n Tug doesn't want to be left alone with 'ol Tag here, you'll either have to stay with him or bring him back down."

As Tag was painfully lifting himself into the saddle, Ivan asked again, "Is what you told me the truth? Are there only three men left?

"No, what I told you was three others, plus Buff. And Buff, he can cause more trouble, and do more fighting than all the others put together. You find him, it's best to just up and shoot him. Needs it anyway. Dang poor leader, you ask me. Sold us a bill of goods. Promised us no shooting. No killing."

"And what was their plan? Those mules can't carry two boxes each for long. The couple of those loaded horses will drop within five miles."

"I don't think Buff can even think beyond those five miles, he's so angry. Heading for Utah is all he said. Everything would be good in Utah. Knew people in Utah. Set up for life in Utah. Made it sound like the glory land, but I've been to Utah. Ain't no glory land, those parts I seen. Bunch grass plains and sand. Dry and cold and miserable. Either that, or so hot you'll be wish'n for the cold again."

"So why did you follow him?"

"Because I ain't real smart, and nothing I ever done before worked out. The deal sounded possible to hear Buff tell it."

IVAN SAT FOR A MOMENT, watching My Way and Dancer as they rode away with Tag sitting slumped in the saddle ahead of them. The forward position didn't mean he was leading, only doing as he was told, sitting listlessly on his saddle. Every move, every misstep, every slight hump of the horse's back sent him into renewed waves of pain and misery. He had no intention of causing the Indians trouble. He would follow their every slightest suggestion if there was a chance the pain would stop at the end of the trail.

RIDING ALONE, following the rest of the escaping group, Ivan moved back onto the trail he had been following for days, hoping to not bump into the gang somewhere along the way. But then, thinking about it and looking ahead, it was obvious where the trail was heading. There was just the one path pointing toward the only visible route through the rocks ahead. He had no need to follow too closely.

Across the near horizon to the west was a solid wall of granite and forest running from north to south as far as Ivan could see. And straight ahead, a narrow break where the trail could pass through. It wasn't a real separation between two sections of the wall. It wasn't a deep valley laying out an easy path to the west, and Utah. It was more of a high-up notch, barely wide enough for a team and wagon to slip through. But there was nothing better in sight, so that had to be where Buff and the others were pointing toward.

The overloaded animals had to be struggling. And looking at the slope they would need to somehow scramble up get to the notch, Ivan was doubtful if any of them would make it. The thought crossed his mind that the men might give up on the gold and light out for freedom on their own. That would put a problem and a question right across his own path. He had clearly said he wasn't concerned about the gold. It was the murderers he wanted. And that remained as his primary target.

But if the law was to mean anything at all. If there was any chance the settlers who came west to build a nation were to live in peace. If the courts and the positions of town marshal, county sheriff, and federal marshal were to mean anything at all, he would be needing to bring down the killers. His thoughts left no room for any other conclusion. But the settlers deserved to have their wares, their possessions, free from theft too. He couldn't just ignore the gold. But first, the men.

It would be difficult to leave all that gold just lying about while he chased the men. But why worry about something he could do nothing about? He couldn't move the heavy boxes any more efficiently than the gang was doing. The wagon team he had led away was miles to the east. There was no chance at all of finding them. And he hadn't seen a wagon at Tug Granger's place, or a team to pull it.

He thought all these things as he half stood in the stirrups, attempting to see over the trailside growth. He needed to see how far along the trail the gang had moved.

Pulling himself back to the matter at hand, he knew that if they got a good run at the notch without killing the horses, the thieves might make time on him, and he'd end up following them into Utah, where he had no jurisdiction. Of course, he had no idea of the distance involved. Utah might be on the other side of the notch, or it might be another hundred miles to the west. But none of it mattered. His thoughts were all speculation. His judgment was that the horses simply wouldn't be able to make the run. Which still left him facing four desperate men.

Then he got an idea. If he could swing off to the side and pass the slow-moving gang, he might get through that pass before he could be seen. That may allow him to set up a surprise on the other side. With no better alternatives standing out before him, it was worth the try.

As he was skirting the struggling thieves, he was close enough to hear shouts. According to the injured Tag, the shouting would be Buff, haranguing the gang members into greater effort and the horses and mules into performing the near impossible. What Ivan had no way of knowing was that the situation was going to be turned on its head within just a few minutes.

When Ivan was near enough to the pass, he turned out of the hillside scrub brush and made a run for it. He whipped his gelding with his hat and dug in his spurs, something he did only rarely. The horse struggled a bit on the loose and broken rocks underfoot, but with a firm hand on the reins and never-ending encouraging words, the rider kept the animal moving.

Holding to the shaded side of the notch, he took no more than a quarter minute to break over the top. He had no real interest in the view to the west, but even a quick glance told him the country ahead was rough but magnificent. Mountain peak after mountain peak. Snow caps alternating with the dull green of old forests. Space. Distance. Was it Utah, or was he still in Colorado? He had no knowledge of where the border lay. There was no time to search out the question anyway, or anyone to ask.

But even that quick glance told him there were no settlements anywhere in sight. No campfire smoke. No noticeable trails. No help for either him or the fugitives. He could see nothing but rough going. Miles upon miles of rough going. And no knowledge about the notched and blazed trail they had been following for days. Did it continue through that bed of rocks he was looking at? Perhaps one day he would find out. But for the moment, he had law business to attend to.

Ivan had pulled the panting animal to a stop once he was through the notch and onto the downward slope, certain he was below the sight line from where he last saw the gold carriers. He swung to the ground to give the horse a break, tying the gelding to a rough bit of growth that had not yet figured out that it was spring. Then he walked back up to the notch until he could just see over the lip.

Squatting and walking further, he managed to gain a better view while tucking himself into a bit of a fold in

94

the wall of granite. Suddenly, he was cold. Then he noticed the wind. In his running, excitement, and fear, he had missed the fact that the wind was blowing. Resting in the shady side of the rocks and crags, there were iced-over snowbanks where the spring warmth had melted the surface, and then the night temperatures had frozen a skim over the top. The wind whistling across that white ice sent chills through his body.

Within a few minutes, the gold thieves broke into the clear less than a half mile to the east. He watched as they cruelly flogged the stumbling animals, wishing there was something he could do to stop it. He satisfied himself with the belief that if they somehow managed to gain the rise of land leading to the notch, there would be plenty he could do.

SHERIFF RORY JAMISON had heard the shouting and noticed the notch. He too, was laying out the situation as clearly in his mind as the visible facts before him allowed. He had also noticed movement at the gap in the rocks but couldn't guess what it meant. For that matter, he still didn't know how many men were ahead of him.

Hoping there was still some run left in the big horses, he decided to push them a bit closer and then whip them up, right into the murderer's camp, if the big brutes would cooperate. He pushed forward to within a few hundred yards of the gang, thinking the bit of noise he and the wagon team were making might be blotted out by the shouting scramble before him. Hoping to time his attack just right, he waited until the shouting voice was clearly audible, indicating its closeness, and then, firing four shots into the air from one of his .44s and voicing the loudest shout he could, he closed on the team. Startled, they broke into a run, holding to the trampled-down trail. Within seconds, they were among the other horses and the two mules. The surprise was total. The resultant chaos a joy to look at for the lawman.

As if it had been rehearsed, the burdened animals bolted and, humping their back, tossed out their hind legs, adding more stress to the bindings holding the boxes to the saddles than the light ropes could tolerate. It wouldn't be long before there would be boxes of gold lying at their feet.

Shouts of alarm arose from several directions while one of the walking men, sensing opportunity among the danger, quickly slashed the cinch on the pack saddle on one of the mules. Thinking only of escape, he swung aboard even as the load was still falling to the other side. He kicked the startled animal into a run and made a dozen or so steps, but once he had figured it out, the big jack was having none of it. He stopped with his front feet digging into the dirt and broken rock and did a quick spin to the right. The rider had no chance at all. With no saddle or stirrups and no horn to grasp, the thief was soon on the ground.

There was still one man mounted. Rory didn't know his name, but he figured the big man with the long hair and scruffy, filthy beard was the boss man. From his startled, "What the…" echoing through the clearing as if from a bull horn, Rory knew him to be the shouter. The man had been riding while the others had been walking, leading horses and mules, all of them carrying more than any thoughtful drover would have asked of them.

He wasn't particularly surprised when the bearded man kicked his horse into a run, ducking into the bush and then heading toward the notch, weaving in and out, making a clear shot impossible, leaving the others to their own devices.

He had seen it before. Under pressure, there really was no honor among thieves, as the old saying repeated. It was very much each man for himself.

Wondering if the escaping rider had enough horse under him to make the climb ahead, he shrugged. He would have his hands full with the other three men. He would have to deal with the escaping man later.

Shouting as he had never shouted before, hoping to be heard over the din created by the angry men and the still terrified animals, he said, "Stand down, men. Stand down or die. Rory Jamison here. County Sheriff. I'd rather shoot you than be burdened with you as prisoners, so make your decision."

Rory was only guessing at what the group had been forced to tolerate to get as far as they did. And knowing Ivan, there would have been some complications along the way. Glancing from man to man, he decided the fight was about drained from them. Drained into the mental pit of fatigue created by the miles of walking, poor food, and a plan that showed no signs of working out. On foot, there was no escape, and the horses were in no frame of mind to be caught.

If none of that was sobering enough, having the very impressive bore of the sheriff's .44-40 aimed their way, swinging from one man to another, may have had a calming effect on their intentions, as well.

"Throw your weapons aside and lie on your faces. You do anything else, I'll shoot you dead."

When the men dropped onto their faces, Rory warned them not to move, and then, keeping a safe distance to the rear of the men, he stepped to the ground. He had lifted his Sharps Big .50 out of its scabbard as he rose from the saddle. He had come to love the powerful weapon since it had been given to him by Lance Newley, a thief and gang leader he had captured some time before. He carried it snugged under his left leg in a scabbard the saddle-maker at the Fort had made for him. It was always loaded and ready.

The weight of the .50 was a challenge to hold steady, even for a man as strong as Rory. But his big gelding was not gun shy.

Turning the animal just a bit so that he could get a bead on the escaping thief, he rested the .50 across the saddle. The time to act was short, down to seconds. The rider would soon be into the notch, then through, and out of sight. Rory had shot horses before when there had been no choice, although he hated doing it. But to shoot a man in the back wasn't to his liking either. Choosing a different path, he would take advantage of the aston- ishing power of the Sharps.

The rider was whipping and spurring his horse cruelly, desperately, attempting anything and everything to make distance. He was almost into the notch. Rory estimated the distance through the notch to be no more than fifty feet. It wouldn't take long for the murderer to cover that distance, and then he would drop down the other side and be gone.

The granite wall was no more than a couple of feet on the deserter's left. Rory squeezed the trigger four times as fast as he could lever and reload. The first lead slug whanged off the granite with a frightening ricochet before the sound of the shot reached the running man's ears. Broken, shattered pieces of rock struck both horse and man.

A particularly painful wound was received as a sharp, broken piece of granite struck Buff on the wrist, tearing flesh away and a bit of the meat under it as it screamed across the top of his hand.

Before the animal had time to react, the second fifty-caliber slug had followed the first, delivering more dreadful sounds, rock chips and terror. Two more shots followed in quick succession.

Although the frightened and hurting animal veered sharply away, there was little room in the notch. The nearness of the opposite wall forced the horse to straighten out again, continuing its run through the small space and toward the steep slope on the opposite side.

SIDESTEPPING FRANTICALLY, as more rock chips assaulted it, the gelding stumbled, its front legs folded, and it fell to its knees, dumping the rider onto the rocky floor, but it was quickly back on its feet. There was blood running down both of its front legs.

With Buff partially blinded by the dust and rock chips, at first appearance, it seemed he would have no chance at all of recovering from the animal's fall. Ivan, observing the action from the fold in the rock on the opposite side of the notch, thought the ending was totally predictable. But Buff somehow still had the gelding's reins locked tightly in his big hand.

Reduced to little more than a terrible need to escape—driven by fear, rage, rock-chips, and streaming blood from a multitude of cuts, but with a death grip on the leathers—the big man was jerked to his knees and then to his feet, by the rising horse. Ivan thought the man must hurt in every bone and joint in his body from the fall and the subsequent tumbling onto the rocky floor of the notch. But he was still moving. Still escaping.

To Ivan's surprise, Buff, all the time reaching out for the saddle horn, took several running steps alongside the gelding, now weaving between rocks and within a couple of jumps of the downhill side.

To Ivan's consternation, Buff was hanging from the offside of the saddle on the running, weaving horse. They had tipped over the edge of the floor of the notch and were clearly on the downhill side. With Buff on the offside of the animal, Ivan had no chance for a shot, although he too gave brief consideration to shooting the horse.

As he watched, Buff somehow managed to get one foot into the stirrup. He was swinging his other leg over the horse's rump, finally rising into clear view, when Ivan reached for his Colt. The Colt came into firing position just as Buff settled back into the saddle, and the animal made a darting turn around a boulder that was partially blocking the trail. Ivan shot twice, but it was hopeless. The gelding was all but out of control as Buff continued to use his spurs, shouting for more distance. Another shot missed when the rider reined to the right, disappearing behind a scattering of broken rock and shrubs. Within a blink of an eye, horse and man disappeared into the heavier grown on the downhill side of the mountain.

LEADING UP TO THE SHOOTING, Ivan had seen the action below the hill. When the heavy team had run among the other horses and the sound of the pistol shots had reached his ears, along with the shouted demand to stand down, Ivan had smiled, knowing it could be no one but his friend, Sheriff Rory Jamison, doing the honors. He watched as a big man he identified as Buff, from looks alone, left the others behind, riding for escape himself. It would be Ivan's job to stop the man. He was just sorting out his choices when Rory sent the first shot from the Sharps his way.

When the big fifty started speaking its special language, any small lingering doubt as to Rory's identity was removed.

Of course, Rory's shooting also forced a change in Ivan's plans. He had no intention of simply shooting the hard-riding Buff, but neither did he intend to allow him to ride through the notch. With lead and rock-chips literally filling the small space, he had retreated to his protective fold in the rock wall. He wasn't about to chance the big .50, so stepping out and demanding Buff's surrender was out of the question. Now what was he left with?

The lead hammered into the notch by Rory's Big .50 had left the escaping horse and the side of Buff's face bleeding in numerous places.

The scattering granite also prevented Ivan from getting into the fray. He turned away from the action as best he could in his confining space and hunched his shoulders, waiting for Rory to cease shooting. By the time he safely stepped into the open, not having heard the boom of the Sharps for several seconds, Buff was over the edge, weaving through and around the rocks scattered on the downhill side and kicking almost suicidal speed out of his injured ride. Ivan got off two shots, but neither had any effect on the gang leader.

Ivan stood forlornly, watching the hillside, hoping for Buff to rein back onto the visible trail. The sound of the big man's shouts off to the right told Ivan there would be no catching him that day. He was out of sight, and his first responsibility would be to ride back down and help Rory gather up the remainder of the thieves.

Ivan ran through his options and confirmed his first decision. It would be best to assist Rory with the captured gang. Taking one long, last look toward where the fleeing Buff had disappeared, he turned back, ready to ride east, down to the flat land where the sheriff had rounded up the gang men.

Knowing it was his friend down below, with the big .50, Ivan didn't want any doubts to remain about his own identity. Rory had never been one for blind shooting, but it still seemed wise to make himself known. He lifted his hat and waved it over his head, swinging it from side to side while shouting, "Hello, sheriff. Welcome to our little party."

Rory lowered the Sharps and lifted his own hat in response. He then turned his attention to the men lying on the ground.

15

SHERIFF RORY JAMISON

"ALRIGHT, FELLAS, ON YOUR FEET ONE AT A TIME. YOU with the blue shirt first."

A tall, rangy rider, all arms and knobby-kneed legs, sporting a scruffy beard and blond hair that had needed cutting for the past year or more, struggled to his knees and then to his feet. He looked defiance at the sheriff. Rory could see words forming in the man's mind that were only moments from being spoken.

"It's best you say nothing. You don't want to give me any more reason than I already have for shooting you. I don't want your name. That would be just one more thing to try to remember. And if you should happen to die up here, there's no way to mark your name on a rock, so what's the point?

"If you somehow manage to get back to town alive, that will be soon enough for names. What I want is for you to empty your pockets. Right down to the lint and tobacco leavings. Then, take off your gun belt and throw it beside your gun. When that's done, you can sit down over by that tree."

The second man to his feet was even more defiant. He stood and burst out with, "When Buff gets back, you won't be looking so smart. Buff'll put you in your place."

"If that was Buff, the coward who left you all behind while he tried to escape himself, you can forget it. Right about now, I suspect he's trying to explain himself to whatever angel it is that has to deal with creeps like him. He isn't going to come back, for you or for any other reason."

"He's dead?"

"You heard the shooting. Now, you do as your foolish friend over there did. Pockets and gun belt. And take off your boots. Show me they're empty, and you can put them back on. Same for all three of you."

When the three thieves were disarmed of knives and hide-out guns, Rory put them to catching the animals and reloading the treasure boxes. With the return of the wagon team, there would be enough horse and mule power to carry the load. Only one horse would have to carry two men. But if Ivan managed to catch the animal that broke over the top of the notch, there would be enough for all. Which was a good thing. It was a long, tiring ride back to the Fort. An animal carrying double wasn't going to make it. That would mean a good deal of walking for someone. Or perhaps for each of them, taking turns, one by one.

Ivan rode into the circle at that time, measuring the scene before him.

"Looks as if I might just as well take a nap, sheriff. You about got this thing wrapped up. It's good to see you, by the way. You'll have to tell me later how it came about that you find yourself up here."

"It's good to see you too, partner. Even better if you could bring in those horses, supposing they're settled down by now. These men tried but didn't do all that well, working on foot."

ALLOWING the now tethered animals to rest and graze, building strength for the return trail. Ivan built a fire and put on the pot. Ivan and Rory both worked over their own horses, pampering them a bit and brushing the bits of broken branches out of their manes and tails. He then broke out the food pannier, taking some himself and inviting the captured men to help themselves to the cold leavings from their breakfasts.

A bit later, with a cup of coffee in one hand and a bit of hardtack and jerky in the other, Ivan said, "I was some surprised to see you, partner. You've done a bit of riding. Found the team too, I see."

"It's more like they found me. I think they were lonesome for someone to tell them what to do. Gathering them up was no problem at all. Good animals. You take your fill of grub from that bundle and have you a sit down. We'll have a coffee, then load up. I'm figuring we're less than a week from the Fort if we put in long days and if these fellas don't cause us any trouble."

For the benefit of the prisoners, Ivan stopped chewing long enough to say, "That one up on the notch ain't causing any trouble."

He let the words carry their own meaning. And their own threat. That Buff was running free wasn't known and wouldn't be until Ivan felt the time was right.

The captive in the blue shirt blurted out, "That true? Is Buff dead?"

Ivan, weary of the whole affair and of these men in particular, answered, "If it should ever be that you escape the hangman and one day get out of jail, you can come back up here and move some rocks. See for yourself."

One of the others said, "That ain't never going to happen, and we all know it. Buff promised an easy life in Utah. What we're going to get for following his foolishness is rope burns on our necks after a six-foot fall."

16

SHERIFF RORY JAMISON

BETWEEN RORY'S TWO .44S, HIS FIFTEEN-SHOT CARBINE, and the Sharps, he had a lot of fire power.

Earlier, when the fugitives had been instructed to throw out their weapons and lie on their faces, after a quick study of the sheriff, they had done so. With his Big .50 back in its scabbard and holding one .44 in his right hand, he had patted down each man, removing knives and any other weapons he found, weapons held back after he had instructed the men to clear their pockets themselves. When that was done, he picked up all the guns and dropped them in a pile beside his own horse. Unarmed, he figured it would be safe enough to ride without manacles or cuffs, even though the fugitives outnumbered the lawmen.

The gold recovery was Ivan's show. He had started it and was well on the way to completing it when Rory had arrived. The sheriff would stand back and allow his deputy to carry the show to the end.

"Lead on Ivan. Let me know what I can do to help."

Swinging into the saddle, Ivan hollered at the lounging men. "Check the loads on those pack animals, men, and saddle up yourselves. And listen up. You're being allowed to ride free. You're to watch over the pack animals and keep them ahead of you. When I say I'd just as soon shoot you, you need to take that seriously. In case you're in doubt about my ability in that direction, I'll tell you I don't even remember the last time I missed a target, walking, running, or sitting. And the only man I know who can shoot better than me is the sheriff here. Now step up and lead out. Just follow the trail you made getting in here. Don't try anything fancy. And stay ahead of the sheriff and me. Don't think you're fooling either of us with any rambling about.

THE HORSES and mules were loaded with the wooden boxes now spread more evenly after the return of the wagon team. There was a shortage of packsaddles. Sore backs could be expected, but there was nothing to be done except watch carefully and treat any bruising that resulted.

The gangmen mounted their horses. Their hands were left free so they could more easily drive the burdened animals. After the final warning about what would happen if they tried to escape, they seemed to be convinced that Ivan and Rory meant the words spoken.

With Buff's escape, they were short a riding animal. One man, switching off hour by hour, would walk.

Possibly, it was the display with the Sharps that had cooled the criminals' attitudes. Whatever it was, it was a silent group that headed back east. Ivan didn't think he saw any sign of remorse for the crimes committed in recent days, but it was a long ride home. Perhaps the reality of prison or the rope might yet work on their minds, if not their hearts.

17

DEPUTY SHERIFF IVAN IVANOV

As if the conversation was due for a change, Ivan said, "Hold here, sheriff."

Pointing toward the plateau, Ivan said, "There's a wounded gang member up there with a couple of temporary deputies I brought on to supplement my little force. Fella named Tug Granger has a cabin up there. I sent the wounded man up, hoping for some help. I'll just go and get him. I'll be two, three hours. You'll find coffee and such in that pannier on the mule."

He turned to the captured men, saying, "You might as well set down and take your ease. What you don't want to take is a careless move before Sheriff Jamison here. He looks pleasant enough just sett'n there, and by rights, he's a calm and caring family man. But that can change sudden like. You just set by an' you'll be all right."

With that, he kicked his gelding back into motion and started up the slope.

Rory had the men build a rope corral on good grass while Ivan was riding up to the plateau.

A HARD TWO-HOUR climb had Ivan riding across the meadow in front of the cabin. Tug saw him coming and stepped to the front of the porch with his rifle cradled in the crook of his arm. Judging faces at the distance could be a chancy thing. Tug would stand guard until he could confirm the rider's identity. Ivan waved his hat, a standard signal of friendship on the frontier. Or at least on the part of the frontier Ivan was familiar with. He pushed his gelding into a slow jog to shorten the time to the cabin and was soon sitting on the porch with Tug and My Way. Dancer was heating water on the stove to bathe Tag's wound again. On the ride to the cabin, Dancer had found some herbs she could pick and use to soothe, if not cleanse or heal, the bullet wound.

The lead had been lodged against the bone in Tag's upper arm. Using the smaller of My Way's two belt knives, Dancer had managed to slit and widen the wound a bit. With the knife plus a whittled piece of wood cut out for her by Tug, she pinched the lead between the two implements and slid it back out. The operation was nowhere as simple as it sounded in the telling. In fact, it took several attempts with Tag screaming and then whimpering, it seemed, a little more with each attempt. But without removing the lead, he was about to die. He may die anyway, but with Dancer's care, he could have a chance.

The wounded man had enjoyed only one day to heal from the extraction of the lead, but Ivan insisted he get to his feet and pull his shirt on. He had already saddled the man's horse.

"There's more at stake here than your hurting, kid. You need to remember that you were shot when you were attempting to shoot and kill my friend. As it is, he broke his leg when his horse fell on the rocks. Your shooting didn't offer one single thing to help the situation. That friend is a deputy sheriff. I'm not seeing anything humorous in any of that. Now, I don't care how much you hurt. Get on that horse. And thank this man who's taken you in and helped to keep alive you for the hangman."

With thanks and handshakes all around, except for the sullen Tag, Ivan, My Way, and Dancer mounted and rode off the meadow and down to where Rory was holding the rest of the gang.

As he had estimated, with the downhill ride taking far less time, Ivan and the others returned in a little more than three hours. The wounded Tag was alive but still hurting. After just the one-hour ride, he was sagging in the saddle, looking miserable.

My Way and Rory shook hands with some surprise while Dancer held back, waiting to be introduced.

Turning his eyes to the woman, Rory lifted his hat and said, "And who is this, My Way?"

"That my woman. My wife. Mother of son. Dancer she be called."

"I'm very pleased to meet you, Dancer. I've heard of you before. Now, it's good to meet you. I'd like to hear how it is that you've met up with Ivan way up these hills, but perhaps you can tell me as we move along. The day is wasting. We need to make some miles."

DEPUTY SHERIFF IVAN IVANOV

ONCE MY WAY AND RORY GREETED ONE ANOTHER AND Dancer was introduced to the sheriff, Rory was ready to prod the whole bunch into movement. But Ivan held up his hand. He hesitated for a moment, as if gathering his thoughts one more time and checking on his already-made decision before he said, "I'm going to ask you to hold up for a short bit, partner. I'm going to move some of these supplies onto my own animal."

"I'm sure there's a reason for that. Care to explain?"

"I'm not going back with you. I've confirmed with My Way and Dancer that they'll stay the course, seeing these birds back to prison. You'll do fine, the three of you. I'm going after Buff. He was the leader. It's him that stole the gold and got men killed. It ain't right that he should just ride away. There're dead men on the back trail and other hard-working men wondering where the gold that's rightly theirs has got off to. No, it ain't right."

"He's got a start on you."

"Don't they usually."

"Utah is somewhere out that way. You won't have jurisdiction. Be careful."

"There's no jurisdiction on right and wrong."

Just before he kicked his gelding into motion, Ivan looked at their four prisoners. He hesitated, then asked, "Buff ever mention any particular town in Utah he was heading toward?"

The men looked from one to the other, not sure anymore where their allegiance should lie. Finally, Tag sat up a bit straighter in the saddle, suddenly realizing that the slippery Buff was still alive.

"Temple. Said to be a one-street shanty town on the edge of the high country. The man lied to us. I have no more allegiance to him. Said there would be no killings. Said we'd share and share alike. Later he was talk'n about a leader's double share. To top it all off, he's a coward, runn'n off on you fellas, car'n only for himself. You go get him deputy. And good rid'n to you."

With no further words, Ivan turned his mount toward the well-worn trail leading to the notch.

19

SHERIFF RORY JAMISON

THE HEAVY FOREST THE TRAIL HAD LED THROUGH ON THE way west now confronted them on the way back east. But many dead and fallen trees had been cleared on the way through the first time. The trail would be more open on the return trip.

But before they reached the forest, there was one more rocky ledge to ride around. The route before them was an extra five or six miles, just to avoid the very difficult and unrewarding scramble up the bare rock. The turn to the east, at the end of the ledge, led between two walls, with the opening not more than fifty feet. There were distinct similarities to the notch Ivan had caught Buff in, except the climb to the notch was much steeper.

They were making good time as evening was drawing near. Rory was leading, followed by the heavy team and then the mules, before the pack horses, which were being driven by the gang members. One man was still walking. They took turns about, but the miles were still long for men in riding boots. My Way and Dancer rode side by side, bringing up the rear.

They were just nicely through the turn and again heading north to where the trail swung to the east when one of the captives hollered, "Hold up, hold where you are."

The riders, including Rory, had been studying the questionable footing for the animals, and had not cast their eyes about them for several seconds. At the shout, every eye turned to the front. There, on a slightly higher ledge and spread completely across the trail, were Indians. Not more than a dozen riders. But a dozen determined men can cause a host of problems if their minds are set on it.

There were areas of the newly settling West where Indian fights were a common problem. Some would go on for years. But where they now rode, there had been no Indian fights or serious problems in recent times. The Ute tribes had generally learned to accept the settlers and ranchers and to build their lives on the reserve lands. But, as in all groups, there were renegades, men who would never be happy, even if they all turned back to the old ways. Those men were simply not content unless they were fighting, showing their bravery, as they thought of it.

The two groups studied each other for a fraction of a minute, each wondering what their next move should be. The group of thieves and their leaders were outnumbered by the Indians by a half dozen head. But that was not enough to assure the Indians of an easy victory. Something else would be required to turn the riders away from each other, to continue on the path of their choice in peace.

Suddenly, Dancer shouted something none of the sheriff's bunch understood and rode at breakneck speed around the pack horses and directly at the Utes. My Way was only a single stride behind her, whipping his horse with the flat of his hand.

Dancer and My Way raced to within shouting distance before pulling their horses to a halt. It was only then that Dancer stood in her stirrups and began berating her fellow tribesmen in their own language.

At least to the whites, listening to the gravel in her voice and the harshness of the words, it sounded very much like she was beating them up with words.

A couple of the Indians began to look uncomfortable, staring about as if to find a quick way into the forest. But the leader, judging by the stance of his horse and his personal demeanor, was not showing any sign of backing down. His horse shuffled a bit where he stood, but otherwise, he was motionless.

Suddenly, Dancer broke into English.

"It is good for me to hear your words in my own language. But they are angry words. It would be better for all if your words were not spoken in anger."

With a quick glance over her shoulder at Rory and the others, she clarified, "This is Limping Wolf. He speaks English as well as any of you. I have been explaining to him that you are a lawman. That you have used your strength and authority to capture these men, and that you have always been a friend to the Ute and others of The People. I have told them about your big gun, sheriff. They know of this gun from the stories of the fight in Texas and from the buffalo hunters. I have also told them it would be best if they were to ride off and go back to the village. There is no good that can come from them riding alone. There is only death and hardships for their women and children if they die in battle. And I have told them that my husband is a big name with the Blackfoot people. They

117

would not accept his death without seeking those who killed him.

"I have promised that none of us will hunt these men or bring any harm to them if they will turn now and ride away. I have also promised that we will only ride through. We will do no harm to the land."

She seemed to be waiting for some response, so Rory rode her way. But only far enough to be easily heard. He still had the captives to guard. As an extra precaution, he spoke to the captured thieves, quietly saying, "You men are better off with us than you would be if the Ute caught you. Stay still".

Rory rode a bit closer to My Way. He raised his hat and laid it on the saddle before himself. He then did the only thing he knew to do. In truth, he had seen very little interaction with the Indians, but he had heard of holding the hand up with the palm facing outward. He did this, hoping it wasn't an insult, or worse.

"Dancer speaks well for all of us. We have no desire to fight the Ute. But make no mistake, we will fight if we have to. And there will be empty Ute saddles when we are finished. Go in peace. We will do the same. Perhaps someday we can meet and talk of old times. Meet in peace."

The leader totally ignored Rory's words. Instead, he turned to My Way and said, "You ride with weak men, my Blackfoot brother. There is no strength in these whites. They will not fight. I think you might be weak too. Afraid to ride with strong men."

My Way nudged his horse a bit closer to the shouting man and said, "I am My Way. I am Blackfoot. This is my woman. The mother of my son. For Dancer and for my son, I will fight. There is no man who stands before me."

Waving his arm to take in Rory and the captives, he

shouted, "Look carefully at these you speak of. I have ridden with this man and with others. We have fought together. We still ride. Those we fought are no more."

To My Way, the talking was done. The threat lay before them all. He intended to say no more. But his hand was on his rifle that lay across his saddle. He could lift it and fire a shot in a matter of a second or two. It was obvious to Rory that it was all understood. There was no more to be said.

The leader, grim-looking as he was, did not bother to consult the others. He neck-reined his gelding to the south and rode down the back slope of the ledge. The rest of the Indians, one by one, reined their horses in the same direction. The last one to leave stopped and looked directly at Dancer. Speaking in their native language, he said, "Ride well, Dancer. Your mother is with the spirits. But your father asks for you. Come. There will be a welcome for you and your Blackfoot husband. I am happy you are doing well."

My Way rode to the top of the rocky ledge and watched the last of the Utes ride into the forest. When he was satisfied that they were not returning, he looked back at Rory and said, "We ride now."

Everyone took up their prior positions, and the cavalcade moved northeast, toward the Fort and home.

As if she had to tell someone by way of explanation, Dancer glanced at Rory before saying, "The leader is Limping Wolf. He is the son of a sub-chief. He would have taken me to wife, but I refused. To refuse a chief's son was to be banned from the village. I left. I walked north. My Way found me. If he would stay home, he would be a good husband. The other man who spoke is my brother."

20

DEPUTY SHERIFF IVAN IVANOV

IVAN SLOWLY, WITH HIS EYES WIDE OPEN AND HIS HEAD turning from side to side, taking in everything within his range of vision, was suspicious of Buff's intentions. Finally, he rode very cautiously into the deserted camp at the base of the hill. He had taken to carrying his carbine across his saddle. He carried it there now.

The rising sun lit the face of the notch. Beyond the opening was a hint of darkness that would soon give way to the glory of the day. For a moment, Ivan reflected on the gunfire and desperation that had taken place at this spot only hours before. The peaceful morning, with the warming sun on his back, might have lulled others into making a careless decision. But not Ivan. He had lived through many beautiful mornings in the high country above his family's I-5 Ranch.

He had always found a liking for sunrise and that time immediately following. He hoped to experience many more mornings such as that. Preferably with the lovely Tempest Wardle riding at his side. Of course, there was still the matter of the gruff Boon Wardle standing in his way, or hoping to, determined that his daughter would be spared from marrying a cowboy with no ranch of his own, or a lawman holding the lowest office in the territory.

Ivan had not yet succeeded in befriending the older man, but he pushed the stern image out of the way and concentrated on Tempest's charming smile. Of course, he had never been quite sure if it was truly a smile or more of a mischievous grin, but he took it the way that satisfied him most.

The question on Ivan's mind now was, would Buff so willingly abandon the boxes of gold to save his own skin? Had he really ridden on into Utah? Or had he returned, hoping to find at least something, perhaps a broken box that hadn't been carefully picked up, to reward him for his efforts? Was it possible that Ivan could be riding into the flaming muzzle of the thief's gun?

A half-hour of cautious riding, approaching the camp through the thickness of the surrounding brush, finally convinced the deputy that the place was truly abandoned. He rode in and dismounted. He had started out before first light, not wishing to show the flames of a breakfast fire. Now, it was time to rest the animal before venturing into the notch and beyond. And a fire would no longer show through the brightness of the morning. He chose his wood carefully, using only that which was desert dry, and placing his small fire beneath the heaviest shrubbery. There would be little smoke. He would settle for coffee and a bite of hardtack. As camp cooks, it was a toss-up between him and Rory over who was the worst. They had often settled for either badly burned fare or cold leftovers. He wasn't a fussy eater.

A bit later, with the fire extinguished and the coffee

pot stowed, he rode to the top of the notch. From there, he had a grand view of the land to the west. A rugged land. A forbidding land. A challenging land. A lonely land. A land showing alternating peaks and valleys, the green of well-watered forest, and dry, brown plains. The half that was standing on edge was compensated for by the half that lay reasonably flat, potential future cattle country. All in all, a beautiful land of promise.

The wind still blew cold, so he didn't stay long. But he was able to see where Buff had broken branches in his mad flight into the bush.

21

SHERIFF RORY JAMISON

SEVERAL SLOW, PLODDING, DIFFICULT DAYS AFTER IVAN had ridden off by himself, the group was nearing the area where Riley Billows held his claim. And just ahead was Lige Bannister's small holding. There had been no further sighting of the Ute riders.

"Should find the wagon somewhere along here, Dancer. Fella named Lige Bannister has taken up some land on the top of that round knoll just ahead. Not much of a man, but he somehow dragged it up that hill he lives on with just the one saddle horse and himself doing the dragging. Most work he's done in years, I suspect. Said he intended to bring it back down. He didn't want to be connected to the theft or the murders. If we find it, we can put the team back to their proper work and have an easier time of it with the wagon carrying the boxes.

"I talked to him on my way out. Said he would give up on keeping the wagon. I'm not sure the man has ever done what he says he'll do, but if he still has the wagon hidden away somewhere, we can scare the information out of him."

After scouting around the base of the hillside Lige lived on, looking behind aspen groves and rocky outcrops, finding neither wagon nor wheel marks, they decided the man had again failed to do what he had promised.

Hoping to ease the remainder of the trip for both men and horses, they unloaded the boxes and put up a temporary rope corral for the animals. Rory worried about leaving just My Way and Dancer with the prisoners, but it wouldn't do to send one of them after the wagon. Lige was apt to start shooting as soon as he saw an Indian approaching.

Finally, after cautioning the prisoners again, Rory climbed onto one of the big horses and, leading the other one, rode up the hill.

Nearing the top, he held his carbine in his right hand and hollered, "Lige. Sheriff Jamison here. Come out where I can see you."

"I ain't want'n to see you nor anyone else. Jest you turn around and ride right back down to where you can be on your way. And I don't care where that is. You go anywhere you want. Jest don't be mak'n no more trouble fer me."

"I'll make trouble for you, you old blister. I'll trouble you right into town and stand you before the judge for stealing a wagon."

"I didn't no way steal no wagon. I jest have 'er here for safe keeping. Wasn't I jest bout to take 'er back down so' you could find it? Well, wasn't I?

"Lige, I was tired of your talk before you even opened your mouth. Now come out here and tell me where you've stowed the wagon. Then you can go hide back in your squalid cabin."

Lige eased sideways from the shelter he called his barn and pointed off to the south.

"Right over there. Big grove of trees. You can follow the wheel ruts."

"No. I'll follow you. And if you lift that rifle, I'll follow you to your grave. Now walk."

At the wagon, Rory said, "You lay that rifle in the wagon and step back. I'll not have you holding a weapon while I'm harnessing the team or driving out of this bush."

Having admitted defeat, Lige laid the offending weapon down, gently, as if it were his one prized possession. Rory dug the harness out of the wagon box and soon had the team in place. With some difficulty, he managed to turn the rig and get it clear of the bush. Just before the horses were to make their first downhill step, he shouted to Lige, "You'll find your rifle down below. The walk down will do you good."

MY WAY HAD BUILT A FIRE. Dancer had dug through the remaining food pannier. Looking with some dismay at the little that remained, as he pulled the wagon up beside the fire, Rory said, "Should have shot that buck we saw yesterday."

The men fed on what little food Dancer had to work with and then remounted their rested horses. With the treasure boxes loaded into the wagon, the extra man now had his choice of riding animals. Or he could ride a mule if he wished. Instead, he chose to ride the tailgate of the wagon, with his legs dangling behind, his seat cushioned by two folded saddle blankets.

If anyone had a sure shot at a buck or an upland elk, they were determined to take it, although it was but a single day's ride to the stage station.

DEPUTY SHERIFF IVAN IVANOV

EVER CAUTIOUS, EVEN THOUGH HE FELT THE FOOLISHNESS of his thoughts, Ivan approached the broken trail Buff had left behind in his frantic bid for escape. There was no doubt that both Buff and his horse had been hurting, but as so often happens, in the midst of uncontrollable fear, they had charged into the brush, leaving a trail Ivan could follow without actually entering into the brush himself. There was no need for him to copy Buff's moves or inflicting the damage to himself or the horse that Buff had.

Following the easier trail, Ivan rode downhill, never taking his eyes off the winding, careless trail Buff had left behind him. Nearing the bottom of the grade, Buff had pointed his gelding back onto the more open way. Even that definition of the trail left much unsaid though. It was true there was no brush, for brush can't grow on rock. But the trail was, in truth, a gathering of rock, both large and small, that had tumbled down from the upper levels over the years. Perhaps over the centuries. Ivan was forced to move ahead slowly or risk an injured horse as he picked his way through the maze. To have an injured or dead horse would put an end to his chase.

There was little to spot on the rocky incline. Nothing more than an occasional shoe scratch on the softer rock or a handful of pebbles thrust aside—in the form of a fan by a moving horse—showing the direction of Buff's travel. With no reason to leave the rocky trail and with every other choice presenting even more difficulties, Ivan moved onward, westward.

About every quarter-hour, he pulled up on a higher point to study the land ahead. Everywhere he looked was rough country. The rugged beauty of the landscape was bordered by the treed mountains to the north and the grey, brownish plains to the south and west. And to his right, below the northern mountains, a range of fluted, folded rocks, forming almost a fence against travel in that direction.

He followed the fluted hills for several hours and missed Buff's turn-off. He hadn't concerned himself when he didn't see a sign for a mile or two, but when he felt he had ridden five miles with no sign, he turned back. There was no turning into the wall of hills. Buff had to have turned to the south. Ivan rode slowly, carefully. When he saw a sign, it wasn't a scratch on the rock, it was a pair of hoofmarks in the sandy mud on the side of a tiny, slow-moving stream.

Ivan had lost more than a full day in taking up the trail, after riding up to Tug Granger's cabin to get My Way and the others. It was possible that Buff had gone to camp beside this stream during that time. Ivan had seen no better option. And it was late in a long day of following and searching. Wearily, he stepped to the ground and reached for his bedroll. The day ahead would go easier for a night's sleep.

23

SHERIFF RORY JAMISON

SOMEWHAT RELAXING AS THE COUNTRY OPENED BEFORE them, they were looking forward to buying a feeding at the stage station, just a few hours down the trail. When they saw a rising cloud of dust in the east a couple of miles away, Rory called over to My Way, "You see that dust? What do you make of it?"

"Men riding. Move this way. No cattle. Riders. Many riders. Much dust."

"We'll keep our eyes open."

My Way saw no purpose in answering the obvious comment.

Dancer, who had been driving the wagon, asked, "You want me to stop or hold steady?"

"We'll hold steady until we see what's going on but be prepared. It's too late in this game to have trouble now."

To be prepared meant having a firearm ready to hand. Because she needed both hands to drive the team, Dancer had her Winchester lying across her lap. By dropping the leathers, she could have it in play in a flash of time. Rory wasn't concerned about My Way. He had never known a moment when the Blackfoot wasn't prepared. Not trusting the man sitting on the tailgate of the wagon and concerned about what would confront them in a matter of minutes, Rory said, "You there on the wagon. Get off and choose a horse. I'll not have you near Dancer if trouble erupts."

~

WITHIN TEN MINUTES, visible forms began to show through the rising dust. Horsemen, for sure. They were still too far away for positive numbering, but Rory thought he could count six. There could be more following behind. It was too many, and they were riding too fast to be casual travelers. Rory hollered, "Could be trouble. Pull up now, Dancer. The rest of you men bunch up. Be ready to drop off your mounts and take shelter. Hold your position, My Way. If any of our prisoners break for the bush, shoot him."

Gathered in a tight knot beside and behind the wagon, they waited. As the oncoming riders came closer, they pulled up in a bunch. Now Rory could see clearly. There were, indeed, six in all. Tough, competent-looking men. All except for the slim-faced man in the center. He rode as if he was untouchable, with no need of lifting a firearm. There was not a smile or a wave of a hat by way of a greeting among them.

The two groups sat in relative silence while the dust overtook them all and then slowly dissipated. Rory became impatient and rode forward. Like My Way and Dancer, the approaching riders held their rifles ready, lying across their saddles.

"Sheriff Rory Jamison here, men. Deputies My Way

and Dancer. And some prisoners. On official business. Clear off and give us the road."

The slim-faced man in the center-front—a smaller man than most of those beside and behind him, who must have been leading through assigned authority or by financial power since he clearly had no physical or facial strength that would call good men to follow him—answered, "I recognize the wagon and team. We'll take those from you now. And the boxes. That's stolen property. We've come to reclaim it. Return it to its rightful owners. I don't believe your claim to being sheriff. I suspect you're the thieves. You and the Indians. Renegades, like as not.

"You'll lay down your weapons and surrender to us now or be shot out of your saddles. And just in case you think we won't shoot, know this, the squaw will be the first to feel lead."

Dancer started it. Referring to her as a squaw had been a mistake, and clearly, she was not in a tolerating frame of mind. Everyone in the group was weary and saddle sore, suffering from lack of sleep and barely suffi- cient food. The miles had been long and rough. They were all anxious for an end to the venture, even if that end, for some of them, would mean prison. Tempers had been held so far. But even a good man, or woman, has a trigger point.

Barely a split second after the derogatory name struck Dancer's ears, the slim-faced man was dead, sliding off his saddle, as if in slow motion, with Dancer's bullet buried deep in the center of his thin chest.

The shock of her actions was total. But the fiddler had struck the starting notes of the tune, and there was no stopping the music anymore. Rory, following Dancer's move, started shooting just soon enough to make the difference. The shock of losing their leader seemed to handicap the others for a breath or two.

In Dancer's way of thinking, since she had triggered once, she might just as well continue.

Rory swung his rifle to his left hand and reached for his Colt .44. His first shot took the hat off the man who had been riding next to the now-dead speaker. As the terrified man was diving from his saddle, Rory was putting the next five shots into the ground beneath the horses. In a steady roll of thunder, he emptied the weapon into the ground under the horses' feet. It wasn't the first time he had done such as that.

Coming to hate the violence and foolish deaths in the law-keeping business, he had, over the past couple of years, attempted to find a better way. One of those ways was to unseat his adversaries. Shooting from the ground, lying on their backs, the men were less risk to themselves and Rory both.

He had found that horses didn't like lead scattering dust and pebbles around their feet, and riders stood little chance of scoring a hit when they were hanging from the leather on a bucking, lurching animal. If the action had its intended outcome, there would be fewer bodies to bury.

My Way kept his eyes on the prisoners who had, to a man, dropped from their saddles and were literally diving under the questionable shelter of the wagon.

It was swiftly obvious that the attacking bunch had not been expecting resistance. Or, at least, not imme-diate resistance. Perhaps they had expected talk, or even argument. They received lead instead. They had yet to bring their weapons into usable positions. The quickness of Dancer's actions and the follow-up from Rory meant that the couple of returned shots, with the riders trying desperately to gain control of their sidestepping mounts, had no possibility of coming anywhere close to Rory's group.

Three riders had landed on the ground when their horses rose on their hind feet while turning to escape the stinging pebbles that had been thrashing their legs.

My Way's first shot took a man from his saddle, not dead, but hurting, before one of the still mounted attackers threw down his gun and held his hands high. Into the thunder of exploding powder, the wounded man could be heard to holler, "No more. I quit."

As if echoing the first speaker's thoughts, the remaining four men repeated the refrain, holding their hands high—from whatever position they held, seated on their saddles, or sitting on the ground after being thrown from their horses.

There would only be the one man to bury, a confirmation, if any was needed, that men mounted on terrified, thrashing horses were both difficult targets and unlikely shooters.

While the melee was settling down, both Rory and Dancer lifted their fifteen-shot carbines and held them ready. With his charges safely cowering under the wagon, My Way rode forward with his own carbine aimed at the dismounted riders. Slowly, menacingly, he rode around the group, taking their faces to memory. He drove off the loose horses as he made the circuit.

Dancer held her position, with the reins grasped firmly in her left hand and her carbine resting across one knee, raised high by placing her foot on the dashboard, but unerringly pointed at the attackers.

Rory shouted, "Now, enough of that. Throw your weapons aside and tell me who you are and what you thought you were doing, pulling a stunt like that."

The demand was met with silence while the four on the ground glanced at one another and then down at the grass.

"I'm going to know sooner or later. You might just as well speak up."

It was Irv, one of the men captured days earlier, who spoke.

"I know who that skinny runt is. Or was, anyway. I know what he claimed for himself and what he and these others really are too."

Rory waited impatiently, but the man said no more. Finally, like a father trying to get information from a disobedient child, he said, "Tell me what you know. We need to get back to traveling."

Meaning the thin man who had spoken earlier, the prisoner said, "Called himself Patrick Quail. I doubt that's his real name. Says he's a businessman. Runs a small supply joint up near Idaho Falls. Not right in the town. More to the north, where no one can keep a close eye on him. Don't know a single person that would trust him."

Rory replied, "Alright. And you said you know what it is this bunch really do."

"They don't want it known about, up at the Falls, but come nighttime, they can be found holding secret meetings. Pride themselves as vigilantes. Ride in the dark. They've hung a few men. Not that they deserved the hangings or had done any thievery themselves. They were hung to cover the thievery this bunch did. There's little enough law in the gold findings, but this bunch are worse than any thieves that ever worked the hills. Shoot them all is my thought. Give me a gun and I'll do it myself. And enjoy the doing."

Rory responded, "Well, I don't think we'll be going in

that direction. You all sit tight now. We've got two batches of thieves and murderers, and I'm not sure which of you is the worst. But I can tell you I'm out of patience. Any trouble from any of you will be met with lead. And don't you doubt it."

24

SHERIFF RORY JAMISON

THE WOUNDED MAN WAS PATCHED UP AS BEST AS THE situation would allow. The dead man was buried in a small gully with boulders rolled over him. My Way had suggested, "Maybe leave for birds eat."

Rory had grinned at the man, shaken his head in a negative response, and pointed out another couple of rocks for the prisoners to roll onto the grave.

With the bunch back underway, Rory and My Way rode to the rear. The mounted prisoners had been given a stern warning that there would be no second chances for anyone kicking a horse into a run or trying to duck into the little bit of brush cover left in the arid land they had ridden into.

As they were approaching the stage stop, Rory rode ahead to prepare the keeper and cook. Both men knew Rory from earlier times, although they hadn't been there long. But Rory was a riding man. A wandering man. After the murders and burning of the station the year before, Rory wanted to know who was running the show for the stage company. It wasn't a long ride from the

Fort, so he had traveled up. He had come to the same conclusion Ivan had come to; the men might have more on their minds than simply seeing to the stage horses and feeding passengers. They would bear watching. But for the moment, they were needed.

"Afternoon, fellas. We're hoping you've got supplies enough to feed a bunch like this. Nine prisoners. Two guards and a lady."

"Got the grub. Take a while to put 'er all together though. Not room-enough inside. Have to squat down in the yard."

"That's all fine. If you don't mind, I'll send the lady in. Wouldn't hurt for her to take her ease a bit. You might have a cup of coffee for her too. You'll be paid by the county for all you do. And receive my thanks along with it."

The men were dismounted and allowed to unsaddle and water their mounts. One by one, under Rory's careful watch, they attended to their private needs and to wash the dust off their hands and faces.

Lined up along the corral fence, they looked like a hard lot. To ease the difficulty of guarding, Rory tied one hand of each man to a corral pole with the threat of serious repercussions if they untied it.

When chow was called, the men moved inside four at a time while the others waited. They had to share coffee time as well, due to the lack of mugs. Rory had refused to allow them access to their own saddle bags, which had yet to be searched, so their mugs remained unavailable to them.

By the time everyone had taken their evening meal, the sun was setting. Rory came from the stage station with his daybook and a pencil in his hand.

"Alright, men. We've gone long enough without

knowing who you are. Now I want names. Real names. Or at least the ones you're best known as. Starting there on the left, speak up."

When the names were all listed and the two groups separated in Rory's book, he ushered the men into the barn. Two men climbed to the loft to throw down enough fresh hay to make reasonable beds for the night. There was some whining about the accommodations, but it didn't change anyone's mind. There were two doors in the barn, the big one at the front and a smaller walk-in opening at the rear. Rory closed the front doors and settled down with his back to where the two swinging doors met. That left the rear door unguarded, except that My Way would be wherever he figured best from his point of view. The men studied the menacing stare from the semi-tame Indian and decided not to chance a sudden break for freedom.

Dancer was given a well-put-together cot in a private room inside. She lay there with her Winchester snuggled close. No one was about to bother the Indian woman or attempt to escape custody that night.

MORNING CAME with the crowing of a rooster. Not knowing the cook kept chickens, the lawmen were awakened with a start. It was time anyway. They took turns washing up and then opened the barn doors. The men filed out, grumpy and unhappy, but they were all there. Tag, who was beginning to feel a bit better from his gunshot wound, was perhaps the happiest to see the morning. Rory figured the young man had finally figured out that life was worth the effort. A date with the state court still faced him, but today, the sun shone brightly, and the coffee was hot. Some side meat and two eggs each set the day up just fine.

When everyone was saddled up and ready, Rory surprised everyone by announcing, "Men, we're not going to the Fort or Stevensville. We're going to Cheyenne. Lead out, Dancer."

A MORNING's ride at the pace of the working team showed everyone Cheyenne on the near horizon. The blast of a steam whistle, accompanied by the roiling black-grey coal smoke from the engine, welcomed them.

Calling a halt, appearing to be working a plan known only to himself, Rory said, "Bunch up, everyone. We're not riding into town spread out like a startled cattle herd. You're to follow the wagon, staying tight between My Way and myself. You know what will happen if you venture off by yourselves.

"I'm telling you this to keep you safe. So, nothing unwelcome happens to you, you know. We're here to protect you. Cheyenne has taken a fierce dislike to men of your sorts. There's' no telling what might happen if you were to fall into their hands. So, stay close and do what you're told."

Dancer, retaking her seat on the wagon, set out for town, figuring the riders could catch up. They did, and the lawmen escorted them directly to the station, gathering the stares of folks on the streets and the attention of one Cheyenne deputy marshal. Rory called the man over and explained the situation. Without a word, the deputy rode off and was soon back with an additional city deputy and one federal deputy marshal. They took their positions and bunched the prisoners even more closely. With the extra escort, they were soon at the depot.

Rory, introducing himself to the conductor as the county sheriff and an unofficial federal deputy marshal, which was a surprise to the deputy who had joined him earlier, commandeered a private car for the prisoners, and space in a cattle car for the horses on a train that would be Denver bound within the hour. The heavy boxes were taken aboard the passenger car, carried by the prisoners, and the doors were closed. The sheriff's deputies were going back to their duties, but the federal man was joining the ride to Denver.

The last thing the sheriff did before the conductor hollered for everyone to board was send a rush telegram to Denver requesting a deputy marshal's escort from the station to the lock-up.

25

DEPUTY SHERIFF IVAN IVANOV

Ivan woke to a beautiful, if chilly, morning. The little water course flowed with just enough water to fill a hollow in the sandy bottom that Ivan dug out with his hands. He moved upstream a few feet to take his morning wash while the gelding dipped his muzzle into the deeper water of the dug-out.

The stream water made good coffee, so Ivan enjoyed another cup while he sauntered slowly around the area, looking for any sign of travel. He ended up on the ridge of the highest close-by peak. From there, he could see to the south and west. The north was blocked by the wavy, fluted rock wall, and to the east was heavier forest.

Studying the land before him and choosing a likely route for Buff to have followed, he thought he saw a way. It wouldn't be an easy way, but so far, what he had seen of the country offered no easy ways. That didn't change his opinion that it was a beautiful and promising country. It would be seen as promising by cattlemen and sheepmen, where the green grass covered the valleys and the plateaus, and by miners or prospectors, where the rock dominated. Altogether, a land of potential wealth.

Assuming that Buff would have been most interested in making miles, he would have taken that easier way. Ivan packed up his camp gear, saddled the rested gelding, and set out, still looking for tracks. He saw nothing until the sun told him the day was nearing noon. And then it wasn't really a track he saw, it was more of a series of tracks, forming scuff marks, where a horse had been led to a short but steep bank that sloped down to a pool of water, surrounded by a few feet of sand. It was obvious the animal had balked at the challenge, leaving behind an easily noticeable scattering of signs—in places, scuffing out the earlier sign of deer, wolf, and other thirsty animals.

Hoping for an easier water source, Ivan slowed, taking in the image of a thirsty but scrambling horse, and moved on, satisfied he was headed right.

The rock wall forced a turn to the south-west. Ivan followed along for several miles, seeing no sign of other travel. Buff was either better at hiding his trail than he had first shown, or he was now taking the time to find a hidden way, whereas before, he was intent only on covering miles.

It was impossible to know for sure, but Ivan had the feeling that the elevation of the land had dropped off a bit. It may have been the quicker, easier step the gelding was showing, or perhaps Ivan's breathing had eased a bit.

It was all still high country though. The rocky terrain didn't allow for enough growth to make firm judgement from, but it was possible the bit of growth that existed was a bit greener. A bit lusher and more spread out.

The trail led through another rock opening on a slight downward grade. Cautiously easing around the bend at the bottom, Ivan's gelding stepped out onto what appeared to be a vast mountain-ringed plain. Not level, but certainly more level than where he had been riding. Here, the grass was green and abundant. The sparse growth of the rockier areas had been put behind him. Then, to Ivan's amazement, he saw smoke. Just a lazy curl of smoke that rose from what appeared to be a hollow in the plain, but from the distance was hard to judge.

With the riding easier, he nudged the gelding into a steady lope, pointing directly to the smoke. It was possible that Buff, feeling he had made a safe getaway, was taking the time for a noon feeding. It hadn't been in the man's character or actions in the past though. But any smoke up here was worth checking out. Cautiously.

The gelding covered the distance to the hollow Ivan was aiming for in less than one-half hour. With the freedom and safety of distance, he rode without fear. As he neared the target area, his concerns for ambush increased. But so did his vigilance. With the lip of the hollow just ahead, he slowed to a walk, holding a tight rein on the horse, lest Buff awaited, perhaps belly to the ground, in the long grass on the downward slope. He turned a bit to the right, watching for any movement, a sun glint off metal, any noise. There was nothing. It was as if he was alone in the universe.

He doubled back to his starting point and turned directly toward the lip of the hollow. The smoke continued, interrupted only by the vagaries of the slight breeze. Trying to see everywhere at once, Ivan stepped the horse to the top of the hollow and stopped.

It wasn't a campfire he had been looking at. The smoke was coming from a bent and crooked metal chimney that protruded through the sod roof of a small cabin. Not far from the cabin was a shed that could pass for a barn, if the user were desperate enough. A creek wandered close by the yard. There was a fenced-in garden area, just coming into green with the early spring warming.

He heard faint voices from the cabin. One sounded like a woman answering a comment that was too low to make out. That voice had for sure been a man. He heard a cowbell but didn't take his eyes from the cabin long enough to locate the animal. Beside the small shed was a pole corral holding two horses. He recognized one.

He had no explanation for the people's presence, except that offered by Tug Granger, as to why he was settled on the much higher plateau, "I first came up here looking for grass and solitude. I found both. I'm a contented man."

Ivan had seen no cattle, although the high plain would hold hundreds, if not thousands.

The first step Ivan's gelding took, as it came over the lip of the hollow and began the short walk to the cabin, brought a fierce barking from a black and white mongrel dog, who charged out of its hiding place under the door stoop. That brought the settler to his door, holding a shotgun and shading his eyes from the glare of the noon time sun. At a word from the settler, the dog hushed and sat beside his master. The animal never took his eyes from Ivan and the horse, greeting them with a low growl and a bit of a snarl on its lips.

Wishing to get off to a good start with these folks, Ivan waved his hat and said, "Ivan Ivanov here, sir. Deputy County Sheriff from over on the east side. May I come down?"

"Come. The dog's alright. Won't bite unless provoked. I might though, if you ain't who you say you are."

Ivan rode to within fifty feet and pulled up. He would remain in the saddle until invited to 'step down and set.' The invitation was soon received.

Ivan stepped to the ground, laid the reins across the gelding's neck so he could graze on the abundant grass, and whipped dust from his pants and shirt with his hat. He replaced the hat and stepped forward.

"Some surprised to see you up here, sir. I've seen only three others, and two of those were pretty close to town, on the other side. Nice place you got here. But lonely if you were looking for someone to play checkers with on a rainy evening."

Ivan had a habit of smiling with his words, so there was no offense taken. Instead, the settler said, "Wife's a better player than me. I'm learning though. Of course, she's been known to tip the board a time or two if she's in danger of losing."

"I never did any such a thing. Don't you be believing this old man. He'll tell you most anything to keep you here long enough for a visit. Come in now, sir. I've just put the pot on."

"That's a welcome invite, ma'am. In fact, it was your smoke that drew me here."

Still holding the shotgun, now in his left hand, while he held his right out in welcome, the man said, "I'm Hubert Kingsley. Wife's Tilly. Good to have company. Come in. Your animal will be alright there. Water by the corral. He'll find it if needs be."

The two men shook hands, with Kingsley giving both Ivan and his riding animal a thorough looking over. "Welcome, deputy. I'll call you that till something tells me you're not who you say you are. Dogs accepted you. Never known him to be wrong about a man. Now, come in the house. We were just about to sit down to lunch. By this time, Tilly will have dropped more of whatever she was cooking up into the pot. It'll be ready soon as you wash up. Basin and towel by the door."

Kingsley stood by while Ivan washed and then pulled the door open, ushering Ivan in ahead of him. He immediately closed the door with a bit of a thud.

"Fearful number of flies, up here, in the high country. I'm told there's fewer flies up higher, but this is as far as we wanted to climb. Tilly has a determined dislike toward the offending creatures, so we keep the door closed whenever possible. I've tried to convince her that they're just one more of God's created wonders. Tilly, though, she says they didn't exist until after Eve ate that apple. It ain't rightly explained in the Book, so who's to say who's right?

"Now Ivan, let's take a seat at the table while I tell you two things I'm pretty sure of. The one is, I'm pretty sure you're who you say you are. The other is I'm pretty sure I know why you're here."

He paused long enough as he studied their guest that Ivan became uncomfortable.

"Well, then, Mr. Kingsley, let me return that with two things I'm also pretty sure of. One would be that you had an unwelcome guest yesterday. The second would be that he held a gun on you while he moved his saddle onto one of your horses, leaving his own in what he called a trade. I recognize his animal out there, along with another that must be yours. Am I anywhere near guessing correctly, Mr. Kingsley?"

With more excitement than Ivan had heard from him up to that point, Kingsley said, "Tilly, she was at the stove, just like she is now. Only yesterday was bread day. Organized, my woman is. Day for everything. Can't seem to change. Doesn't want to, far as I can tell. But no matter.

"Anyway, I was in the garden hoeing weeds, which grow up here as if it was their last chance to amount to something. My rifle was leaning against the fence not ten feet away. But that was just twenty feet too far. Fella on a half-dead horse come over the brow of that hill over there, not too far from where you came yourself. Still a whopping on the horse with his hat, even that close to the house. You'd a thought Ol' Scratch himself was sett'n on his tail feathers, whispering threats in his ear.

"Well, he drove that animal right to the corral and leaped to the ground. More agile than I would have thought for a big man like he was. He immediately pulled the cinch loose and lifted his entire rig, saddle, bedroll, and all, onto the top rail. Takes some strength to do such as that. Gave his horse a slap on the neck and waved him away. The poor beast didn't go further than the water tank. Dipped his muzzle and held it down for so long I thought he'd drown himself.

"I wasn't no way concerned about that, but I got mighty concerned when the fella opened the corral gate. Didn't take no schooling to know what he had in mind. I ran for my rifle, shouting a warning. He answered with a pistol shot over my head and another into the door frame of the house. It was a warning to stay low and keep quiet. I did. And so did Tilly.

26

SHERIFF RORY JAMISON

Sheriff Rory was sitting in Donavan Gaines' office at the Federal Marshal's Denver Headquarters, prepared to give a detailed report of the search and capture. My Way and Dancer had made plans of their own. Rory, with a knowing grin, had slipped a few dollars to Dancer as pay for their assistance. He knew from before that My Way had little use for money, but like most women, Dancer had carefully eyed the many stores as she drove the hired freight wagon from the railway depot to the downtown livery. She would find use for the money, even if her husband didn't. Rory encouraged them to enjoy the city and told them to be careful. Not everyone on the streets would welcome an Indian couple in their midst. They were to meet him at the hotel in time for dinner. My Way would remember which hotel they had stayed in last time.

Deputy Marshal Gaines and Rory had become some-times associates, very nearly enemies, and on a rare occasion or two, friends.

The telling of how My Way and Dancer had assisted

in the arrests and transport of the prisoners brought a smile from Donavan. The head marshal laughed right out loud when he was told that the Indian couple were deputized and put in charge during much of the long trail.

"You have been noted for using some unconventional methods and even, on occasion, unconventional people, sheriff. And I had heard a bit about My Way from some work he did with Deputy Ivanov a while ago. But to bring a lady such as you tell me this Dancer is into the dangerous picture you have described to me this morning is a whole new thing.

"But I must say that they seem to have carried a considerable share of the load on this venture. So please thank them both for me. I would appreciate if they would stay in the city until we sort out the story and try to figure out which of those prisoners did what. We will very likely need all of your testimonies, including Ivan's, of course, when he becomes available.

"When we need My Way's testimony, if we can make this thing move forward quickly enough, I'll send word down to the hotel, all the time praying the court will take the testimony of an Indian. And an Indian woman. They speak good English, you say?"

"They do. Dancer especially."

The conversation seemed to lag a bit, as if Donavan was thinking up his next comment. Finally, he said, "Rory. There are some who have doubted your methods, but I no longer do. And I know of no one who would question your efforts or your successes. So that's all to the good. But now you have brought us a dog's breakfast of criminal activity. It may take half the lawyers in the country to try to figure it all out. Now, let's try to sort out who it is that we have in the lockup."

Rory interrupted with, "Before we move into that question, let's agree that we don't need any lawyers messing with this situation until we're comfortable with it all ourselves. I don't want any book learners telling me what I can and can't do. And I don't want anyone telling me when or how I get information from these birds. And in any case, there have been no charges laid yet. There is nothing for a lawyer to do until there are charges to defend.

"I still don't have a clear understanding of how they got that wagonload of gold out of Idaho Falls and all the way up past the Fort without anyone giving chase. The frightening thing is that, except for the two murders, which brought on unwanted attention, they might have made it all the way into the hills and disappeared. Into Utah or wherever they wanted to go. It was the murders that brought attention down upon them.

"And then to have the Idaho Falls' vigilantes arrive on the scene is just too much. How did they know about the heist? Or is it all really one larger gang rather than the two they claimed to be? There was certainly no time on the trail to question anyone or sort all of that out."

Donavan hesitated, but finally nodded his head.

"Alright. Back to the question. Who are those men sitting behind bars, and what is each one accused of doing?"

Rory waited to be sure Donavan had voiced his thoughts before he said, "This was mostly Ivan's arrest and chase, Donavan. And a good job was done of it too. I think the steam kind of went out of each group of men when their leaders were shot and killed, although Ivan wasn't with us when the vigilantes were first confronted.

"Ivan laid a brilliant trap for Buff. And although it

didn't work out quite as he wished, that's mostly my own fault. But I'll tell you about that sometime. Maybe.

"The other four settled down pretty quickly. We had no trouble with them after that. They were exhausted from walking and driving overloaded animals, from lack of sleep and barely edible food. They even sat up and took notice of my cooking. And that's saying something. I'm not suggesting they were happy about being caught. But I am saying they knew they couldn't go on the way they were. That string had played out.

"Later, when the bunch of vigilantes rode up on us, we were ready for them. Judging by their actions, I suspect they were placing too much confidence in their reputations or their past successes. The word that came later—from Irv, one of the gold thieves—was that the leader, known as Patrick Quail, had been leading the gang of thieves and murderers, masquerading as civic-minded citizens. In fact, they were vigilantes, taking out known or suspected thieves, but doing it in the secrecy or night, and in whatever way they thought would bring profit to themselves."

Rory held off when Donavan picked up the cooling pot, refilled his coffee mug, and then reached to fill the sheriff's. Donavan's only comment was, "It's like one of those tangles of hibernating snakes. Hard to tell what tail belongs to which head."

"You're correct on that. So, you can see why we need help. Ivan and me. Add to that, the other reason we're here, Donavan, is that the thefts and vigilante matters took place outside our jurisdiction. Now, we've done work before where we didn't have true authority, but that was either along with the marshal's service or in unsettled areas where we were working under the permission of the state government. Up in gold country, the growth in population is outreaching the law, but we do what we can. But in something as clear cut as this, our Judge, Anders P. Yokam, would, almost assuredly, refuse to hear the case, except for the two murders. But how do we separate those murders from all the rest of what went on?"

Rory took a slurp of the lukewarm coffee and shuddered. He had never found coffee at that temperature to be to his liking. He pushed the cup aside and continued.

"To help in sorting it all out, Ivan learned a bit during the chase and arrests of the gold thieves, and I added a bit on the long drive home."

Reaching into his vest pocket, he fingered his little book. Inside the book was a folded piece of paper. He drew it out and looked back up at Donavan.

"I've got Ivan's list of the names of those he was initially following. It may help some. Names didn't matter much in the high-up and far away. I knew they were thieves and murderers. That's enough for an arrest. I couldn't separate them for private questioning without inviting more trouble than we could handle. We were too short of guards for that. So, I didn't bother questioning them further. Where they were from or what their daddies called them didn't seem important right at the time.

"We do know that the leader of the gold thieves was known as Buff. No one seemed to know another name for him. Everyone just called him Buff. We can be sure that wasn't the given name his mother would have known him by. He adopted it when he was buffalo hunting. Or so the men told me.

"There's no telling what his family name was. Don't much matter now anyway, unless Ivan captures him and brings him back down. We let the gang believe that Buff was dead. We might get further with the investigation if we leave it like that.

"The man carrying the bullet wound in his arm and shoulder is Tag Miller. Same name as the pastor up at the Fort carries, but I doubt as how there's any relationship.

"Another was called Vern. I heard the men calling him that, although I don't know his last name.

"The fourth fella answered to Rudolph, or Rudy.

"Then there was Irv. He didn't say ten words the whole time. Don't know what information he might have to add to the investigation.

"According to Tag, who, we have to remember, was trying to save his own skin, it was Vern and Rudy who did the killing of the original guards. Vern is a big, rough-looking man, the kind of man you wouldn't be surprised to hear lived outside the law.

"Rudy, on the other hand, is shorter, thinner. Kind of a pinched face and small, almost delicate hands. Doubt he's ever had to shave. Looks more like a barroom singer than a killer. Have to be careful with these types. They can fool a man, catch him off guard. You get to trusting a man like that, you could end up dead.

"Buff was the only other one who would have known the truth of who the killers were, and he isn't here to answer the question.

"It's doubtful if Vern or Rudy are going to step up and confess. Probably best to just hang the bunch of them. That way, we'll know the guilty ones were punished properly."

Donavan studied the sheriff for a length of time, with a small grin forming on his lips, before he said, "That may happen if you take them back up to the Fort and try them before your own judge. But here, in the city, there's sure to be lawyers who will question that rather brief, all-encompassing, totally effective form of frontier justice."

Rory had only been half-joking about the hangings. He knew it wasn't going to happen, so he made another suggestion.

"I've been thinking on the long ride home, Donavan. This might be the perfect place to invite Block in. He's been designated as the marshal's in-house detective, examining evidence and such. This might be a perfect fit. And that would leave me free to return to the Fort and attend to my own work. I could come back down for the trials if I was needed."

Donavan tapped his teeth with the end on his pencil and studied Rory.

"I'll give that serious thought. You just may be on to something."

Rory stood and made motions to indicate that his part of the meeting was over. As a parting note, he said, "I'll be claiming the horses and gear and any rewards offered and collected—for the county working fund. I'll have the livery hold the animals until after the trial."

Knowing the sheriff had accumulated considerable funds in the county treasury using exactly that approach, a resigned 'fine' was Donavan's last word for the afternoon meeting.

27

SHERIFF RORY JAMISON

THE HOTEL HAD BEEN SOMEWHAT RELUCTANT TO welcome My Way and Dancer as staying guests, but with Rory's help, they worked it out. Meeting for breakfast early the following morning, Rory asked, "What's for you two now? Do you wish to ride back up to the Fort with me, or are you heading directly out to the Ute villages?"

Dancer answered, "My brother said that my father lives yet. I would like to see him. I think it would be best if we did that now."

"Your testimony may be wanted for the trial."

"We will come to see you before we ride back up to our Blackfoot village. You can tell us then if we are needed."

Agreeing on that, they went their separate ways, with Rory making a quick visit to the county office before venturing out on the three-day ride home. He considered the use of a rail car for the horse and the cushioned passenger car for himself, putting him in Cheyenne, just a single, long day's ride from home. But he needed to see to some things in Stevensville on the way. A visit to the

Double J Ranch would be in order as well. Even though he no longer held an owner's share in the ranch, it was still run by his family, and it had been too long since he had sat at their big kitchen table.

IT WAS ALSO TOO long since he last shared a friendly cup of coffee with Anthony Clare, the sheriff in the adjoining county to the one that had voted Rory into office. Anthony hung his hat in a small roadside village that might someday grow into a town. Or it might die out. Or be swallowed up as the big city encroached on the area. When the townsfolk had discussed it in times past, Anthony hadn't seemed to care one way or another. He had a small office with a single iron-barred cell that was seldom used. He ran his own operation as he thought it should be run. The single complication in Anthony's life was the gold country. As Rory had, Anthony had deputized a couple of men to try to hold the peace and report to him if he was needed.

ANTHONY WAS a good and wise lawman, but perhaps a bit more casual than Rory. He wouldn't look past any actual lawbreaking, but if a criminal was simply riding through the territory, he was content to let him ride. All that had held well for him until recently.

ACROSS THE NORTH-TO-SOUTH trail and up in the hills above the village, there was a lovely series of hilltops with green, well-watered valleys between. The valleys were small, not well suited for ranching or farming. They had attracted no settlers. That changed when a group of families who had wagoned across the country looking for new homes arrived a couple of years earlier. Old country folks, familiar with just getting by and expecting little of life except struggle against authority and what they saw as their right to live as they wished and to be let alone. To them, the series of small valleys was perfect. They had taken possession, built their shacks, stayed to themselves, and come to town only for their necessities. Their few beef animals, bacon-producing hogs, milk cows, chickens, and gardens provided for them, while also putting some tradable produce into their hands.

None of that was out of the ordinary except that most settlers came one family at a time. This bunch came as a group and were determined to stay and live as a group.

Trot and Glad-Lilibet White owned and operated the small general store in Highland, which was the name finally settled on by the folks who made their homes in and around Anthony's village. The name had arisen from a good-natured discussion, with some arguing that the village would dry up and blow away within the year, so it didn't really need a name, while others laughingly suggested it would soon rival Denver in importance. When one of the cranky old timers—who was constantly whining about the elevation and how hard it was on his 'constitution' as he called his hard-pressed lungs and heart—suggested High Land, it was agreed upon, but the city clerk, a lady who kept the town meeting minutes in a school scribbler stowed in her kitchen cupboard, just to get the last word, and to show her sense of humor, reduced the two words into one and authoritatively wrote Highland in her book, and the deed was done.

The uplanders, as they had been named by the village folk, were not unfriendly, but neither did they invite interaction with others. For some, there was a language barrier, mostly with the women, who seldom left their homes and remained untaught in the ways of a new country. When a few of the men, thick in the shoulders and jaws, their arms bulging with muscles, their suspicious eyes challenging everyone they saw, ever carrying their rifles, as many men of the era did, came to town, they had the singular purpose of escorting their women to the general store. Their shopping would be done quickly and quietly, with the men standing by.

Trot didn't seem to notice anything amiss during the visits, but Glad-Lilibet certainly did. She said nothing, only remaining watchful. Glad was a lovely lady, attractive in face and form and not altogether unfamiliar with unwanted attention. She couldn't help notice that the lascivious eyes of one uplander, a man who had lost his wife some months before, never seemed to turn away from her while the shopping was being carried out. Even at that, nothing might have come to a head except, as if he had finally reached the edge of his lustful thoughts, and urgings, when he had stepped forward to pay, he had reached across the counter, touching Glad on the shoulder.

Glad yelped in fright and surprise and jumped back, out of reach. Trot took the few steps required to cross the small store, intending to come between the man and Glad. But before he could get a word out of his mouth, he found himself backed against his own counter, with a large belt knife held to his throat. Glad screamed again, this time in fear for her husband, but it had no effect on the attacker. While the other uplanders, men and women alike, watched in fear, the man twisted the knife just enough to bring on a small prick of blood. The two men stood there in silence, eyeing each other. Trot, startled that this could be happening in his own store, in their small, peaceful village, with the uplander looking as if this type of confrontation was all old hat to him, wasn't sure what his next move should be.

Sheriff Anthony walked into the store about that time and immediately took in what was happening. The door had been held open by one of the shoppers, so there was no tinkling of the bell to warn of someone entering. With quick steps, Anthony crossed the floor while he lifted his heavy Colt from its holster, flipped it so he was holding the barrel, and laid the butt with considerable force to the back of the uplander's head. The single blow was enough to lay the man on the floor, out cold. The cocking of two rifles warned Anthony. He spun on his boot toe and put a single shot into the door jamb between the two rifle-carrying men.

"Stohp", a word that was close enough to the English word that held the same meaning, came clearly from one of the older ladies. A woman of some stature in the settlement, her words were heeded. The men slowly lowered their rifles and Anthony dropped his weapon to his side. But he didn't holster it. He eyed each man and woman as they slowly started filing out of the store.

Anthony, without taking his eyes off the men whose rifles still hung from their hands, spoke to Trot.

"Trot, you relieve that fella of anything harmful he might be carrying. Then you take these cuffs off my belt, and you put them on his wrists. Do it quickly now. And the rest of you, go back to your hills. Your shopping is done for this one time. You make trouble again, and we'll go around and around."

～

WHEN SHERIFF RORY JAMISON, just two hours later, turned off the northbound trail and entered the small village, he rode right into a weeping, angry crowd in and around the front of Anthony Clare's office. He found himself staring into the muzzles of several rifles until someone recognized him and hollered for the rest to back off.

When he got closer, he dismounted and asked, "What's this all about?"

A man he had never seen before answered, "It's the sheriff. He's been shot."

Rory dropped his reins and hurried into the office. The cell door lay open, and on the floor beside his desk was the dead sheriff, Anthony Clare. Mrs. Clare was on her knees, weeping and stroking her husband's face. Several others were crowded around. Rory took a quick look and turned for the door. Outside, he asked the man who had spoken to him when he first rode up, "What's going on? When did this happen and why?"

"It was the uplanders. They'd come down to the store for some shopping. One fella, him who it was said had an eye for Glad White, grabbed her, scaring her halfway to the grave. Trot, he run to her defense, but the uplander, he pulled the biggest knife ever seen and threatened Trot to shut up. That's about when Anthony happened to walk into the store. He arrested the knife man and told the rest to go back to their hills and homes. Never did know no names for any of those folks. Never caused no trouble before. Just kept mostly to themselves, is all.

"Anthony locked the fella up here. The rest, they loaded their wagons with purchases, women and kids, and turned for their homes. It was maybe an hour later when three of them rode a storm'n in here, burst into the jailhouse, and shot Anthony. Broke the other fella outa the cell, although it seems—since there's blood enough on the cell floor—as if Anthony, he got a shot off. Them fellas, they took up their man and run back to their hills with him. But not before one of them, don't know who, he went and scooped Glad right off the street and rode away with the screaming woman laid across his horse's neck."

"Did anyone follow?"

"Took a few minutes to round up a saddled horse, but then Trot, he took out after the bunch."

"I don't know the area. Show me where they went."

Pointing, the man said, "Why sure. You just go to your left down the trail a few hundred yards, back toward the big city. You take the offside trail and keep riding. Into the hills."

"Alright. Did anyone else ride with the woman's husband?"

"No, sir. Not that I know of."

Rory found that strange, but he accepted it as fact and said, "Alright. Don't any of you follow now. I'd not want to shoot you by mistake."

Rory was in the habit of carrying his Sharp's .50 at the ready, cleaned and loaded, but with the hammer down. He only had to draw the weapon, cock it, and fire. He did the same with his multi-shot 44-40. With that armament and his two .44 Colts, he swung aboard his gelding and was immediately at a run, heading toward the trail that was pointed out to him.

The first few miles of the trail were taken at an easy

161

upward slope, leaving behind the openness of the village area and weaving into the first of a series of divisions in the trail. Rory figured these trails would lead to other settlers' small holdings. To take the wrong turn would be to waste precious time. There were hoof and wheel marks aplenty leading into all the trails, but the most recent marks in the dust indicated the runners had taken the hard left choice. Rory followed, his every sense alert for ambush. He expected to catch up to Trot first, depending on the stamina of the horse the man had commandeered. He also suspected there would be shots, shouting, or some other such noise to narrow in on. But so far, he had been riding through silence.

Accepting the clear fact that the Sharps would be of little use in the winding, forested area, he would concentrate on the use of the .44s. He had previously found that he saved a second or two if he had thought these things out. He couldn't say for sure it had ever saved his life, but he liked to be ready, and there was no harm in having simple decisions made before there was a need.

Very little time had been lost between the shooting of the sheriff and Rory's rush into the hills. With the quality horse he was riding, he could easily gain on most other animals. He had to be getting closer.

The first sound he heard was of iron-shod hooves rattling across rocky ground. Even that sound was dim, almost more of an echo as it made its way through forested country, as if it was far ahead and higher up. Then, much closer by, he heard a shot, almost the popping sound of a small caliber weapon fired at a close target and muffled by clothing or such as that. It wasn't the type of weapon most men would be carrying. But if it was one of the small pistols collectively referred to as derringers, it could easily be secreted in a woman's skirt pocket. The thought made him wonder.

That first shot was followed quickly by a man's shout, garbled by distance and poor pronunciation. There was a short pause, then another shot, this time a louder, clearer bang, and the terrified scream of a horse followed by a low, gurgling shout of alarm and, finally, a woman's scream of pain.

Rory pulled his gelding down to a walk, listening carefully for any noise on the trail, and then eased forward carefully. Within seconds, there was a shout. A man's voice hollering a single word, "Glad".

The sounds of horses higher on the trail were now clear and seemed to be moving away, as if they were leaving whatever was happening on the trail below them to be dealt with by the man who had scooped up the woman. His two accomplices had disappeared, melding into the group of other settlers.

In the rush of words coming his way from the man at the sheriff's office, Rory had the impression that the man who killed Anthony Clare and the man who grabbed the woman were one and the same person. But with the possibility that Anthony had wounded the man with his final effort, he couldn't know that for sure.

What he did know for sure was that the situation on the ground couldn't last. There were possibly only seconds remaining before someone else was shot. And not shot with a pop gun.

Trot White had quickly followed after his wife, but was he even armed? Did he have the courage to actually draw down on the perpetrator? Was he more than a simple store clerk? Or was the armed upcountry rider the one who would, sooner or later, do the inevitable?

~

WHAT RORY COULDN'T and didn't know was that although Trot had been too young to wear a uniform in the war, that didn't mean he was unfamiliar with firearms or their use. He had traveled with his family across the weary wagon miles as a teenaged young man. He had hunted to fill the stew pot, and he had stood shoulder to shoulder with his father, fighting off white raiders who had been terrorizing waggoners traveling either alone or in a small group. On that one occasion, when the powder smoke cleared away, a single raider, wounded and barely able to sit his horse, rode away. Four of his fellow thieves lay in the grass. Trot's mother had been struck once, causing serious bleeding from her upper thigh. His father and older sister were caring for the woman while Trot climbed onto the wagon seat and shouted the team into motion.

The dead men would remain lying on the grass, their life's blood nurturing the soil and the grass that brought life to so many. They would lie there unarmed. Trot couldn't see that they would need the guns where they were going. Better he should have them in the wagon. Stripping the bodies had taken only a few minutes, time enough for his mother to struggle into the back of the wagon. The memory was fresh in his mind. The captured weapons were displayed on the wall of his little supply store. All except the single Colt .45 that he now wore on his right hip.

28

SHERIFF RORY JAMISON

Rory, using his raised arm to fend off the low-hanging spring growth, brushed past a bush and around a sharp corner. He burst into an almost tragic/comic scene of fear and fight. The woman, who could only be the captured store clerk, lay on her back, half pinned to the ground in a large pod of blossoming Plains prickly pear, a high country rocky-ground plant known, not for its height, but more for its spread, and its yellow flowers. And, of course, for the sharp spines that protected it and allowed it to live its solitary life.

The woman was screaming in pain, with the pear covering virtually every surface she lay on. Each squirming move she made in her desperate attempt to escape the pear was making things worse for her.

Foolishly, a man, no doubt her husband, had turned his back on the uplander who was lying on the ground where he had been thrown from his horse. His every intent was the rescue of his wife. But that could change abruptly, with tragic consequences, if the uplander managed to regain his consciousness, turn over, and get his hand on a weapon.

From his position atop the gelding, Rory could see the uplander was bleeding, but the wound was barely visible. And judging from a very quick glance, it didn't appear to be serious. Perhaps it was a minor injury inflicted by the small weapon that had created the popping sound he had heard only seconds before. The derringer was well able to kill at close range, but the shot would have to hit a vital spot, and that was not easy or likely with a running horse and frightened, frantic people riding for their lives.

Leaving the others to their own devices, Rory stepped down from the saddle and went to the downed uplander. He was lying on his face while still gripping his rifle. The sporadic bending and stretching of one leg, as if digging for leverage with one boot toe, told the sheriff that the man still lived, although obviously in pain. He bent and grasped the rifle. The man's grip firmed up, and a very brief tug of war was required before the weapon slipped firmly into Rory's hand. He threw the rifle aside and turned the man onto his back. Clearly, he was hurt much more seriously than Rory had at first suspected. Whatever weapon had caused that much damage had carried a shell powerful enough to do serious work. And the shooter had found his, or, perhaps, he thought, her mark. The man's jaw was half blown off.

Lying on his face he had been able to at least breathe. On his back, he was choking on his own blood. There was also, visible beneath the half-torn-off shirt, an unseen, vivid streak of blown-away flesh across the man's rib cage caused by the first shot. No one would pay much attention to the chest wound until the undertaker was preparing him for burial. The streak of missing flesh had been caused by the first shot, the one where the derringer was pressed hard against his body, with his clothing muffling the sounds of the exploding powder.

Bowing to the demands of mercy Rory didn't particularly feel, he turned the suffering man back onto his face. He would die there on the trail. There was no need to make his final moments worse than they already were.

Before turning back to the woman's plight, Rory's last thought was that the dying man was not the one Anthony had shot. He had no way of sorting out the other wound, but for sure, the man could not have ridden so far with that facial wound. This was the man who had scooped up the woman on their rush for the hills. The loosed prisoner must be further up the trail, aided by others.

As he stepped toward the now whimpering woman, the man looked at him with wordless suspicion. Rory said, "Sheriff Rory Jamison here, fella. You can accept that or not, but while you're thinking about it, let's get the lady out of the cactus patch."

Trot studied Rory, all the while holding one of the previously captured Colt .45s trained on the sheriff.

"Put the gun down before you make a serious mistake. I told you who I am. Now grab the lady's feet. I'll take her arms. We'll lift her right up and out."

Trot, not totally convinced who this other man could be, was nevertheless thankful for the help. He holstered the weapon and turned to assist Glad-Lilibet.

Hesitating, seemingly more concerned about his wife's modesty than her overall well-being, Trot took the lady's two ankles in his hands. Rory took a firm grip on her wrists and then slid his fingers down her arms until he was holding her elbows.

Sometimes, being gentle to spare the victim as much misery as possible can, in fact, cause serious additional pain and discomfort. Rory lifted with considerable energy and effort. Trot, hurting almost as much as Glad, in sympathy with her misery, pulled gently. Her scream could very likely be heard back in the village and throughout the hillside, in the uplanders' small shacks. Rory held her upper-half clear of the cactus while her bottom and legs sagged, once more, onto the spines. Realizing what he had done, Trot again lifted his wife and held her clear of the dreadfully sharp needles. Hundreds of the little demons pulled off the plant, stuck firmly in the woman's skin and flesh. The two men stood, with Glad stretched between them, looking at each other as if asking, "What next?"

Trot said, "Sorry about that, Glad. Sure, didn't go to hurt you worse."

Glad was silent, perhaps unconscious. There was no time or reason to sort that all out right at the moment. What they needed to do was get out of the pear patch themselves and down the hill, before they had unwanted company.

Both men, wearing boots, were protected from the worst of the pear. Rory quietly said, "I'll back away. You come along. Don't lay her down, or we'll drive those spines in further."

In a moment, they were out of the patch and standing in the clearing alongside the trail. The three horses were grazing side by side nearby. It was time for one of the men to take charge with a workable plan.

Tired of indecision and weary of muscle from holding the woman clear of the ground, Rory said, "Stand till I get a better grip."

Standing behind her, one by one, and slowly, he

worked his hands further up Glad's arms, gripping tightly enough to slow the blood flow, avoiding the spines wherever possible. When his big hands were gripping her underarms, hoping he was strong enough to do the job, he said, "Alright. Come toward me slowly. Set her feet on the ground. I'll lift and hold her up."

Trot was set to object to Rory's fashion of gripping his wife, but Rory got the first word in with, "Do it. Do it, and then bring your horse over here."

The strain of holding most of Glad's weight, as her semi-conscious mind failed to instruct her legs to stand, was more than most men could have accomplished. Rory though, had long been known as an extraordinarily strong man. Still, by the time Trot had a horse standing near, Rory was shaking with strain, his teeth clenched with the effort. Glad finally firmed her legs somewhat, relieving the strain for Rory, he quietly spoke directly into her ear.

"Good girl. Stand if you can. I'll keep holding you."

With the spines Glad was carrying, it would be inhuman to try to have her sit the saddle. Forcing the words through teeth, locked firmly with effort, Rory said, "Hold that animal. Don't let him move." Then, with a supreme effort, the sheriff bent at the knees, straightening his arms while holding the burden upright, gaining several inches in height. He slowly straightened back to a full-standing position. Glad's feet were now eight inches off the ground. With one more heave, Rory lifted and flopped her face down across the saddle. It was not a gentle move. Trot, figuring out the plan quickly, grabbed her shoulders from the other side of the horse and pulled, while Rory dropped his hand to Glad's knees and lifted. With a bit of wiggling and adjustment, mostly done by Trot, she was as settled and balanced as she would ever be.

Through his heavy breathing, Rory said, "Grab that rope off my saddle and tie her firmly. A fall could kill her. And then listen carefully to me."

Before he could continue, Rory bent at the waist, placing his hands on his knees, and took a dozen deep breaths. The effort to lift the woman at arm's length had been a severe test for his usually more than adequate strength. But it was done. To keep her there was her husband's responsibility.

During that interlude, Glad awoke enough to ask, "That...that other man. Wha...what happened to him?"

Trot was hesitant to tell the truth. Killing a man was no small thing. But finally, he decided she would eventually figure it out anyway.

"You got free by yourself somehow, Hon. I was still back down the trail some way. Not here yet. I heard a shot, then a man scream, and then another shot. And then you were screaming. I haven't tried to sort that all out."

As if she could say no more, Glad lay her head back down and remained still and quiet.

WHAT NO ONE was to know until Glad was recovering in the hospital and could tell the story was that she had managed to reach the two-shot derringer she was in the habit of carrying in her dress pocket. She had lifted it to shoulder height, raised her head, pressed the small weapon tight against the man's chest, and squeezed her shot off. But with the bouncing of the horse, she had managed only to graze his ribs. His startled yell was what Trot and Rory had both heard, quickly followed by the second shot.

It was that second shot was that took the captor's jaw and half his face away. It was also what startled the animal into a full run. Glad, now fearing for her life, reached for the side of the horse's face, grabbed the bridle cheek strap, and pulled. Hard. The animal had no choice but to turn its head, causing it to take a stumbling twist to the right, throwing Glad into the cactus patch before completing its turn, dropping the rider by the side of the trail.

FITTING the last loop of rope over her shoulders, snugging it down tight enough to hold without causing more injury, Trot, seeing that his wife would speak no more, said, "Whatever happened, you did well, my love. Just these cactus spines to deal with now. We'll get you down to town and figure it out from there. You lay balanced if you can, but I'm going to tie you to the horse. I couldn't lift you back on if you should fall. Not without hurting you worse anyway. Once I'm mounted behind the saddle, I'll lay my hand on your shoulder so you'll know I'm here, and I'll be able to know if you're sliding off."

Glad twisted her head to the side as if she was trying to see the second man. Rory stepped nearer, saying, "I'm Sheriff Rory Jamison, ma'am. From up in the next county. Your husband will take you downhill. I'm going after the others. Sorry about your troubles."

Looking now at Trot, Rory said, "I'm riding uphill. Here's what you need to do. Take your wife to the village. Leave her where she is right now until you secure a wagon and team. Load it almost to the top with hay. Lift the lady and lay her face down on the hay. Don't turn her over. Leave immediately for Denver. Make the best possible time, stopping for nothing. Switch the team out for others if chance offers. Take some food and water for her. Get her to the hospital. Removing those spines is beyond the ability of anyone here.

"Also, and this is important, send a fast rider to Stevensville and on to the Fort. Tell the law in both places what's happened. They need to be alert until this is settled. Someone in the Fort needs to tell my wife where I am.

"Send another fast rider to Denver. He's to bang on doors no matter what time of night it is. Get someone from the federal marshals up and active. The county office too. Tell them we have a dead sheriff. Tell them I need at least two marshals up here by morning. Other help, if it's available. They need to ride up the hill as soon as they get here. Tell them my name. Remember it now, Sheriff Rory Jamison. Now go. I'll be praying for the lady's well-being. And for some justice for her and your sheriff."

With that, Rory mounted his gelding and turned uphill.

29

SHERIFF RORY JAMISON

THE FUROR IN HIGHLAND WAS DISTURBING THE ENTIRE settlement without accomplishing anything much, until the widow of Sheriff Anthony Clare shouted for silence.

"What's the matter with you people. Stop all that jabbering nonsense and do as Trot told you. Alvin, open your livery and bring out the team. Fill the wagon with hay. Don't mess around. I'll see that you're paid.

"And two of you men, take the best horses you can find and ready them for a long night. One of you ride north and one to the city. Write Sheriff Rory's name down if you can't remember it. Now get going. You've already wasted more minutes than enough. I want to see the tails of your horses within one minute. Now go."

As if they had been waiting for someone to take charge, the men responded immediately to the usually quiet, somewhat withdrawn widow. Readying the wagon took an additional few minutes, but it too was soon underway, with Alvin, the livery operator, handling his own team while Trot and one town lady sat cross-legged on the pile of hay, hoping to comfort the now awake Glad-Lilibet White.

Even with the best they could get out of the horses, they all faced a long night of travel.

SHERIFF RORY RODE UPHILL CAUTIOUSLY. He was riding into unknown territory with the aim of confronting equally unknown men. And he reminded himself that he would have to watch the women too. He knew little of the old European cultures. Most of what he knew had come from either Ivan or his family. And a bit from the old man known as Kiril, whose mystery he still had never fully solved. What he had learned was that when circumstances commanded, the women wouldn't hesitate to take their place on the field of battle. He suspected that attempting to arrest one or two of the men just might be seen as provocation enough to move the women to action.

His temptation, and wish, was to set by and wait for the deputy marshals to arrive. But that wasn't going to happen until the sun had set, risen, and crossed the distance of the sky again. Too long. Too much could happen in that time. He would have to do it alone, again.

DEPUTY SHERIFF IVAN IVANOV

Ivan stayed, visiting the lonely couple only long
enough for lunch and a friendly second cup of coffee.
Hubert Kingsley, a well-put-together man that Ivan
guessed would be in his early forties, and his wife, Tilly,
a few years younger, slim, and attractive, were eager for
talk.

It had always made Ivan smile a bit privately to hear
remote settlers talk of their love of aloneness and the
silence of nature. And by that, they weren't putting aside
the bird song or the soughing of the wind through the
leaves of the never-resting quaking aspen. What was
usually meant was the noise of human activity, the
rattling of wagon wheels on rocky ground, the shouting
of teamsters, the faintly heard arguments of husbands
and wives who were sorting out matters of their own
and doing it in the most destructive way, the joyous
screaming of playing children. He had been that way
himself under the tutelage of his immigrant family until
Sheriff Rory dragged him to town and deputized him.

And yet, often, when company arrived, these folks

were prepared to throw all that aside and stoke up the fire to heat a fresh pot. His own family, who had chosen a somewhat remote spot to settle on, were no different. And Kiril, that cranky old reprobate who had filled Ivan's young mind with foolish tales of how the men ran the world and their own homes, ruling over the women back in the old country. Nonsense, of course, that Ivan finally managed to tear from his mind as painlessly as the removal of an impacted tooth by an inexperienced dentist, making room for the realities of modern life.

Even on this law-keeping venture, he had met other settlers, men who lived alone but who hated to see company come and then leave again.

Aloneness wasn't all it was cracked up to be, no matter what the single settlers had to say. They, or the folks like the Kingsleys, who at least had each other but were still anxious for visitors.

With a final wave and a promise to return their stolen horse if the opportunity presented itself, Ivan left Hubert and Tilly Kingsley standing in their yard, shading their eyes against the westerly sun as he pointed his gelding in the direction Buff had been last seen riding.

Ivan was a full day behind. That didn't surprise him. Ivan's task of first importance had been to assist Rory in gaining full control of the captured thieves. He had stayed at that matter until My Way and Dancer had come to replace him. Only then was he free to pursue the fleeing gang leader.

Buff had used his head start to good advantage. He had also shown he was prepared to abuse or even kill his horse if it would add minutes to his lead. Ivan had no intention of harming his own animal. They had traveled too many miles together and seen too much country to be parted now. He hoped to see even more miles before either he or the animal wore out.

His experience too, as a lawman, was that the criminal was almost certain to make a mistake, aiding in his own capture. Sometimes a deadly mistake, driven to that point by his own self-confidence and his low thoughts of his pursuer. Buff would be caught when the time was right, with the circumstances pulling the knot together inch by inch.

The trail of the single horse was clear. The spring grass had risen to a height of about ten inches. The hooves of the running horse had left a trail of broken stems and trampled ground all along the way.

Ivan had no idea how much more growth the warm weeks could draw out of the grass, but he could see that there was great opportunity here for wise and prudent cattlemen. There would be some winter snows to deal with, but from the grass, a rancher can make hay when the summer sun brings it to maturity. It could all be managed if a man had a mind to.

But all he was personally interested in was the bent and broken, grassy trail that headed in an almost straight line to the southwest. He rode with confidence, watching the horizon. Nowhere nearer than one-half mile was there any cover.

Ivan had heard of Indians who could lie still in almost no cover at all, lying in wait for an adversary, without being seen. But Buff was no Indian, and he had shown no sign of that kind of patience. But when Ivan reached the hazy, shadowy hills he could see to the west, caution would, again, take precedence over speed.

The trail over the grassy high-level bowl stopped abruptly at a rock-strewn, downhill slide. The grassy trail had led unerringly to the slide, almost as if the rider knew the country. That was a totally new thought for the deputy. Was it possible that Buff knew this country well? That would put the advantage firmly on his side and help explain how he had unerringly followed the notched trees over so many miles.

The hazy hills had turned into mountain peaks of solid rock, rising over one thousand feet above the lower benchland, showing no way through or past, except for the slide. Ivan was reminded of the slide hill leading down to the Lander's BL Ranch.

AFTER PROWLING around the hills above his own family ranch, the I-5, he had known of the BL Ranch before he led Rory there. That was when Ivan was first riding with Sheriff Jamison, and they had captured Mike Wasson, the sometimes town marshal and full-time cattle thief.

Thinking little of the problems the slide had represented and having done such many times, Ivan had pushed his animal over the brink and onto the steep grade. Having little choice but to follow, all the time fearing it was a suicidal move, Rory had spurred his gelding over the steepest portion of the narrow trail. The led animal that was carrying the prisoner had no choice but to follow. As he broke over the top and first saw the path ahead, Wasson screamed in terror, but Rory had no sympathy. He dropped the reins of the prisoner's horse and concentrated on his own ride, leaving Wasson to the mercies of the trail and his loose riding animal. There was no way of turning back, and with Wasson's hands tied to the saddle horn, he was simply along for the ride. There was no doubt they would all meet again at the bottom.

The sheriff had ridden the treacherous trail, but he had also sworn 'never again'.

~

Now, here sat Ivan, staring at the only visible way west, the way Buff had taken, wondering if there might be another way. A hidden way. Was he losing his courage, or was he growing more smart as time went by? There was no answer to that unspoken question, so he studied the trail one more time.

He knew Buff had ridden that way from the recently disturbed rocks, identified by the displacement of their lichen growth. And a careful study showed a bit of white horsehair and blood on the sharp edge of another rock. Little more than an hour away from his home corral, and the animal was already injured.

He would find no better place nor any better opportunity to examine the way ahead. Ivan backed off into the shade, dismounted, dropped the reins, and dug the field glasses out from among the rest of his gather. Staying in the shadows, he took a full quarter-hour to study the slide and the way ahead, carefully assessing each choice of direction, each possible hiding place, each feasible camping site. He studied it all as if his life were at stake. And it could be if he made a mistake.

To find Buff making coffee by the stream, he could see in the distance was too much to ask. But his mind dwelt on the possibility anyway, just for a moment. Knowing there was no chance of that happening, he would settle for an indication of the easiest path. Buff had shown his liking for quick and easy.

The slide remained straight for a hundred yards and then took an abrupt bend to the left, which would be south, all at a steeper than comfortable downward angle. Straight ahead, past the bend, was a sharp drop off that nothing could survive if the turn were missed. It wasn't a trail he would wish to be on in the dark.

With his mind made up, there was no more time for dawdling or wondering. He stepped into the leather and nudged the animal forward. The much wiser gelding snorted and pulled back, reluctant to face the way ahead. Ivan grinned inwardly again at the thought, repeated many times over the years, that horses were in some ways smarter than men.

He wondered if he had ever ridden worse terrain but pushed the thoughts out of his mind, and with just a light touch of the spur, the horse started down. He managed to hold a tight rein for perhaps half the run, but when the trail steepened, there was no holding the animal. Doing what seemed to come naturally to the gelding, he soon straightened his front legs in an attempt to slow the downward slide while folding his hind legs till his haunches were almost on the rocky ground. All Ivan could do was plant his feet firmly but carefully in the stirrups and watch for the upcoming corner. If the horse showed signs of missing the turn, he was ready to bail off, rocky landing or not. But again, the wise and steady animal took his rider where he needed to go.

Settling in at the bottom and moving forward, Ivan resisted the urge to look back. Rocks and dust the gelding had disturbed continued to tumble down the steep path. He could hear the crashing of the falling rocks and smell the drifting dust. But he did wonder if the Kingsleys came this way or was there a better path.

~

THE LITTLE STREAM he had seen through his glasses, from the top of the hill, was even more inviting once he rode right up to it. Although he would not normally go to camp that early in the day, there was no telling where he would next find water, and the gelding would benefit from a few hours rest after sliding and jumping down the treacherous trail. He staked the horse out on fresh grass in easy reach of the water and then treated himself to a pot of coffee.

There followed three days on the trail, and two nights, hunkered down beside flowing water, with one camp showing all the signs of recent use. With so few riders crossing the country, it almost had to be one of Buff's camps. Pulled back, away from the fire and the water course, tucked under or behind whatever brushy cover he could find, trusting the gelding to awaken him if unwelcome company approached, Ivan slept.

Awakening with the sun the next morning, Ivan took a more careful look around him. There was grass enough, and the trickle of water appeared to be a steady flow, enough to care for a small herd. Close by were the remnants of older growth, poplar, willow, and a few struggling pines. One big, old poplar had been lightning-struck and burned half-through. The butt and twenty feet of scarred trunk still stood, bare of branch or leaf. But all around, for many yards in all directions, were young poplar trees, some only now sprouting and some ten to twelve feet tall.

Walking over to the burned tree, Ivan marveled at how it had re-seeded itself over the years of its life. With the steady flow of nurturing water, there arose a nice grove of the moisture- loving trees. But he pushed those thoughts from his mind when he noticed a weather-worn and nearly grown-over notch, at shoulder height

181

on the dead tree. It was the first blaze mark he had seen in many rocky miles. The fact was that he had put the axe marks the fugitive group had been following out of his mind when they reached the rocky country. Now, here was another. What could it mean? Was it the extension of the original trail or something else altogether? He would never know, and it no longer mattered. What mattered was getting back on that trail. But with Buff leading the way, he had no more need for blaze marks.

DEPUTY SHERIFF IVAN IVANOV

It was the following noon when Ivan rode up to a man sitting on a shade-covered rock on the side of the trail. Beside him stood a badly abused and worn-down horse. The much-abused animal was nibbling on the poor offering growing around the base of a small group of trees. Whatever life-sustaining water the trees enjoyed must have come from deep down, drawn up by roots that had dug down that far, working their way through one split rock and then another. There was no sign of surface water. Approaching cautiously, Ivan loosened the weight of his sidearm just a little, never taking his eyes off the man. With his peripheral vision, he was scouring as much of the area around as possible, watching for an accomplice the sitting man might be fronting for.

As he drew near, the man rose from the rock and stepped into the sunlight. Ivan could easily see that he was armed with a Colt, and there was a camp knife hanging from his belt. Evidently, the man had judged Ivan correctly, noting his reluctance to ride closer. With his hat raised in greeting, the man shouted, "Come in, stranger. Ain't nothing you can do to me to make things worse, except shoot me. And I expect if that was your plan, you might have done it already. And I ain't got no reason to harm you. No reason to harm anyone at all, sept'n the fellow who held a gun on me while he switched his saddle to my horse and rode off, leaving this much abused gelding in trade. But since I suspect the gelding is stolen, it really wasn't much of a trade. Come in and share my little bit of shade. Perhaps you can tell me where I went wrong in life all those years ago. So wrong I find myself in this forsaken rock pile, leaving Mormon country for my own health and welfare, to say nothing at all about happiness, while I move forward into the unknown. Or at least I was, until I found myself with a lame horse for both company and transport."

With that, the man stepped out of the sunlight and back into the shade, retaking his seat. With some lingering doubts, Ivan put his horse back into motion. He rode toward and then past the man, then turned swiftly so he could see his backtrail, glancing between the seated man and the rock and brush country he had just crossed.

"That's a good move, young fella. Have to remember that one. Course, it ain't likely to be required of me if I ever find the utopia I'm hoping to somehow locate. You see any water back to the east you was coming though?"

Still seated on the gelding, Ivan said, "Stream eight to ten miles back. Small, but enough. You could walk it, leading the animal if you were to desire water bad enough. It's for sure, judging by looks, that the horse could use some."

"That's a far walk on a hot day. Perhaps I'll wait for the cool of evening. Horse drank up all my canteen, so he'll be alright for a few hours. Should turn the beast loose. Ain't my animal. Stole, I'm thinking, as I've already said. I get caught riding a stole horse, I'm likely to find myself in worse shape than I am now."

Ivan stepped to the ground and went to the injured horse. Walking around until he could see the offside hind foot, he paused. Thinking of where he had seen the bloody rock with the white horsehair dried into the mess, he compared it to the injury he was looking at. The skin was broken, and flies had gathered. Making no comment, he went to his own saddlebags, rummaged around a bit, and came up with a tin of salve and a rolled rag torn from a worn-out hotel bed sheet, brought along for bandage material. He wiped his hands on his pants legs and talked gently to the horse while he turned the lid off the tin. He scooped out a large dollop of the salve on his index finger and, with the other fingers, twisted the lid back into place. He dropped the tin into his pocket and reached for the gelding's leg. A nervous twitch warned him to go slow and easy. Talking gently to the animal, he rubbed his hand along the upper leg, and then, when there was no reaction from the horse, he worked down to the wound. Still speaking gently, he said, just a bit louder, "Bring me the canteen off my horse."

The stranger did as he was asked and then retook his seat in the shade. Ivan washed out the wound, brushing the flies away at the same time.

"Come hold this animal's bridle. Hold him steady."

Still carefully watching the slight movements of the hoof, wary of a kick he knew could be fast and devastating, he dabbed the ointment into the broken skin. Speaking to his reluctant helper and a bit to himself, hoping the horse would take the words as a comfort,

Ivan said, "Nearly done. Just get this wrap on to keep the flies off, and we'll have done all we can do."

Another minute and the tin of salve was back in the saddlebag, and Ivan had joined the other man in the shade. He was no sooner seated when there was a hand thrust out at him.

"Chad Stanton, recently of Salt Lake, until the heat became a bit much. Previously from St. Louis and points east. That's a good job on the horse. Whoever owns the animal owes you his thanks. I do too, supposing I'm left to ride the beast, stole or no."

"Ivan Ivanov. Stevensville, Colorado. County Deputy Sheriff. Looking for a man."

"Well, I'm hoping it's not me. Of course, it seems everyone I ever met was looking for a man, one way or another. Knew a lady over west a ways. That was her goal in life too. Outspoken about it. It was her favorite subject when we were together. I got to figuring there was a whole lot of country I ain't ever seen yet, and if I was to correct that situation, I had best be on my way. I've had a week to think about it and haven't found a reason to question my original decision. I have no objection to her looking for a man. There's no doubt some out there who might even rise to the bait. But beyond losing my freedom, I had some doubts about a Mormon lady fitting into the life of a Methodist man, or vice versa. So here I am. Near enough broke and waiting for the cool of night so's I can lead a stolen horse to water."

Ivan was silent for a few seconds, trying to assure himself that Chad Stanton and Buff weren't one and the same man. Finally, remembering the tumble on the rocks Buff had suffered, which had to have left marks and bruises, adding in the bulk of the man and the worn and filthy clothes he had been wearing, he had to admit to himself that the two could not be mistaken for each other.

"You backtrail me, Chad. Over east three, four days ride, depending on how this horse holds up, you'll find a steep slide hill. Miserable trail coming down. I expect it's worse going up. But you take that trail, cross the miles-wide meadow at the top. You'll come to a place. House, barn. Couple of other small buildings, shed, and such. Corral. Place of Hubert Kingsley. Wife's name is Tilly. Good folk. This is their horse. The fella that pawned him off on you forced a swap on them too. The one he pawned off might be stolen too. There's no way to know and no one up in that high country to question on it. You make the swap and ride on to Colorado. Enquire at the nearest livery if anyone knows the brand or had reported him gone. There's only a couple of settlers along the way in that high country, so you'll maybe not see anyone at all. Small bunch of renegade Utes. Try to see them before they see you.

"Now, tell me about the rider who took your horse. Then tell me about the country ahead."

DEPUTY SHERIFF IVAN IVANOV

WITH HOURS OF DAYLIGHT REMAINING IN THE DAY, IVAN tightened his cinch and moved off, heading west. Chad Stanton confirmed that he would wait out the heat of the afternoon, maybe even take a nap in the shade, and push on to the east in the cool of the evening. Ivan wished him good riding. Neither man expected to ever see the other again.

Chad had provided two pieces of information that were destined to be helpful to Ivan. The first was that the Utah border, although there was some disputing exactly where it lay, was no more than fifty miles to the west. The trail was reported to be winding and twisted, difficult in some spots, but passable.

The second bit of information was that the first settlement to be encountered across the border was a dust-covered, fly-infected, single-road blister of misery known as Temple, run by a renegade Mormon who had vowed to give up the faith, but not the three wives who currently spent most of their days seeing to his comfort and working in his various business establishments. One of those business establishments was a saloon serving forbidden alcoholic beverages, both a threat and a promise to any Mormon vigilante who attempted to close him down.

Another enterprise was the small mercantile outlet offering for sale most of the things needed for survival in that bleak, desperate corner of the world.

The renegade's name was Quillan. He offered no explanation for the single moniker. Nor did he explain if Quillan was his first or last name.

The advice received from Chad Stanton was that Quillan was a live-and-let-live sort of man, but it was best not to cross him or question him too closely. And to leave his wives alone. Ivan found no issue with that advice and expected no trouble.

He pushed on, figuring he had made twenty miles before he found another of Buff's camps. Admitting that the man knew how to choose and establish a good camp, Ivan picketed his horse and prepared to settle in for the night. After burying the mess Buff had left behind, he gathered wood for a long night. High mountain nights could get cold. He would keep the fire burning low during those hours, but he wouldn't be sleeping too close by. Offering a target to Buff or any other wanderer was not part of his plan.

The next day, he thought he might have made thirty miles, although much of the trail was taken at a walk. It seemed he was either climbing a hill or sliding down the other side. Slow going. But there were clear signs of passage in the recent past. It almost had to have been Buff. He had seen no sign of other movement. And to confirm his initial thoughts, he stopped and compared the hoof prints in the dust. It was clearly the same horse going both directions. A reasonable assumption was that

Chad Stanton had left the prints going east, and Buff had left the identical prints behind him, riding Chad Stanton's horse, returning to the west.

As weary as Ivan was of the whole matter, he had no intention of catching up to the man. He wasn't sure he wanted to confront Buff where there were so many options for setting up an ambush. It might be best to take him when he had settled into some comfort in Temple or another town if he should choose to continue on, deeper into Utah. If he could avoid gunfire, so much the better. His hope had been to arrest Buff, put him on a train, and return him to Denver for trial. The second option was, of course, to bury him.

THE FOURTH DAY after leaving Chad Stanton, Ivan saw a twisting, broken rise of smoke in the west. He continued to the top of the hill he was climbing and dismounted behind a short rocky bluff that forced a bend in the trail. Leaving the horse on a bit of sparse grass, he climbed the rock wall and lay so that only his head protruded over the top edge. He had brought his glasses but didn't really need them. The layout at the foot of the hill was clear. It had to be the settlement Chad had named as Temple. Studying the place, Ivan couldn't imagine anything that would entice anyone to settle anywhere nearby. It was a rocky, dusty, miserable place, virtually without green growth or any other visual promise unless a man was an admirer of endless grey and brown rocks, with a few leaning toward red thrown in to add color.

To see the activity on the street more closely, Ivan lifted the glasses to his head and adjusted the crude focus wheel. There was just the single horse tied outside one of the buildings. It looked like a saloon, although he couldn't be sure. Across the way stood a barn. Probably a livery, although it was too small to hold more than a dozen animals, at best. The big door in the end was open. Two men stood there. One was dressed in farmer overalls. He looked comfortable and at home, leaning on one door-post. The other man was much larger, bulky of shoulder and chest, as Buff had been, with a mop of unruly hair protruding from his wide-brimmed hat. Ivan thought the hair looked black, but at the distance, he couldn't be sure. He also thought the man was Buff. But of that, too, he couldn't be sure.

Now, the question was, would Buff recognize Ivan. There was no doubt the man knew he was being followed. His actions on the trail confirmed that. But would he remember the man who stood at the top of the pass, miles back to the east, while Rory dusted the horse and rider with rock pellets? If he had taken note of Ivan at all, it would have been a brief part of a second, and even then, Buff was cowering for his life at the time. It seemed doubtful that he could pick Ivan from a crowd. But with so few riders in the area, perhaps he didn't have to. A stranger in town would be a noteworthy event. Buff could make guesses like anyone else. The chances of him being fooled were slim.

Ivan clambered back down the rock face and tightened the cinch. He lifted the 44-40 and checked it for loads. He ejected one shell to check the movements of the mechanism and then reloaded to full capacity. He was even more careful with his Colt, unloading it, carefully wiping any dust from each shell. He worked the hammer and trigger several times, then re-loaded. With a last, careful thought about what he was doing and how he would respond to whatever arose, he stepped into the leather.

~

A HALF-HOUR LATER, he rode into the north end of Town. Nailed to a stunted tree was a poorly hand-painted sign announcing, to anyone interested in knowing the name, that they were entering 'Temple. A free town for free people.'

Ivan grinned to himself. He was looking forward to meeting this Quillan. A man willing to put it all right out there where there could be no doubt about where he stood, challenging all who were of a contrary mind, was a man to meet and know. He might not be the man you depended on to be standing beside if things came to a head, but until then, he seemed interesting. And safe enough.

The small livery Ivan had studied from the top of the hill was the first building the traveler came to, at the north end of town. He turned in and dismounted at the door. The man in overalls was nowhere to be seen, so Ivan led the gelding into the cooling shade and stalled him after first leading him to the water trough. There was already hay in the manger. Ivan unsaddled, threw the leather across the top of the stall planking, and dusted himself off. As he was turning to leave, a voice called him back.

"Howdy, stranger. See you took the liberty of stalling your animal. You here for long? Need anything else? Shoes alright? Any stiffening in the legs?"

Ivan stopped and turned around. He grinned at the man and said, "You talking about me or the horse?"

"Well, mostly the horse, I guess. But I could let you

have a bit of liniment for your legs if you felt the need. Have to put it on yourself though. Danged if I'm going to do it for you."

"We'll let it go for now."

"Staying long?"

Ivan maintained the grin, saying, "You already asked me that. Answer is 'I don't know', not exactly anyhow. Thought I saw another man here earlier. Big fella. Bushy hair. Broad chest."

"That's what you thought, is it? Fact is, if I were to answer every personal question that came my way, I'd be a mighty poor liveryman. Or man of any sort, far as that goes. You want'n gossip, you need to take yourself across to the café. Lady what runs the place is a regular blizzard of information and opinion. Once in a while, she even gets something right."

"No. I'll let it go. I expect he'll turn up. When it's his time. No one's born before their time, and no one lives beyond their time."

"And are you father time, announcing the beginning and end of all things?"

"No, sir. I'm just a simple man riding the country. Seeing what I can see. Always wondering how things will turn out."

The liveryman studied Ivan for a moment, spat into the manure pile, and responded, "And I'm the King of Peru."

"Ivan grinned even wider, saying, "I'm not sure Peru has a king. Never did think about that before. Might be an opportunity for you."

"I'll think on that, lawman. While you go get yourself some vittles. Saloon or café. Both offer good fare. Quillan's wife, she that waits tables in the saloon, is better looking. Easier to look at as she goes about her duties.

Just don't forget that she's Quillan's wife. Quillan sure ain't about to."

"Thanks, pal. I'll be careful. Always am around other folks' property. You go ahead and rub down the gelding's legs. Pay you a bit extra. And if you happen to remember what direction that other fella, the one neither of us noticed, rode out in, I'd pay for that information too. Just between two horsemen, you understand."

IVAN ENTERED THE SALOON, hesitated a moment for his eyes to adjust to the dimness of the place, then pulled a chair back from one of the three small tables. There was one man standing at the bar, with the toe of his riding boot resting on a brass railing, nursing a stein of beer. He had a cowboy look about him. On his head was a typical, big-brimmed hat. His canvas pants showed the signs of many hours in the saddle. On his hip, he had strapped an ammunition studded belt with a holster holding a bone-handled Colt. The weapon looked used but well cared for.

He glanced Ivan's way, squinted as if seeking a memory or recognition, and finally settled for "Hot enough, stranger? Depending on what yer used to, is what I mean to say."

With that, he turned back to his beer, not seeming to need an answer or a greeting.

It was either the scraping of the chair on the floor or the man's speaking, but something gained the attention of a young woman. She stepped through an open doorway between the bar and café area and what Ivan presumed was the kitchen. She wiped her brow with the tail of her apron, indicating that the little room was stove-hot and uncomfortable to work in.

She made her graceful way over to Ivan's table and greeted him with, "Welcome. Are you needing a drink? Food? Or just some time out of the sun?"

Her smile as she was asking turned away any thoughts that she might be intruding into personal matters.

"Food. And a drink if it's spring water or coffee."

The beer drinker laughed and said, "Best you take a beer fella. The spring water runs across a half mile of cow pasture before 'Ol Quillan gets around to scooping 'er out fer the table. Gets a bit heavy time to time, if you should take my meaning."

The woman said, "Hush up now Nathon."

She turned back to Ivan, saying, "Some who down-play our little settlement enjoy telling strangers that foolish tale. But It's not true at all. Oh, the stream runs across the pasture alright, but we gather the water in milk cans, right out of the rock, you might say, before it ever reaches the grass. You're safe enough to drink it."

"Then I'll have a big glass, along with whatever it is you've got on the stove. Coffee after I've eaten, if that's possible."

"It's all possible. And good too. That is, if you like steak and eggs along with fried potatoes."

Ivan smiled and said, "Nothing better."

When the woman returned to the kitchen, Ivan spoke to the beer drinker.

"Why don't you bring your beer and join me, Nathon?"

With a question on his face, Nathon picked up his mug and took the few steps to Ivan's table. He pulled out a chair and sat. He lifted the mug but held it just below his lips as he said, "I gotta wonder. Ain't many come this way. Even fewer face that trail you came down. There're easier paths. Gotta be a reason. But here you are, the second in this here one short day.

Ivan studied the man before he said in response, "You didn't see me on the trail from in here."

Leaving the unspoken question hanging in the air, he waited.

Nathon twirled a squiggly image in the moisture that had dripped from the sweating stein while he thought up his next words. Saying no more would be the safe route. But he had never been one to take the safe route. On the other hand, to speak up might tip his hand. That thought held no promise either.

Before he spoke, Ivan jumped in with, "I wonder if it could be you stepped out back to study the trail after another man rode into town? A big man. Broad shoulders. Head of hair."

"That's 'Ol Buff. Everyone over on this side knows Buff. He's got no friends, you understand. It's just that folks know him."

"Is he a Mormon? And as far as that goes, are we in Mormon country here?"

"Him? Mormon? No. Buff, he don't think on or believe in anything but Buff. It's just that he hangs out around here. Must feel safe or something. Not much else to attract a man. As to your second question, the whole matter is a question. Some from the faith claim it, but Quillan and some others hereabouts argue we're still in Colorado."

"And what's attracted you here, Nathon?"

"Now, that's the question, isn't it. It's kind of like I fell off life and don't know if I want to get back on or not. Days are easy here. Don't need much money. Drink one beer each afternoon. Pay a dime for dinner come evening.

"I'm contented until I see someone like you coming along. Young. Well suited up. Good riding animal. Badge in your pocket, I'm guessing, giving you authority and purpose. Makes me wonder if I could have done the same before so many years went past. Makes me wonder what Buff did this time too, that got you on such a long trail. Most give 'er up long before they cross that rock pile."

"Has Buff got a history of doing, as you say?"

"Goes away for months sometimes. Rides back with someone on his tail, like as not. Goes back into hiding. Sometime later, it all starts again. It'll end someday. Maybe tomorrow. Man, never knows. Could be today."

Ivan responded, "Strange. I was just having the same conversation with the liveryman. You fellas' thinking seems to be following along the same path."

"Nothing much to it, stranger. Just pondering is all. Just pondering."

Nathon tipped the last swallow of beer to his mouth and pushed his chair away from the table, making motions to stand. Hoping to hold him for another minute, Ivan asked, "I suspect Buff rode off to the north. Liveryman didn't see him leave, so he couldn't say. Or wouldn't. What's to the north from here?"

Nathon was already wondering if he had overplayed his hand. If his appearance of loneliness and hunger for talk had loosened his tongue too much. But the answer to Ivan's question would divulge no secrets. An hour's riding would answer the question anyway.

"What you saw from the livery door is about what there is. Rock. Sand. Cactus. Snakes. Enough growth to gather a bit of firewood if a fella should find himself

197

with a desire for a cup of coffee somewhere along the trail, which you're not likely to find to the west of here."

"No settlers?"

"There's a high valley. Maybe three thousand acres all told. Decent grass. Water. The only such in many a mile. Mighty rough country up there. Surrounded by rock and high cliffs. There's a ranch. Like this here settlement of Quillans', it could be it's in Colorado. More likely in Utah. Won't know until a formal survey is done, and since there's no great rush to settle this rock pile, that ain't about to happen today. Or tomorrow. Rancher up there holds the land. Raises beef. Runs a regular little village. Men come, and men go. A lot of jack Mormons, or so the story is, although most look as if it'd been a while since they were seen in any kind of church setting.

"Some stay and work for wages for a month or two. Some take a meal and a night in the bunkhouse and pull out in the morning. Some hang around a bit while their horses and themselves rest up or heal from some mysterious wound picked up along the way. They all appear to be broke. You'd think it was a stage station, what with all the activity. Just who all the men are is never discussed."

"And does Buff find a welcome there?"

"That's just the thing. Everyone finds a welcome there, no questions asked. Until someone brings trouble down on the ranch. Then, the sparks fly. Of course, if it should happen to be a gentile making trouble for a Brother, that changes the rules. The Bishop, him who owns the ranch and is said to be on the downside of the faith himself, he'll tolerate no annoyance from gentiles. It's all kind of confusing. Mormons of convenience, I'd say."

"This Bishop, as you called him, he got a name?"

"Just Bishop. Won't answer to any other name or title.

Rightly, he ain't no bishop of anything, Mormon or no. It's just a title he hung on himself. Kind of like back east, where there seems to be more fellas going by colonel or major than there ever was in the war. Who's to stop a man from calling himself anything he wants, right?

"The church will take a hand in all that, clean it all up, sooner or later. But it's still early days. A lot of men are doing as they please. That won't last.

33

DEPUTY SHERIFF IVAN IVANOV

IVAN HAD HIS MEAL AND RETURNED TO THE LIVERY. HE spent an hour grooming his horse and putting his packs back in order after hurriedly breaking camp for several days. He had negotiated one night in a small shack Quillan called a cabin. He would rest, let his horse rest, and be prepared to ride north with the next sunrise.

The following morning, when Ivan was set to swing into the saddle, hoping for another bit of information that may be helpful, the liveryman was as close-mouthed as ever. As Ivan laid a couple of coins in his hand, the old man, knowing what Ivan was wishing for, held off except to say, "An hour with Nathon, and you've about heard all there is to hear. Mighty free with his information, that man. But not with everyone. Might pay to think of just why he chose you to gain from his opinions.

"There's them that don't much take to him, but so far, in the few weeks he's graced us with his presence, no one's challenged him. Peaceful enough, far as that goes, but he carries that hip iron as if it growed there. Ain't ever seen him use it, but you gotta assume. Yes, sir, to stay healthy and breathing, you gotta assume. Ride well, Sheriff."

Ivan paused before nudging the horse into motion. He glanced at the liveryman and said, "I've never said aye, yes, or no about being the law."

"Right you are Sheriff."

Putting the sounds of the man's voice and the folks of Temple behind him, he headed north, not knowing what to expect. But in the back of his mind, he pondered on Nathon. Who is he, and, more importantly perhaps, what is he?

Anyone watching from the height of the surrounding hills might accuse Ivan of dawdling. But it was taking some time to sort out what Nathon had said about Mormons and jack Mormons, about loyalty among the brothers, about being secretive. It was a whole new world to Ivan. He coupled that information with what little Chad Stanton had said about his short time in Utah. Then there was the Bishop's ranch. And that raised more questions. Questions about the Bishop, about the ranch, and about how Buff might fit in the picture. It didn't sound like the kind of place he could simply ride into and declare the law or arrest Buff. There was a good chance the Bishop would see the intrusion as a challenge to his authority.

His slow ride was also giving him time to look the country over and ask himself some questions.

Were there better or easier routes east than the one Buff had led him over? Nathon mentioned something about easier paths. What did he know, or was he simply guessing? And where was the start of the trail Tug Granger had used to freight his supplies in?

How far was it to the nearest rails? Figuring that might be Salt Lake City, he wished he had asked Nathon or the liveryman. Or perhaps the woman who served his meal. He had no real desire to ride the many miles back across the top of Colorado to return to the Fort. He would much prefer to ride the cushions, preferably with Buff handcuffed in the seat beside him. But the distance to the rails might cause him to reconsider.

Were there escape routes from the Bishop's ranch, or hiding spots Buff could stow himself away in?

Did the Bishop merely wink only at smaller crimes, or would he protect Buff once it was known that he was a murderer?

Finally, accepting that he would never know all the answers, he stepped up his pace and headed directly for the ranch. There was no clear trail. Rather, there were a multitude of slightly used paths, any of which might take him to the ranch headquarters, or to a different part of the ranch, or give it a miss altogether. Selecting the track most used and hoping it led to the ranch yard itself, he moved on.

In that country of rocks and scattered forests, there was always a way to slip off the trail and take a careful look at what was ahead. Figuring he was getting close to his target, he found such a spot, raised a bit above the trail itself, settled into the best shade he could find, removed his hat, and lifted his glasses. There before him lay the Bishop's ranch. He could see cattle spread across the grass, with a few riders in attendance. But most likely, the animals were fenced in by the rock walls, as Ivan's own family's I-5 Ranch was.

The big house was easy to identify, as was the main barn. Several outbuildings left him wondering, but he settled the glasses on what looked like a bunkhouse and cookhouse together, a low, squat building with a lean-to structure at the back, most likely the kitchen. A chimney protruded through the roof of the larger building, and another through the lean-to roof. A covered porch ran across the front. There were two men sitting on chairs on the porch and another who had settled in on the short series of stairs rising from the dusty yard. None of them looked like Buff.

He lay still for an hour, watching the movements, trying to place the people and their responsibilities. There had been no sign of anyone he could name, by looks or bearing, as the Bishop. There was much activity in a corral attached to the big barn. Three men appeared to be working with young stock. From the distance he couldn't be sure.

Several men rode in, switched their saddles to fresh horses, and walked to the cookhouse. They stood, leaning on porch posts or the cookhouse wall, visiting, until a man clad in a once-white apron appeared. He clanked the iron triangle for three or four seconds and returned to the building. The men followed him in. More men were walking up from the barn, and two rode in from the north. Buff sauntered up from one of the smaller outbuildings, looking exactly as he had when Ivan had seen him through the glasses, as if he hadn't bothered to bathe or change his clothes. There was no guessing what the building Buff emerged from was used for, and it didn't matter to Ivan.

What mattered to Ivan a half hour later, was that Buff was the first to leave the lunch table and walk back into Ivan's view. Without stopping, as if he had a planned destination, he jumped off the end of the porch and walked quickly to the lightly treed area surrounding the ranch. Clearly knowing where he was going, he ducked under some low branches and disappeared into the bush. When he didn't return in five minutes, Ivan slid down to his horse, mounted, and quick-stepped around the hill-side and in the direction that should intersect Buff's movements.

Ivan, ranch-raised, was not the best roper in the coun-try, but, on the other hand, he wasn't the worst either. Wanting to be prepared for whatever opportunities presented themselves, he first checked his Colt. It moved easily in the holster, confirming there was nothing to deter a draw if the need arose. He then loosed the tie-down on the saddle rope, taking the coils in his hand and fingering out a small loop as he rode closer. The timing was next to perfect. Ivan was only one hundred yards away when Buff hurried out of the brush, turned around a rocky edge, and fell to his knees. He immediately pushed some dead brush aside and started scooping dirt with his hands. Ivan had no way of knowing what the man was digging up, but what he did know was that he had his back to the sheriff, and his head and shoulders were easily seen and available. Resting the reins across the gelding's neck, Ivan kicked the animal into a bit more speed while forming a loop big enough to do the job.

Buff finally heard the footfalls of the horse and turned his head, but it was too late. The loop sailed at him with a slight whirring sound and dropped over his head, slid off one shoulder, and down to his chest. Like any good ranch horse, the gelding dug in his hooves and came to a complete stop. Ivan gave a tug on the rope and, with his knee, turned the obedient animal away. Three quick steps took the slack out of the rope and held Buff's arms tightly against his sides.

Just to be sure Buff understood the situation, Ivan allowed the horse to drag him a few additional yards before pulling him to stop. When the pulling stopped,

Buff immediately attempted to gain his feet. The horse, without instructions from his rider, put more tension on the rope, putting Buff back on the ground.

In desperation, Buff managed to get a hand on his Colt. He had just enough freedom of movement to grip the handle and lift it from the holster. But with the horse doing what cutting horses did, accurate aiming would be close to impossible. Wildly, frantically, Buff rolled, trying to turn the weapon on Ivan. The best he was able to do was fire one shot into the air before Ivan put the spurs to the horse, yanking Buff out of his sitting position and laying him out flat on the ground. He continued to drag, saying, "Drop the iron, Buff. I'll drag you back to Colorado if I have to. Drop it."

Buff threw the weapon a few feet and lay still. Ivan dismounted and started walking down the rope, with the gelding keeping a good tension on it the whole time. He managed to throw another loop over Buff's chest and was reaching for his handcuffs when three men ran through the brush, and another two, riding all out, approached from the rocky trail. When they saw Buff on the ground with a stranger looping him with rope, they all reached for their weapons.

Quickly, Ivan tied off the rope and stood. With his hand hanging close to his Colt but not yet touching it, he hollered, "Any of you pull iron, you're going to see what's on the other side of sunset. There's no need for shooting here. Or for anyone dying. Just hold up, fellas. This man is under my arrest. Sheriff Ivan Ivanov here, county sheriff and deputy federal marshal. No need for anyone else to get involved. Just back off and let me go about my business."

One man, sitting tall on his gelding and assuming

command of the small bunch from the ranch, said, "We can't let you do that. Not until the Bishop has his say."

"The Bishop gets no say on federal murder charges."

"We'll just take y'all over to the big house and find out."

"I'm advising you to ride away and let me do my duty."

"You know we're not going to do that. Now I agree. There's no need here for shooting or dying. Not yet, anyway. But we're going to see the Bishop. You can come with us peacefully, or you can bleed to death right here in the sand."

Ivan couldn't see that he had a choice against five men. But he had no intention of turning Buff loose. The tension in the rocky enclave told him the situation could deteriorate quickly. He had to give something to get something.

"I'll walk over with these three. One of you riders bring my horse. I'm going to cuff this man. And I'll be leaving the rope in place."

When no one objected, he snapped the cuffs in place and completed his tie in the rope. He then followed the men who had run through the brush, leading Buff with a hand on his arm while the riders gathered up his horse and rode around the rocky trail to the ranch yard.

When the walkers appeared out of the brush, there were several other men watching. From barn doors and the cookhouse porch, they watched. And on the raised wrap-around veranda at the big house, Ivan could see a man who could only be the Bishop. Tall and wide-shoul-dered, with a well-groomed look about him, he held all the appearances of a man ruling his domain.

Beside the Bishop stood a man in range clothes, almost certainly a rider. Perhaps ranch foreman or manager. He stood close, but not close enough to suggest anything but a working relationship. Behind the Bishop and close to the fancy front door stood two women, silent but watching.

The two riders appeared, leading Ivan's horse, approaching the yard fence before Ivan and the others could walk the distance. One of them, judging by hand motions alone, was speaking to the Bishop, but Ivan was still too far away to hear the words. The silence then held until the walkers stopped at the white picket fence.

Sitting his horse, mostly hidden in the surrounding bush, Ivan noticed a rider with a rifle in his hands. No one else seemed to notice the man or at least pay him any attention. He was too shadowed to recognize, although there was no reason for Ivan to know who it was. After just a quick glance, he turned back to the big house.

No one said anything for a count of ten or more. Then the Bishop spoke.

"You, sir, have intruded on my home. You have attacked a man and made claims against him, claims I have no way of knowing the truth of. You have imposed yourself into our peaceful life with violence. Explain yourself."

Ivan grinned at the man, perhaps a bit insolently. He had little patience for self-important men.

"I suspect, sir, that your rider here has already told you who I am and who this man is. The fact is the man is my prisoner. He likes to go by the name of Buff. I have followed him and his gang of thieves and killers from Colorado. The gang are all either dead or under arrest by my associates. The gold they stole is in our custody. But no one can return life to the men they killed.

"I suspect Buff is well known throughout this portion

of your state. He seemed to feel right at home here as I watched from up on the hill and down in Temple. You already knew that I have arrested him for murder. Multiple murders, to be more precise. I have done my duty this far and intend to continue until this man is in jail or hung. You and your men have only to stand back and allow the law to do its work."

"And how do I know you are the law and that this man is a murderer?"

"Oh, I think you know, alright. You're a smart man. You've got it figured. Now, just give the instructions for your men to back off, and we'll be gone. There'll be no need for either of us to bother the other again."

The Bishop stood stoically, majestically. Every part the potentate, the king of his own domain. Ivan could see the struggle. To give in to this lawman, to allow the man to come right onto the ranch and take one of his people, was galling and embarrassing. Yet, to try to stop the arrest was sure to lead to gunplay and death. And who was to say the death wouldn't be his own? He knew well enough that the federal deputies were not known for quitting or backing down. He would also know there were a lot of other deputies who would descend on his ranch if harm were to come to one of their own.

Without warning, one of the Bishop's riders said, "Let me take him, Bishop."

As he spoke, not waiting for the Bishop's reply, he was already lifting his handgun. But before the weapon came level, he was flung violently backward. Then, as his boots were gripped firmly by the stirrups, preventing more backward movement, he folded forward, smashing against the horn, and began sliding sideways, clutching his chest, as the roar of exploding powder was echoing off the house and other buildings. That single shot set it all off. Ivan was sure the shot had come from that rider shadowed in the fringe of brush.

Some men ducked for cover. Others reached for their Colts. There was a thunder of shots, screams of pain, and running horses.

Ivan dropped to the ground in a squatting position, finally getting his own Colt into action. A man was riding toward him, with his weapon already spitting fire and flame, but having no effect except for moving some road gravel around. Ivan shot him off his horse and then turned when he heard the click of a hammer being drawn back. One of the men who had walked Ivan and Buff through the brush had a Colt in his hand. But it wasn't aimed at Ivan. Suddenly, the weapon flared with fire and sound. The action was pure murder, with Buff's hands still manacled at his back. Buff fell to the ground, shot from three feet away. The shooter holstered his weapon with a satisfied grin on his face. Ivan heard the words, "Thought you could take what was mine, did you?" He was never to know what the man was referring to, for the next instant, the shooter, himself, was felled by a shot from another ranch hand.

Ivan looked at the dying man, wondering what his motivation was and what was to come next. The other two men who had walked with Ivan were nowhere to be seen.

There were riderless horses running in panic. At least three men lay in the dust. Two more were staggering toward the bunkhouse, bleeding and broken, the fight having been shot out of them.

Then Ivan realized that most of the firing had come from the edge of the yard, not from the gathered men. Still hunched low, he turned side to side, taking in the carnage. He then glanced up at the veranda. The Bishop was lying in a pool of his own blood. His second in command was lying beside him, his weapon pointed toward the cookhouse, with a trail of smoke still whispering from the barrel of his colt. Clearly, he had died trying to save the Bishop. The women were nowhere to be seen.

The shooting had stopped. Most of the men had disappeared, either frightened or seeking shelter from the law.

Ivan struggled to his feet, bent again to unlock the handcuffs from the dead Buff and unwrap his rope. He rose up, in time to see Nathon and his horse ambling into the yard, with Ivan's mount in tow.

Not understanding all that had happened but knowing that with the death of Buff, his work was done, he mounted his own gelding, coiling the rope as he hit the leather. All the questions that needed asking and answering were in the look he flashed at Nathon.

"Let's go home, Sheriff."

Instead of answering immediately, Ivan took one final look at Buff, the man who had caused so much hurt and carnage during his lifetime.

As he had in times past, the sheriff wondered what Buff was seeing right at that moment. Ivan had been struggling with his beliefs ever since meeting and riding with Rory. The young sheriff had challenged him, more by the way he lived and acted than by his spoken words. Still, he couldn't discount the words. They had always held a ring of truth. Was there something out there that Buff had now become sadly aware of? The thought bore much thinking. Later. Right at that moment, he had a job to wrap up and a long journey ahead of him. And he had to find out just who Nathon was.

34

DEPUTY SHERIFF IVAN IVANOV

IVAN RODE OVER TO NATHON AND SAID, "YOU DID A pretty good job, keeping your identity from me. So, what do I call you, county sheriff or federal deputy marshal?"

"Like you, a bit of both, I suspect."

"And I suspect you're not going to be able to work undercover again the way you did down in Temple."

"Not much need for it anyway. I try to hold close to the Salt Lake office, unless something big is underway."

Ivan studied the man. He had somehow managed to ride right onto the ranch without drawing notice, and when the first threat had presented itself, he shot the man out of his saddle. It was more than possible that he had saved Ivan's life in the process.

"There's a couple of things I have to do, before we leave, Nathon. I need Buff's saddlebags and the gather from his pockets. Then I'll be wanting to ride out and finish digging up whatever it was the man was scrapping out of the dust when I threw a rope on him."

At Nathon's nod of agreement, he stepped his horse back over to the yard fence and stood down beside the body of Buff, who everyone else was ignoring. It took only seconds to strip the valuables from the body, including the gun belt, which he slung from his own saddle horn.

Remounting, he headed for the big barn. There were men gathered inside when they arrived. Three of four ducked out the back door. A couple of others looked on belligerently. Among them was a man Ivan had seen only once back at Temple. He had not heard a name for him.

"Which saddle belonged to Buff?"

No one answered with words, but one man, probably the ranch hostler, pointed to a well-worn black leather rig. Ivan stepped to the dirt floor of the barn, and soon, the saddle, with saddle bags and bedroll intact, was resting across the gelding Buff had stolen from Chad Stanton. He remounted and trotted from the barn with the gelding in tow. He circled the yard and out the narrow rock-lined opening, not stopping until he was at the spot where Buff had been digging. Nathon had followed along silently.

It took little additional digging to clear away the debris and lift a small wooden box from the soil. He snapped the catch, holding the lid tight, and looked inside. He then held it so Nathon could see.

The Salt Lake deputy simply said, "Gold. Dust and nuggets. You'll never find its owner."

Ivan stuffed it into his own saddlebag and mounted without comment. As they walked their horses away from the carnage of the ranch, Ivan said, "I saw one of those men in the barn yesterday. Down in Temple."

Nathon came back with, "Name's Quillan. Owns most of Temple. Always had his eye on the Bishop's ranch."

"It's possible he's the one who killed the Bishop. I didn't see where the shot came from."

"Neither did I. I was a bit busy right at that moment."

Ivan hesitated. The whole thing was rubbing a sore spot, creating friction between the morning's happenings and his thoughts of right and wrong. Finally, accepting that he was out of his jurisdiction, no matter that he had claimed federal authority, and accepting that he had best be getting home, he said, "Some things will have to be left for another day. Now, how far is it to the closest rails?"

When Nathon provided the answer, Ivan considered the hours required to ride that distance, plus the many hours on the rattling, frequently stopping train, and then had another question.

"You have any idea where there's an easier trail to the east?"

SHERIFF RORY JAMISON

SHERIFF RORY JAMISON, WISHING WITH ALL HIS HEART that he had never stumbled on the current situation, or more truly, that the current situation had never occurred, mounted his Double J Ranch bred, blood red bay gelding and cautiously turned to the uphill trail.

Until he had stopped to say hello to Sheriff Anthony Clare, his single goal was to ride home as quickly as circumstances allowed. Now, the young wife he hadn't seen for far too many days would again be waiting. But duty also called, a situation he and Julia had discussed at considerable length before their marriage.

In the current situation, extreme caution was called for. Someone had shot and killed Sheriff Anthony Clare. That someone was still on the loose, perhaps wounded, and desperate. And the man originally jailed by the sheriff had been freed, but not before Sheriff Anthony had, perhaps as a final act on this earth, put lead into him. The blood on the cell floor confirmed that.

Now, there were two men on the loose and running. Were they hoping to find shelter within the cabins and small stables of the uphill settlers, or were they intent on escape that only distance would assure? And how seriously wounded was the one man? Would his wound prevent him from running?

All of that brought up the question of how the community of settlers would react to Rory's attempts to capture and arrest one or more of their own. Would they shelter the culprits, or would they, for the benefit of the whole community, turn them over to the law?

With the woman rescued, but hurting, and on her way back down the hill in the comforting protection of her husband, Rory had no need to rush. Caution would be the order of the day. As he rode, he thought of Ivan. Where was the deputy? He had undertaken a dangerous and difficult task in rough country he was unfamiliar with. How was it with him now, after so many days had passed? Further, Rory wished he had the deputy riding beside him. There was every likelihood that Ivan's skills with his native tongue and his understanding of the Eastern European culture would aid in communication with the uplanders, even if they weren't from the same country as the Ivanov family.

And that got him wondering how it was that the uplanders had settled this close to the Ivanov family, seemingly without either knowing of the other. Then there was Kiril. Yes, what about Kiril? Being dead the past many months, Rory no longer concerned himself with the mystery man. But he did concern himself any time there seemed to be more than the normal number of coincidences.

Now, here he was again, working outside his jurisdiction, hoping Oscar Cator, the state government administrator, would back his actions as he had in the past. Anthony Clare was dead. There was no other law in the county. So, Rory had stepped in. But would the higher government folks see it that way?

Now, how far was it to the village? If village there was. No one from the town below seemed to know. Perhaps the uplanders lived their own solitary lives, coming together in social community, but relying on the town for the bit of shopping their gardens and ingenuity wouldn't provide. So many unknowns.

Rory was at ease in ranch country. Even in hill country. At least where he felt he understood the culture. But he had no experience with what he now faced. There would be no help in making decisions. Decisions that could easily mean life or death, to himself or to others.

He continued up the one-track trail with serious questions swirling in his mind. Two things were critical to the lawman. One was who had triggered the shot that killed Sheriff Anthony? Was the released prisoner seriously injured in the escape was the second. And a third question, one he hadn't asked himself before, would the villagers support and protect the killer?

He saw the first cabin, down a narrow side trail, a bare half-mile above where he had pulled the woman out of the cactus bed and boosted her over the saddle, and, more importantly, where the kidnapper had been killed. He paused and studied the layout before moving on. He had seen no sign of activity around the setup.

The main trail turned into a steeper, two-hundred-yard climb and then leveled out. There before him lay three cabins and what looked like a small community house or gathering place. Perhaps it was a schoolhouse. Or a place of worship. Or, more likely, it served all those purposes.

In front of the building were several saddle horses and one wagon, with the team staked out where they could graze. Behind the wagon and easing into the brush were several children. Being half-hidden, he couldn't count them, not that it mattered. From the distance, they seemed to be watching him with wide-open eyes, suspicion and wonder obvious in their looks and their childishly protective stances, appearing as if they were ready to run, to disappear into the denser brush.

He turned and studied his back trail carefully. Seeing no one anywhere near, he stepped his horse into the slight cover of some trail-side bush. He knew he could be seen from the one window in the building, but he could do nothing about that. Nor did he want to. It was time to meet these folks and confront the issues. He had lifted his 44-40 into his hand as he rode up the steep incline. Now, it lay alongside his right leg, easily visible, as he wanted it to be, and available for action in a split second if the need arose. So he waited, listening, watching.

The first sign of activity he saw was the shadow of a face in the window, obscured by the bright sunlight. He returned the look, pointing his eyes at where he supposed the looker's eyes would be. The face remained still for a few seconds and then was gone. And Rory continued waiting.

WHEN THE DOOR to the building finally eased open, it was a woman who stepped out. He couldn't see her clearly, but as she made her way down the steps and then onto the trail, walking toward him in sturdy, black lace-up shoes, he could see that she was young. She walked with confidence, coming within easy talking distance. It was then that Rory could see this girl was young enough to be a daughter to one of the others. He guessed her age at no more than seventeen or eighteen. She was pretty enough, in a sunburned manner, to catch most young men's eyes. Her blond braids were coiled on the top of her head, partially obscured by the scarf she wore, which he later found out was called a babushka, or something close to that, depending on the language used, that draped from her head down to her shoulders. While he waited for her to speak, the thought crossed his mind that living in the uphill settlement, closeted away from the larger community, isolated socially, offered only a very narrow life for one such as her, or for the other growing children.

"My name is Gretchen. I have been sent to talk to you."

"Hello, Gretchen. My name is Rory. Sheriff Rory Jamison, if you wished to know full name and title. I am sheriff in the area to the north. I was simply riding home from the city when I stopped to visit my friend, Sheriff Anthony Clare, and found he was dead. Now, with the local sheriff murdered, I am the temporary law in this area.

"I know nothing at all about you folks. I only know a good man was murdered. A man with a wife and children. And a woman was kidnapped. Although the woman was grievously wounded, she is now released, and the kidnapper is dead. Another man was arrested earlier for molesting that same woman. He was wounded in the jailbreak."

Rory paused for a moment, letting his words sink in. He thought he saw fear in the girl's eyes and was sorry for that. Unless it was because the others didn't speak English well enough, he couldn't imagine why one of the men hadn't been the one to approach him. But as he had learned over so many similar situations, you work with what you have in front of you.

"I have no intention of bothering anyone here in your settlement. But I most certainly intend to arrest the man who murdered the sheriff, and the one who molested the lady at the store.

"Do the villagers intend to hide and protect these two men, or can I expect your support?"

"The men asked me to talk with you because I speak the language a bit better than some of them. They wish you to know that we are a peaceful people, wishing only to live our quiet lives. It is true that suspicion of police and governments runs deep in our culture. That is why everyone ran away when the sheriff arrested Otto. It is also why the men wished to bring Otto home from the jail. There was no intention of hurting anyone."

Rory studied the nervous young woman, again feeling sorry that she had been put in the position of speaking for the others, for people who would have much more life experience than she could possibly have. He finally said, "Alright, Gretchen, let's assume all of that is true. Unfortunately, it changes nothing. Perhaps he was thinking he was doing the man you refer to as Otto a favor. But whatever the reason, one of your men kidnapped a woman, forcing her onto his horse. He ran uphill, hoping to bring her here, I am supposing. But whatever was on his mind, we will never know. That man is now dead.

"The woman had serious injuries and is on her way to the hospital in Denver. Another of your men—Otto, you named him—was shot, judging by the blood in the jail cell. I have no way of knowing how badly he is hurt. And, worst of all, the sheriff is dead. Shot and killed by another of your men. None of that is going to be forgotten. I have two men to find and arrest, and I intend to do just that. Quickly and without more trouble, if possible. So, the question stands. Are you going to turn the men over to me, or are you going to stand in my way? There is every chance that others will be hurt, and could even die, if the villagers oppose me. And if I am hurt or killed, more lawmen will come. Many more."

"The people are going to ask what you will do with these men."

"I will arrest them. I will take them to jail in the city. After that, it is up to the court to decide what will happen. I do not make those decisions."

With her sun-strained, blue eyes taking a hard study of the sheriff, but with no further questions, Gretchen turned and walked back toward the cabin. Rory sat his horse, waiting, watching, and listening. Listening in case someone was tempted to come up behind him.

The wait was shorter than Rory had expected. But instead of Gretchen emerging from the front door again, the door on the back side, close to the bush, cracked open. For a moment, the door stood ajar with nothing more happening. Then, with a rush and the clump of boots on the wooded steps, two men ran out. One of them was limping, falling behind the other as they ran desperately, disappearing behind the building. Soon, the pounding of horse hooves was heard over the din of voices now sounding from the cabin.

Instead of running after the escapees, realizing they would know all the trails and could easily outpace him. Or set up an ambush, if that was their intent, Rory rode to the front of the cabin. He dismounted, tied the gelding, and walked through the still-open door. Immediately, there was a hushed silence in the twenty or so adults, mostly men, gathered inside. After looking around the room, trying to take in every face, every attitude, every thought aimed his way, he felt he saw fear. Fear and mistrust. Every eye seemed to be focused on either the 44-40, still hanging from his right hand, or his belted twin .44s.

Initially unsure how to proceed, he hesitated. Then, hoping these folks were, at heart, as Gretchen had suggested, peace-loving, but suspicious of authority, a built-in, lived experience brought with them from the old country, he decided to keep it brief and unthreatening.

"You have come to a country where we respect the liberty of individual people. You may live as you wish, as long as you don't interfere with others. But we are also a country where we respect the law. And, most certainly, we respect our women. There are few things anyone can do that will upset us more than abusing our women.

"Now, you may say what your man, Otto, did in the store was a very small thing. But to the lady he touched, and to her husband, it was not a small thing. But it would not have led to violence or even jail time, if your other men had not broken him out of the sheriff's keeping. And the fact that someone shot and killed the sheriff turns a small thing into the biggest thing it could be.

"I saw the two men run from the back door. I saw one of them limping. I suspect that was Otto, who was shot during the jailbreak. I am going to find those men. And when I do, I will arrest them and take them to jail in the city. They will be taken to court to stand before a judge. What penalty they suffer is not up to me.

"You could help yourselves and your men if you were to either tell me where they are hiding or take me to them yourselves. Are you prepared to do that?"

When there was only silence in response to his

words, he wondered if their command of the language was adequate for understanding or if their silence meant they would not be cooperating.

Gretchen, showing poise far beyond her years and experience, stepped forward and repeated much of what Rory had said. When she was finished talking, the gathered people turned their heads silently, this way and then that, as if each was looking for guidance and decision from the one standing near them. Finally, one man stepped forward. In broken English, he said, "We understand. We cannot help you. We will also not try to stop you. We are community. We are as one." He had to have Gretchen find the word community for him.

The speaker, an elderly, dignified gentleman, spoke rapidly to Gretchen and turned to the door. Gretchen spoke as she stepped near the sheriff.

"Come with me. Joseph wishes to talk with you privately."

Gretchen and Rory strolled leisurely across the packed earth of the compound, following the slow-walking leader. There was no talk until Gretchen said, "Joseph is our leader. It was he who put the plan together to escape the old country. The people depend on him and believe in him. What he says is like the law in our community."

ENTERING JOSEPH'S SMALL CABIN, Rory was surprised, but somehow pleased and at ease with the simplicity of the small home. There was everything they needed and nothing they didn't need. Simple. Easy. Satisfying. Joseph was clearly a leader who had not taken advantage of his position. He lived as simply as everyone else. From the neat, circular stove wood stack at the side of the house to the order and cleanliness of the interior, Rory was impressed.

Now he waited, anxious to be on the trail, while the old man took his seat in a home-built rocking chair. Gretchen, with a slight wave of her hand, said, "Please sit here, Sheriff." Gretchen herself stood where she was, behind Rory, but where she could face the man named Joseph.

Joseph carefully, meticulously, filled his pipe, pinching all the stray bits of tobacco off his shirt and placing them back into the leather pouch. Only when he had retied the strings holding the pouch closed and lit his pipe did he turn his eyes to Rory. Rory appreciated the care with which the man's feelings were being gathered. He could see the whirl of competing thoughts in the man's eyes as he prepared and then lit the pipe.

When he was ready, Joseph spoke to Gretchen, all the time looking intently at Rory. Gretchen repeated the words as if they were her own. Joseph paused to give her time to relay his message.

"Otto is a lonely man. Since his wife died last year, he has had no woman. All our women are already married, and" here she paused before saying her own name, "Gretchen is the oldest of the new generation. There was no one suitable for Otto to wed. Still, Otto was wrong in what he did. He knows that and wishes he could live this day again, where he could stay home and not go to the store.

"Your sheriff shot him in the leg. It is not a serious wound unless it gets the illness from not being kept clean. Otto would go with you if Samuel were not pushing him to run."

Rory desperately wished to interrupt. To find out

where the men might be running to. But he waited, holding his silence.

"I want a promise from you, Sheriff. I want you to promise that you will arrest Samuel in whatever way you must. But that you will allow Otto to surrender to you. We are not fond of the law or the police, but also, we know murder is wrong. Samuel must pay the price for what he did. Only when you promise me that will I tell you more."

Wishing for more and hating the idea of making deals he may not be able to complete, Rory pondered for a few moments. When he had made his decision, he said, "It is impossible to know how the men will respond when I find them. But I will promise to do as you have said if it is possible. I will not put my life at risk to keep that promise. If Otto fights me, I will do what must be done."

The two men had hardly broken eye contact from the moment they had taken their seats. Now, it appeared that Joseph was looking right into the very soul of the young man before him, looking for trust. Finally, he said, "There is a man. Far from here. A man not of our village but of our country. He has a place in the hills. Samuel and Otto will go there."

"Who is this man, and where is his place?"

"The place is in the hills above another town, many miles to the north. The man is known as Kiril."

Rory was stunned into silence. Kiril. The name he had hoped was wiped from his life forever. The man who had been at the beginning of months, no, years, of searching, traveling, wondering. The man whose troublesome mystery Rory had believed solved. Or solved enough, at least. The mystery that had involved law enforcement from every level, from Colorado to Texas to Washington. And now that name had been spoken again. Would it never end? Would he never be gone for good?

Fearing he would choke on the words, Rory carefully said, "I know this man, Kiril. But how did you come to know him? Did you search him out when you arrived here?"

Joseph continued, "I am not totally surprised to hear that you know him. He is a man to know. And to wonder about. We did not search him out. We had never heard the name. He came to us. He seemed to know things. He somehow knew a people from his own country had settled here. He came to us with gold coins to welcome us and an offer of help if we ever needed it. He said he was happy to learn that we were living in the old ways. But we are not following the old ways, as Kiril meant. It is the old ways that made us want to leave the place we knew. Our old homes. We have traveled far. Farther than we knew was even possible. We did not bring the old ways with us. We came seeking new ways. New life. New freedoms."

At the mention of gold coins, Rory slid to the edge of his chair, coming near to jumping to his feet. He got control of himself again and, almost dizzy with apprehension, asked, "Do you have one of these coins, or did you spend them all?"

With a rattle of words that Rory didn't understand, Joseph spoke to Gretchen. She quietly walked to the small table Rory could see in the next room and pulled the single drawer open. She appeared to be pushing other items to the side, her hand finally settling on an item Rory could not see. Gretchen lifted her hand from the drawer and, with it, a small wooden box. She lifted the box out, closed the drawer, and walked toward

Joseph. Seeing that she was about to hand him the box, Joseph indicated, with the pointing of his pipe stem, that she should take it to Rory.

Rory accepted the offering, huddled it carefully on his lap, and lifted the hinged lid. Inside were three gold coins. He didn't have to even lift one out to know it would be stamped with the same lettering as the ones that had stirred up the previous hornet's nest. What was he to do now? If these were put into circulation, eventually to be seen by some sharp-eyed banker, the troubles and questions of the past few years could swell up again. He couldn't let that happen.

The theft of federal gold had been more or less solved. Or at least as solved as anyone cared to think about. Or concern themselves with. The middlemen had gone to trial and were serving their sentences. Several men were dead. And in Washington, a simple, well-planned theft had become a political quagmire that might take months or years to sort out, and there was no telling how many heads would be on the block before that was put behind the nation's political watchdogs. *Better to let those sleeping dogs lie*, he thought to himself.

"Sir. May I ask why you have never cashed these coins?"

"I feared they may be stolen."

"And that was a good guess. But there is nothing to fear anymore. I worked on this case. It has all gone away. No one wants to open that topic again. But you must not spend these coins. No one must see them again. What I'm suggesting you do is melt these coins down into an ingot of gold. Gold that no one could trace. The gold alone will be worth as much as the value of the coins.

"Send a trusted man, or perhaps Gretchen, here, with an escort, up to Idaho Falls. There, you will find bankers who deal in gold every day. They will not think it strange that you have a small ingot. Sell the ingot, and you will have spendable money, money to help your settlement, and Kiril and his gold will be a thing of the past.

"And before you ask, let me tell you that Kiril is already a man of the past. Kiril died many months ago. I was the one who found him. He died at his own home, sitting on his chair outside, with his rifle across his lap. He died of a heart attack or some such thing.

"He had been dead for several days when I found him. His horses were starving in the corral. His chickens had already died of thirst and hunger. I fed his dog and took him home with me. He still lives with me and my wife. Kiril and his mysteries are no more. But his cabin still stands, and I well know where it is. If it is there your men will seek refuge, I will be there to greet them.

"I will leave you now with my thanks. I will keep my promise to you, if at all possible. Melt the gold down and say no more about it. Some day, I will ride back up here and tell you how it was with your men.

"I now suggest that you go down to the village and try to make amends. Try to be friendly. And remember that the lady was very seriously hurt. That is no small thing. She will be in the hospital in the big city for many days, I believe. Hopefully, she will one day forgive all of you for what one man did to her. The villagers will be good friends if you allow them to know you."

With no more to say, Rory stood and nodded to Joseph. He turned and said, "Thank you, Gretchen. Hopefully, we will see you again soon."

SHERIFF RORY JAMISON

Instead of running, the men he sought, desperate for escape, may have decided to set up an ambush in territory they knew well. Rory stepped into the saddle and, without allowing time for anyone close by to take a sight on his back, touched the spurs lightly to his gelding and ducked into the bush behind Joseph's home. There were several trails leading away from the settlement. Rory trusted none of them, pressing instead into the deepest bush available as his exit from the small settlement. Within a hundred yards, he was completely enclosed in heavy forest and the lower underbrush.

He had no intention of trying to follow the two escaping men. Whether they had hit the trail already or were hiding within the settlement, they would, sooner or later, have to face the wrath of Joseph, as well as the widow and children of the man killed on the trail. There was no doubt the two would be seen as the source of the trouble.

The escaping men were not hardened criminals. They could more likely be called accidental criminals.

Men who had set out to do something and had it all go completely wrong. They would be frantic for escape. Desperate. Unpredictable in their inexperience. And with them knowing the trails, it was prudent for Rory to not travel any of the known ways.

He continued pushing a new trail through the forest. Within a few miles, he came to an opening around a bit of a slide area. Studying the options, it became clear that the slide was the easiest and most likely way forward. Probably the only way forward. All else was near enough to vertical. An unclimbable rock face. There were many such places in the mountains. It was as if all the weathering and the pressures of time focused on this one release point. Over an unfathomable number of years, the trickle of loosened rock had formed the fan-shaped slide, like a moraine at the base of the larger hills.

To turn back would defeat his purpose. Tackling this slide would not be the first for either him or the horse. Before he stepped into the open, leaving the safety of the forest, he slid to the ground and took a careful look around, all the while holding the gelding as silently as the high-strung animal ever was. Five minutes of looking and listening gave Rory all the assurance he was likely to get. He was alone in the vastness of forest and mountains.

He swung back onto the saddle and nudged the animal forward. As always, the gelding hesitated, pulling back and digging its front feet in, not in total rebellion, but simply showing sensible caution.

With a click of his tongue on his teeth and a slight touch of spurs, Rory encouraged the animal onto the slide rock. Some mountain slides were larger, broken-off rocks, all jagged edges holding the threat of further sliding, if one of them was disturbed from the gravel it rested in. The slide Rory was facing was smaller, made up of shattered shale, burned red in color, causing Rory to wonder if it was of some value in this mineral-laced country. He only had a second or two to allow those thoughts to wander through his mind when the animal's forward movements reached the tipping point and, with the gelding's four feet all on the sliding mass, there was no turning back. The very earth was moving beneath the gelding's feet. All he could do was go with it, remaining as steady as possible. Rory's single goal now was to somehow steer the animal across the slide at a gentle angle, aiming for the easiest exit point, no simple matter at the speed they had suddenly flashed into.

Dust and noise, almost a tinkling sound as the small rocks slid and tumbled into each other, accompanied man and animal to the bottom. They missed the exit target by a few feet, but a touch of his right spur and a quiet word encouraged the animal to extra effort. With three awkward jumps, as the shale slid past and all around them, the horse stepped onto grass growing over firm footing. It was clear that there would be a lot of misplaced shale left at the bottom. Thinking these thoughts, and with a silent word of thanks, Rory and the gelding moved into the enclosing bush.

As had long been his practice while riding difficult trails, Rory stopped at the first trickle of water he came across and loosened the girth, removing the saddle and allowing the horse to drink, roll, and graze while he took his canteen and found some comfortable moss to sit on under an old tree with the shade of overhanging branches to welcome him. The horse had earned a break from his daily work and an understanding hand.

It was slow going through the forest, but Rory now felt safe. There was little chance the escaping men would find him there. His original plan had been to angle across the lower part of the mountain slope, hoping to make his way to the bottom safely and onto the trail to Stevensville. But his plan changed after a few miles when he heard the rhythmic creak and screech of what could be nothing but an ungreased windmill. The windmill meant people and, most likely, a ranch. It might also mean he was back in his own elected jurisdiction. Not that it really mattered now that Sheriff Anthony Clare was dead. He still had a job to do. And that job would move him through the hills from one jurisdiction, one county, to the next, as need dictated.

SHERIFF RORY JAMISON

THE FAN OF THE CREAKING WINDMILL PROVED TO BE THE highest point, rising above a cluster of trees huddled around a small cabin. It had the look of a nicely positioned line cabin, with a small barn, a corral, and an overflowing stock tank feeding a growing pool of mud. A dozen head of mixed-breed cattle were gathered around the tank, no longer thirsty, but with no particular desire to move.

In answer to Rory's shout of 'hello the cabin', a man with a white apron wrapped around his middle emerged from the door, shading his eyes against the now-setting sun.

"What's fer ya," shouted the man.

"That depends on what you're cooking up," answered Rory.

"Aint no matter", answered the cowboy cook, "It comes at ye on a take er or leave er basis."

"Well, I'd most likely take 'er, as you say, supposing I can figure out what it once was. But first, I'll have to find my way past this fence."

"Suppos'n you was ta ride a quarter mile ta the east, an ifn'n yer pay'n attention, like ya should be, you'll find ye a gate. Don't ferget te close it after yerself."

Rory waved his thanks and turned to the east.

AN HOUR LATER, after Rory had unsaddled, watered, and picketed his horse out to graze and then cut and split three large armloads of stove wood, the cowboy cook called him to dinner.

"Set yerself down anywhere ye likes, suppos'n it's not on thet chair with the cushion on it. I'll be need'n thet one fer myself. Get almighty sore now 'n then. Hep yerself ta my mystery stew. Plate up there on the shelf. Spoon in the drawer."

Rory grinned and filled his plate. He had eaten many a meal welcome meal, stopping over at campfires of traveling men or ranchers offering a night's sleep in the loft. Many of the meals set before held a question or two. It was common to question what brand was on the animal before it was skinned out and reduced to steaks and stew meat. But that was a question best kept to oneself, for a man avoiding trouble.

Range riders were seldom noted for their culinary skills. He took the first spoonful and chewed slowly, a new question in his eyes. He swallowed and smacked his lips. Then, grinning again, he said, "I'm thinking the real mystery here, partner, if this stew is an example of your daily fare, is how you keep on being alive. I like some spice now and then, but you've set a new boundary. The question is whether this stew will ruin your stomach first, or will whoever once owned this beef get a clear shot at you."

"Wall, I'm notic'n yer scooping 'er down alright, Sheriff."

"Good stew. Spicy but good. And what makes you think I'm Sheriff?"

"Wall, fer the one thing, yer almighty curious. An' fer another, yer all dressed up an' fitted out, carry'n enough armament to refight the battle a' the Alamo, an win 'er by yerself. An', fer another, I seen ye once down te town."

"That's interesting. I don't remember seeing you."

"Didn't see me. I made a point of it."

Sitting in the outside shade after washing up the dinner pots, the two men were easing around one question and then another, working up to what Rory really wished to know. Finally, he said, "You neither asked nor offered, so I'll tell you, I am Sheriff Rory Jamison, County Sheriff. I know these hills fairly well, but not completely. I'm not sure anyone knows them completely. But if I was to guess, I'd say your place is tucked into the hills behind the Triple T. I know those boys at the Triple T. Good fellas. Slim, the foreman, has done me a favor or two. Do I about have your holdings placed right?

"Close enough. Good neighbors, those fellas. Hire me on fer their brand'n, suppose'n they were ta need an extra hand. Puts a bit a' the silver inta my hand, if'n ye were ta take my mean'n."

"And when they hire you on, what do they call you?"

"Cole. Thet's enough. Jes' Cole."

"Well, Cole, I'm sure you're wondering why I came at your holdings out of the forest. The fact is that I'm searching for two men. One is a murderer. The other broke jail. They might be desperate enough to hold you under their guns while they clean up that mystery stew. They're not woodsmen either. They might be looking for a place to get out of the night air if they find your ranch. They're up in the forest somewhere. I know where they're heading, and I hope to get there before them, so I'll be leaving you now. But you take care tonight. And thanks for the meal."

Cole remained silent while Rory saddled the gelding. As he was leading the animal away from the corral, Cole said, "Com'n ta nighttime. Yer welcome if'n yer wish'n ta stay."

"Thanks. But I can make maybe five or six miles before dark. Having those miles behind me will help in the morning. Like I said, you keep your eyes open for the next day or two."

Rory mounted and lifted his hat in farewell. Cole simply nodded and continued sucking on his dead pipe.

DEPUTY SHERIFF IVAN IVANOV

Ivan found a better trail. It started out heading east. As he stepped his gelding along, his hope was that it would continue in that direction. Deputy US Marshal Nathon described the trail for him and promised that if he held to it, he would soon be firmly back in Colorado Territory. It was a wide trail, showing signs of work. Someone, most likely a settler, perhaps several settlers, had cut trees and rolled rocks to the side. Two horses could easily travel side by side. With just a bit more work, wagons would be able to make their way into the high country, carrying those things settlers required for comfortable living.

Ivan's work on the gold theft was done. He had hoped to stand Buff before a trial judge, but that decision was taken out of his hands. Buff had already stood before a much sterner judge.

As he pushed along, his mind went to Sheriff Rory, My Way, and his wife, Dancer. They had headed back east with a considerable challenge. One wounded prisoner, the others, and several spare horses would need a lot of guarding. A lot of feeding. A lot of patience.

When Ivan had first pinned on the deputy badge or, in his case, put it in his pocket, he had never considered what it would mean to make a capture and arrest far from town or village. Taking charge of men who would do almost anything to escape had proven to be a considerable challenge several times. And that brought back the stories he had heard of lawmen who had found the job easier and just as effective by bringing in the prisoners slung over a saddle, rather than sitting upright, gaining the reputation of shooting first and only arresting when someone surrendered.

THREE DAYS after leaving the Bishop's ranch, switching his saddle between the two horses, Ivan saw the smoke of a breakfast fire on the eastern horizon. He lifted the gelding to an easy trot, following the trail until he came to the plateau he recognized from his first ride up to Tug Granger's cabin. As he angled his steps, approaching the cabin from the new direction, he started seeing cattle. The animals were in the dozens, rather than the hundreds that the more settled ranchers held on the grass of the open grazing lands. Still, as Tug had said before, it was a start.

Ivan was too late for breakfast, but the coffee pot still held some dregs, and Tug soon refilled it and set it back on the fire.

As the two men took their seats on the porch, Tug said, "I'm told you left here alone, trailing a man. Your friends came for the wounded man and headed back east. And now here you are back, still alone. That means one of two things. Either your suspect gave you the slip in Mormon country, or you found him, with the result that he is now in his grave."

"He didn't give me the slip."

Figured that since there's few other explanations for second horse and saddle.

Knowing that was enough talk on the unpleasant subject Tug moved on, asking what Ivan had seen on the trail.

"New folks coming in regular now. You might have seen some stock, or a cabin or two."

Ivan nodded, saying, "I didn't see much stock. Pretty rocky along the trail. I expect if there's stock, it's mostly back in the hills. But there were three or four cabins. Three, for sure. The other might have been a campfire. I didn't take time to ride in or enquire."

Smiling at Tug, he added, "You'll soon be run over with folks. Might even be a good-looking lady show up, seeking out an opportunity to capture and tame a fellow."

Tug merely grunted and reached for the coffee pot.

ANOTHER THREE DAYS of fast travel, Ivan was spending the night with Riley Billows at his Red Feather Lakes Ranch. A single long day followed that enjoyable meeting, ignoring the temptation to ride up the hill to see Lige Bannister. He didn't figure the cranky recluse would have anything to say that would be helpful.

Ivan, still suspicious of the two men running the stage station, nevertheless put his boots under their table and cut into the steak and potatoes laid out before him.

The next noon, he was stalling the gelding in the livery barn at the Fort.

He spent most of the afternoon explaining about the happenings along the way. Assuring Julia that her sheriff husband was fine and well the last time he saw him was his first priority. Then, with Cap brushing off any suggestion that he couldn't ride and uphold the peace in the territory, even with his still-healing leg, Ivan rode on to Stevensville, where the explanations started all over again.

39

SHERIFF RORY JAMISON

RORY, WISHING WITH ALL HIS HEART THAT HE COULD DIP down to Stevensville, which was so close by, for a short visit and report on his doings, instead stuck with his original plan. That plan took him to the upper trail that eventually would lead to MacNair's Hill and Deputy Buck Canby, although he couldn't take the time for a visit until the current mess was sorted out.

MacNair's was located on the outer fringe of Rory's county and fell under his jurisdiction. Buck had done a commendable job of holding the fragile peace, with the assistance of a couple of men he had hired to back him up. Rory really needed to visit and be brought up to date on the recent happenings, but the diversion might put him behind the escaping men. He was convinced that any deviation from his plan could lead to unwanted gun play.

From the MacNair's Hill trail, there was a narrow, barely seen pathway through the brush, created by the young and unpredictable Arch Majeska and his brothers.

The brothers and a couple of accomplices were thieves who had very creatively formed a shelter in the rocks and ridden out the winter months without being found. When spring came, they may have escaped free—with their loot—if it weren't for the hatred one brother had for the lawmen at Stevensville, and the foolish urge to hold up the small bank there. The resulting carnage left the banker dead and half the town burned to the ground. But it also left the younger brothers dead, leaving only the older of the boys, Addison himself, to be brought down, in a tense situation, by Julia, Rory's young wife.

It was hunting down the rocky shelter, seeking whatever might be hidden there, that led Deputy Ivan on the twisted trails. He found the shack without too much trouble, and along with the several trails, he found a young woman who had spent the winter cooking for the Majeska boys. Cooking and nothing more, she insisted, with the guarantee of Addison, that he would hold his younger brothers and the couple of others under careful scrutiny. With Ivan's help, she was now at MacNair's Hill cooking in the café, and Rory now knew the location of the trail.

He swung the gelding downhill, picking his way carefully through the bush and around fallen boulders, some of them large enough to hide horse and rider. With two slow, watchful hours behind him, he came to the opening in the forest that led onto the second MacNair's Hill trail, the one accessed through the I-5 Ranch. At the bottom of that trail stood the lonely and empty cabin Kiril had left as the only remembrance of his existence. But then, thinking that through, after talking with Joseph, Rory corrected himself. *There was obviously more to you, Kiril. Much more. But we will never know what it was.*

Or who you really were. Or why you did what you did. Or where you got your information.

~

RIDING DOWN THE HILLY TRAIL, he held his eyes to the left, where the cabin would come into his view immediately after clearing that last curve.

Even moving downhill carefully, the gelding's iron-shod hoofs occasionally struck rock. The sound wasn't loud, but it was loud enough to be picked up by the ears of an observant man. Confident that he had reached the cabin before the two fugitives could have possibly done so, he was momentarily careless, ignoring the click of the animal's hooves. That carelessness, so rare in his life and habits, came near to costing him his future.

When he rounded the final small bend in the trail, bringing the cabin into view, a shouted warning, causing Rory to turn his head just a bit, came a breath before the buzzing sound of a bullet, missing his head by bare inches, followed immediately by the crack and bang of a large caliber rifle. Before there was time for a second shot, Rory was off the saddle and dropping, prone to the ground, with his .44-40 in his hand. The horse ran a few paces to the side and stopped, dropping his head to graze.

The shout and the shot told him the runners were not in the cabin. In fact, they were in the bush on the far side of the trail. They were probably more hidden there, and safer, than they would have been in the cabin. Perhaps Samuel had figured that out. He doubted if Otto, the loner whose desire for another man's woman had ruined his life and gotten men killed, was bright enough to do it.

Embarrassed that he had opened himself to such risk, Rory rolled over twice before crawling further into the brush until he was thoroughly hidden by undergrowth. He rose to his knees, hunched behind a mountain pine. With all the intensity he could muster, he listened. But there was no further sound. No shouting. No running footsteps. No hoofbeats of escaping riders.

And then there was. In a difficult-to-understand mix of English and another language, the angry words reached Rory's ears, starting with what he figured was most likely a curse. Unfortunately, he couldn't understand all the words, but he managed to sort some out.

"You are a fool. Your shouting warned him. I could have got him. Now what do you think will happen?"

"It is not right you shoot that man, Samuel. You said we would get away. You never said we kill anyone."

Distilling the mix of angry words he could pick out from among the language he didn't understand, Rory decided that Otto was not going to be a problem if he could be separated from Samuel. But how he could bring that about was in no way clear at the moment.

What was becoming increasingly clear were the silent words that had been bothering his own consciousness for the past few weeks. Words he didn't welcome or want to figure out. Each time he heard the very faint voice in his head, he first tried to deny it's existence. Then he tried to push it down. To silence it. Finally, in desperation, he ignored it. The problem was that every few days, the voice spoke to him again.

Frustrated with the whole matter as he hunched behind the tree, facing two armed and desperate men, he thought, *not now. You're about to get me killed.*

Knowing nothing else to do now that everyone knew where the other was, he shouted, "Stand down, you two.

You're under arrest. And you have been warned. If you come out now, I will simply arrest you and take you to a court of law. If you shoot at me again, I will shoot and kill you. Now come out."

The men probably didn't understand any more of what Rory said than he understood of their language, but there was no time to fuss about that.

Suddenly, from the trees, a man limped into the clear. With the limp, he could only be Otto. He ran awkwardly with his arms in the air and with one leg not performing well. As he ran, he shouted, "Sorry. Sorry, Mr. Sheriff. I no—"

At that point, a bullet brought him to the ground. He fell, groaned, worked his legs a few times, as if he was still running, and lay still. There was no blood showing, but Rory knew there soon would be. With disgust at the murder, he shouted, "Samuel. Come out. You can't win."

Rory's shouts brought three shots, one after the other, as fast as the shooter could work the bolt action rifle. The action was much slower than the new lever action carbine Rory carried, but it was effective, just the same.

Bolt action, multi-shot rifles were rare, largely experimental, and held for military use, primarily in Europe. In fact, Rory had never seen one. But Samuel and his folks came from the old country, and there had been many arms invented and used there in their numerous wars. Arms that had not been on the western shore of the Atlantic. With rifles being manufactured by the millions and the various militaries recruiting men from wherever they could be found, it would not be impossible that Samuel had served in one or another army and brought his weapon home with him.

Those thoughts were nothing more than idle brain

chatter as Rory waited for the fusillade to end, feeling fairly secure in his tree-lined enclosure.

When the immediate firing stopped, Rory shouted again. This time, there was no firing, but there was the sound of crashing through the underbrush and then the flap, flap of smooth-soled boots running on the mixed grass and gravel of Kiril's yard. He took a chance and slowly rose to a squatting height, turning his eyes here and there until he spotted the runner. With Samuel's back to him, there was no risk to Rory, so he stepped onto the trail and raised the carbine.

"Samuel. Stop. You can't get away. Stop."

When the shouted warning brought no response, Rory raised the carbine and put three quick shots into the ground around Samuel. The lead struck grass or rocks, glanced off, and whined into the distance. The sound alone had brought fugitives to a point of surrender in the past. But not Samuel.

Rory had seen no sign of the men's horses, and now, with the direction of Samuel's run, he assumed they had been hidden in the barn. As the runner reached the corral and stretched for the gate to open it, Rory but a bullet into the top log, not three inches from Samuel's hand.

Samuel released his hand as if a whole hive of wasps were attacking him and turned to take another shot at the sheriff. As he was raising his heavy rifle, Rory, weary and exasperated at the foolishness of men, squeezed his own trigger. He was again shooting at the pine logs Kiril had built the corral of, hoping for the man's surrender, but the lead glanced off the wood and struck Samuel just below the eye. He fell onto the rubble of the corral, dead, with a large part of his skull blown away.

Rory dropped the butt of the carbine to the ground

and hung his head in defeat. All he had planned, the chase, the capture, the trip to court in Denver, all he had hoped for and imagined had ended in two more dead men. As he was wondering how the two had arrived at the cabin before he had, the silent voice spoke to him again.

40

DEPUTY SHERIFF IVAN IVANOV

IVAN, AFTER BRINGING CAP AND JULIA UP TO DATE ON HIS travels and those of Sheriff Rory, still had time to ride to Stevensville before the sun would disappear. He considered the miles the gelding had traveled and decided the horse still had enough steps left in it. Both man and animal could rest tomorrow. In any case, the gelding had only done half duty, sharing the time and the burden of Ivan's weight with the horse Buff had stolen from Chad Stanton. Ivan had brought that horse back with him on the chance that Stanton may, one day, show up at the Fort. Returning the man's riding animal would provide one small victory from among the tribulations of the past few weeks.

With the decision to keep riding, Ivan again swung the saddle and bedroll onto his own animal, leaving the other with Kegs at the livery. He was in no particular hurry, so the normal three-hour ride stretched out a bit. When he put the gelding into the new barn in Stevensville, built by Tippet after the fire had destroyed the old one, night was well upon the scene.

The talkative Tippet had a whole head full of questions for the deputy, but all he got for answers was, "Another time, my friend. I'm for bed and a long rest."

THE HOTEL MAN mumbled under his breath when he was asked to heat water for a bath so early the next morning, but Ivan's smiling response was, "Tig, you've done nothing at all during your night shift except sleep in that tipped-back chair. Do you good to stoke up a fire and haul a little water. Kind of set you up for the day, that bit of exercise will. In any case, Ma won't let me in the café, what with me carrying the various odors of near-enough a month's gather from riding hundreds of miles, sitting at more fires than I care to remember, and the sweet aroma of more than just the one horse. Now, I'm going to go over to the office and kick Key Wardle out of the sack. It's time our local marshal was up and pacing the streets, making sure us citizens will be safe. I'll be back after that."

Tig had no response to any of this nonsense, so he lit the fire and went to pump water.

Later, taking his breakfast at an uncustomed late time, Ivan brought Key up to date on as much of the adventure as was necessary before asking, "And what's been happening here?"

"Seems like nothing compared to your story."

"Well, I'd not mind having a bit of nothing for a while."

IVAN WANDERED the town until noon before he finally approached Tempest in the ranch supply store.

"I'm back."

With a teasing grin, the lovely young lady said, "Oh? Have you been away?"

"You ain't going to fool me with any of that pretend stuff, young lady. I know your heart's been pining for me the whole time. Pining and worried. Now, I'd like it if you could take the afternoon off. I'm riding up to the ranch. Ma always asks about you. It would be best if you were right there to visit with her as I catch up with Pa and Pavel. I have your horse saddled and ready. Tied to the rail out front. Just tell the boss you'll see him in the morning."

"Just like that! Go tell my boss I'm taking the afternoon off!"

"He'll understand."

WHEN THE YOUNG couple cleared the last short rise of the hilly trail to the I-5, Tempest was, like always, delighted with the expanse of green grass and the surrounding forests beneath the backdrop of the larger hills. A shout from Ivan brought his mother from the house with a scream of delight and his father from the barn with a pitchfork held in his constantly busy hands. Within minutes, Tempest was holding down a chair in the shade of the porch overhang, visiting with Mrs. Ivanov, while the three men wandered the barn admiring the two foals born in the past month and exchanging stories.

It was a bare half hour later when Tempest rose to her feet, shading her eyes with her hand, studying the distant image making its way across the grass. It was sure enough a rider. That much couldn't be questioned. But he appeared to be leading two heavily packed horses. A wanderer from the hills? A gold seeker giving up and heading home? They all, sooner or later, seemed to find the back entrance to the I-5, crossing the miles of Ivanov grass, hunting for a way down to town. As she watched, she at first wondered and then became sure. Almost sure, anyway. Sure enough to call the men. At her holler, Ivan came first from the barn. He followed her pointing finger, studied on the shadowy movements out on the graze, and then called his father and brother.

The older man, taking only a quick look, said, "The Sheriff. He comes. With bodies again. With trouble behind him."

Ivan, knowing his father was correct, didn't bother saying anything.

Mrs. Ivanov rose from her chair, saying, "I make coffee. The sheriff, he always likes the coffee."

Tempest walked into the little house with her. Without asking permission, she went to the cold pantry, pulled back the wooden door, studied the contents for a moment, and then reached for the tail end of a cured and salted ham sitting on a plate, covered with cheesecloth. She carried that to the table, cut off several slices, and then returned to the pantry for eggs.

Mrs. Ivanov watched the efficient, unquestioning actions and smiled, thinking this girl would be a good woman for her son, if he should ever be smart enough to ask her to marry him, and said quietly, "Is Goot."

Rory pulled to a halt beside the barn. There was no need of parading the two laden horses where the women would be upset by their burden. With sparing words, the sheriff explained the experience of the past few days to Ivan. Of course, the other Ivanov men listened intently, especially when Kiril's name came into the tale, and the fact that the dead men were from a group of immigrants from the Ivanov homeland, or, at least, close by.

Rory was intent on riding downhill immediately, but the entreaties of the women were enough to have him dismount, tie the horses out of the sun, and head to the water trough for a wash. The stories of Rory's venture, followed by Ivan's, both told quickly and with a sparseness of words, were enough to cause a morbid silence around the midafternoon table. Ever worried for the safety of her son, and the sheriff, Mrs. Ivanov silently prayed for their protection.

When the mention of returning the bodies to the uphill community came up, Ivan immediately said, "I'm coming with you."

"You just got home yourself. You don't have to do that."

"I said nothing about have to. I'm coming, that's all."

"Come then. And welcome."

Speaking to Tempest, Rory said, "I'd like if you would do something for me. We'll ride together down the hill, and then Ivan and I will peel off south. You'll return to Stevensville. When you get there, I'd like if you could find a man to ride to the Fort. He's to find Julia and tell her where I am. Also, tell her that I want her to ride to Cheyenne and catch the train to Denver. She's not to ride alone. But I'm sure she can find someone trustworthy to side her. She's to check into the hotel in Denver and wait for me. That's all she needs to know for now. Can you do that, Tempest?"

Without even a thought for her job, the young lady said, "No, I can't do that. In fact, it's a poorly thought-out plan. A man's plan, not considering the needs of his woman. How would it look, the sheriff's wife riding across the country with another man? But no mind. I'll ride with her to Cheyenne and be on the same train to the big city. We'll meet you men at the hotel when you get there. I'll have hotel rooms set aside."

At the questioning look on Mrs. Ivanov's face, Tempest grinned and said, "One of the rooms will be for me, Ma."

"Ya. Is goot."

41

SHERIFF RORY AND
DEPUTY IVAN

SHERIFF RORY HOPED TO SLIP PAST THE VILLAGE WITHOUT being noticed. The pain of losing their own sheriff so recently would still be vivid in the community. He and Ivan both made a point of not studying on the short business street, but they couldn't help seeing a few folks stop on the boardwalk and turn their way. There was no disguising the burdens the two led horses carried. No one called out to them, and the two lawmen didn't stop.

When Rory turned onto the two-track trail leading to the uphill community, Ivan spoke his first words in nearly an hour.

"So many trails in this country a man couldn't ever ride them all. Where does this one go?"

"To the homes of what the villagers have come to call the 'uplanders'. I suspect they're either from the same country as your folks or one close by. They knew Kiril and could speak with him well enough that he turned the heads of some of the men. Caused more trouble than these folks needed. Cost lives too. I do believe the whole country would have been better off without Kiril ever having been here.

"I'm troubled too by the fact that we'll most likely never know the whole Kiril story. Four men are dead, and one woman is grievously injured. That's more trouble than enough from one man. And that's without going back to the gold coin mess, which I hope to never hear another word about."

Reflecting on how he himself had bought into Kiril's story at the beginning, Ivan chose to hold back any comment he might have had.

A BARKING dog welcomed the lawmen into the fringes of the uphill community, followed by a shout from a child whose play had been disturbed. It all combined to cause the children to disappear, like rabbits, into the bush. Several screen doors opened and then slammed shut, leaving men standing on their porches, watching the riders approach.

Rory pulled to a stop, a respectful distance from the schoolhouse, hoping, as he had at the village, to protect the women and kids from the sight of the body- draped horses. He and Ivan sat silently, expectantly, knowing inquisitive men would soon appear. Within seconds, it seemed, one young man leaped off his porch, ran around the side of the house, and down the path leading to Joseph's home. As the leader of the small community, Joseph would take a hand in dealing with the situation.

After a five-minute wait, Joseph, trailed by several other men and a few women, walked into the center court beside the schoolhouse. Hanging near him was Gretchen. Quiet enough so that only Ivan could hear,

Rory said, "That's Joseph, their chosen leader. The girl is Gretchen. She speaks excellent English. I didn't ask how she came to know the language. Don't matter anyway. She speaks for Joseph."

The walkers paused for a few seconds, whispering among themselves after noticing the burdened horses, and then came forward again. Joseph and Gretchen stopped within speaking distance while the other men came forward. Rory held out the reins to the led horses. Two men covered the few feet necessary to reach them and took one each, ready to lead them away. Rory quietly said, "Take them where the kids can't see."

As that activity was playing out, Joseph never took his eyes off Rory. When the leader began to speak, it became clear the man was unhappy. Not angry, perhaps, but certainly holding questions back in his study of the two lawmen. It was also clear that Rory and Ivan were not going to be invited to step down or to come to Joseph's house. What Rory saw in the old man's visage was more like disappointment than anger. There were no weapons in clear sight, but Rory had no doubt they would appear quickly enough if tempers should rise and wisdom diminish.

Without first referring to Joseph, Gretchen said, "You have brought back our men. Was the shooting necessary? You made a promise."

Rory quickly answered, "I made a promise only to do what I could to bring them in alive. When men take up weapons, there is no promise that can guarantee the outcome. I didn't shoot Otto. He was trying to surrender to me when Samuel shot him. When I called on Samuel to surrender, he shot at me several times. I had no choice. And it may interest you to know that they were hiding in Kiril's yard when I found them. Joseph needs to warn the other young men about the poison Kiril was filling their heads with.

"This matter ends here and now. I would have rather seen your men standing in a court of law, but it is what it is. Please make sure there is no next time."

Rory was ready to turn and leave, but Ivan shook his head slightly, calling Rory to wait as he listened while Gretchen translated Rory's words for Joseph and those who stood around him.

Joseph was seen to nod a couple of times as he took in the sheriff's message, translated by the young woman. Although the leader's strained appearance remained, he showed no sign of anger. But a couple of other men were grumbling and speaking out. Joseph turned and wordlessly warned them into silence. When Gretchen completed the telling, Joseph said, "Tell the sheriff 'Thank you for trying'. I will speak to the men. Please, go now. This is a very sad time for the people. We would be alone."

Again, the men behind Joseph spoke out, but this time with shouting and pointing their fingers at Rory. The sheriff couldn't understand what they were saying, and Gretchen was given no opportunity to speak.

Ivan listened carefully to the shouted words and then, raising his arms to silence the crowd, said, in his native language, "The sheriff speaks the truth. I knew Kiril. I was a follower at one time too. The man was wrong. And he was a troublemaker. If you men follow his words, you will end up like the ones on those two horses. And you would have been proven to be fools. I am Deputy Sheriff Ivan Ivanov. I can tell you the people of this district will welcome you. But you will have to learn to live in a new way. The old ways were poison.

"By the looks of your homes, you have been here for

some time. So, you have already been welcomed. You may live here like anyone else. But live in peace. I am of your people. But I am first a lawman. Make no mistake. We will have law in this land. And we will have peace."

Into the silence following this short speech, Ivan glared from one man to another and then, at Joseph last. Nothing more was said. When Ivan turned his horse to ride away, Rory followed, with his right hand on the cantle of his saddle, his shoulders twisted to the rear, his eyes watching for any unfriendly movements.

42

SHERIFF RORY AND
DEPUTY IVAN

AFTER A SHORT VISIT WITH THE WIDOW OF SHERIFF Anthony Clare and a night in the tiny hotel in the village, Rory and Ivan had little to say on the long ride to Denver. They had quietly exchanged stories of the past few weeks as they sat over dinner the evening before. The matter of the high trail to Utah was incomplete. There were many questions hanging in the air with no answers to support them. Nor none in sight. It had often been that way when a crime that started many miles away wound itself into another jurisdiction. Communication across the miles was slow and unpredictable. The lawman who ended the case often enough knew little, or nothing, about the beginning of the case. Like the details of the stolen bank gold coin issue, perhaps some matters would never be solved.

In addition to all of that, he recognized the bare truth that few lawmen of the era, including Rory and Ivan themselves, knew much about the law, and little to nothing about investigation methods. There was more a 'find them and arrest them' type of law. Or, if matters turned that way, 'find them and shoot them'. Again, Rory thought of Block and his title of investigator. Sorting out this multi-county mess was a job for the deputy marshal.

There really was little more for either man to say about the long chase through the high country. But the mention of the early settlers they had met along the way was a subject that brought more light, and hope, into the conversation than the constant shooting and dying, brightening the men and setting them up for a more hopeful look at the future.

For many more southward miles they rode in silence. But during the previous night, Rory had again been visited by the voice in his head. The visitations were becoming more frequent. And more insistent. Just short of demanding. He had that to ponder on as the dusty miles rolled past, beneath the horse's hooves.

Denver was coming into sight, down the road, before Rory had sorted it all out. Tell Ivan or hold it to himself? In the end, he said nothing. It was only fair that he should first share his inmost thoughts with Julia, his long-suffering wife.

The two weary lawmen were riding down the familiar main street of the city when, with no gentle lead-in to the subject, Rory asked, "What are you going to do about that woman?"

As if he had no idea what his friend was talking about, Ivan responded, "What woman?"

"What woman indeed. The one you seem to believe is going to wait forever for a saddle-worn lawman to think beyond a pleasant Sunday afternoon ride and a picnic beside the river. Now what woman would that be?"

Stubbornly, Ivan came back with, "I have no idea what you're talking about."

Rory let the discussion die, but he knew Ivan was thinking about it.

～

THE FIRST STOP was at the livery. With the hard-ridden animals treated to a little kindness and a good feeding, the men walked the couple of city blocks to their usual hotel. A simple inquiry confirmed that the women had not yet arrived. Rory booked the rooms, putting one in Tempest's name. After each had enjoyed a mid-day bath, they met again in the dining room.

It was a toss-up if they should report to Donavan Gaines at the federal marshal's office or Oscar Cator over at the state building. The decision was made when Ivan suggested, "There's just no telling what the federal folks are going to make of all this. I may or may not have crossed the state line. Folks out that way seemed unsure exactly where the survey posts were. Or claimed to be unsure, anyway. And it's certain they didn't care. I took it as a matter of convenience for them. In fact, I got the feeling most were glad to claim Colorado as home. No one was wishing to be under Mormon rule.

"And, of course, I had no interest in knowing. All I wanted was Buff. Buff handcuffed and sitting a saddle, heading back east. That didn't work out, but the ending was somewhat the same. The goal was to put an end to his criminal activities and let the lawyers and a judge deal with the past.

"Since there can be no doubt the federal lawyers and judges would have had him climbing those thirteen steps, where a loop tied in a sturdy rope was there to greet him, the ending was about what could have been expected. My pursuit just shortened the matter, is all.

Still, I'm in no real hurry to explain all of that to the lawyers. Anyway, I'm thinking they're going to want you to dig into the whole stolen gold thing more than dealing with one thief, no matter what his role was in the crime. There's more than just the one unanswered question there."

Rory listened and considered as Ivan talked. After a bit of consideration, he said, "Let's go see Oscar over at the state office. He'll want as much information as I can give him on the murder of Anthony Clare. He'll see the other thing as being county too, if the Feds haven't bumped him out of the way. We'll have some questions to answer."

A walk of a few blocks delivered the two lawmen to the county office and a greeting from the ever-diligent and often belligerent Bertha.

"Afternoon, Bertha. I'm hoping you're keeping these lazy bureaucrats under control. Ivan and I have some news to report. Do you figure Oscar is awake and available?"

"And when is it that you do not have news to report?"

After laying out that unanswered question, she looked at Ivan and, with a serious countenance, asked, "And where is your Indian friend, Mr. Ivanov?"

"My Indian friend, as you name him, is somewhere around. In fact, he and his wife with him, were a great help to our recent investigation. Without them, you may have been hearing about our demise rather than enjoying the pleasantness of our company. Don't you be thinking small of My Way."

Catching her breath after this stern speech from Ivan, wondering if she had overstepped her bounds, she glanced back at Rory and, with a wave of her hand, said, "As for Oscar, go right in. So far as I know, he hasn't had any bad news yet today. I'm sure he can handle yours."

By the time this banter was over, Oscar was hollering over the top of the low office wall, "Get yourselves in here, my northern friends. I expected you last week. But late is better than never, I suppose."

Rory had sobered a bit by the time he turned the knob on Oscar's office door. The thought of having to talk about the death of a fellow lawman was depressing enough, but to have that man be Anthony Clare, a good lawman, and a better husband, father, and friend, put a pall of sadness over the report.

With no need to come out with a detailed question Oscar said, "Sit down, men. Tell me what happened."

Ivan, who knew Anthony mostly by reputation, having met him only once, sat silently while Rory told the bare bones of the sad tale. Oscar's first response was, "And how is Mrs. Clare holding out?"

"It's soon to tell. She's mourning, obviously, as are the kids. She'll need money to either relocate or to hang on where she is. There's little chance of work in that tiny village. And as far as that goes, a woman with no experience outside the home, and with children to care for has few opportunities. I'm hoping the state office can help."

Oscar had trouble taking his eyes off Rory, knowing the risks his sheriffs and deputies regularly took. He cringed inside every time he heard the story or read the report of a chase and arrest of some desperate man. Or, on rare occasion, a woman. Rory and Ivan had become especially important to him and to the state, as they had so successfully policed the vast, often enough remote northern portion of the land.

Turning his eyes to the ceiling for a short spell, as if sorting out the possibilities, Oscar finally said, "We have a small fund. Too small, in my estimation, but then, I'm not a politician, so I don't get any say. I'll do what I can for Mrs. Clare. I don't often bend the rules, but…

Oscar's hesitation after making that statement was allowed to sit in silence. There was nothing either lawman could add that would improve the unfinished sentence. Oscar finally dragged his eyes off the office ceiling and looked again across his desk.

"Now, what's going on in mining country, and what's the rest of the tale on how it impacted y'all up north?"

As if it was a practiced move, staying to one subject before moving on, the report on Anthony Clare was completed before the subject was turned back to the gold theft and the murders of the wagon guards. Both Rory and Ivan sank back in their chairs. Rory took a deep breath and said, "It's a long story, Oscar. It ended well enough, considering that Ivan and I came out of it alive. As did My Way and Dancer. But you already know my part, and My Way's. I wrote a report on all of that. I'll write a report on the chase and deaths of the uphill men who caused the incident that cost Anthony his life. But first, to complete the stolen gold matter, Ivan has his own tale to tell."

Ivan held the floor for a quarter-hour while Oscar took notes on a pad of paper. More familiar with, and preferring, Rory's extensive written reports, Oscar was struggling a bit to keep up with Ivan's telling. Several times, he waved his hand, pleading for a few seconds break while his writing caught up with the words Ivan's droning voice had packed into his immediate memory. Ivan paused, waiting for the signal to continue. The story ended with, "And here we sit, wishing some things had been different. And more than one question still hanging out there begging for answers. But most criminal matters seem to end that way."

The room fell to silence. Each man was thinking his own thoughts as the seconds ticked past. A full minute of silence is a long time when others are waiting to hear your voice, your thoughts. Knowing that, but unsure where to take the conversation, Oscar fidgeted as he studied the ceiling again. Studying the ceiling was becoming a habit.

Rather than ending the silence with words, he shuffled his chair away from the desk and stood. After a short pause, Rory and Ivan also stood. The silence held for another few seconds. The tales of struggle, death, and desperation were becoming difficult for Oscar to hear. They seemed to come too frequently as sheriffs from other parts of the state were doing their part to gain and then maintain peace under the law in the growing, wealth-hungry population. He finally eased his hand forward, toward Rory. During a firm handshake, Oscar said, "Men. I couldn't do what you do. Like so many other lawmen, you're a breed apart. The country is fortunate to have such as you. Thank you.

"Although the sheriff up in Idaho Springs will take a part, this latest gambit is over to the federal jurisdiction now. I caution you to be watchful of what they try to work you into. They have their own agenda. You are a state employee. Don't lose sight of that."

He then turned to Ivan with another handshake.

"Ivan. For my part, there will never be anymore said about the Utah border. Like you did, we will be assuming you never left Colorado. And thank you."

With a flip of his jacket to expose the watch chain hanging beneath, he lifted the large, silver instrument from the little pocket sewn there for the purpose. After a glance at the time, he smiled and said, "It would be the state's pleasure to take you two to dinner."

Making the decision for Ivan and himself both, Rory answered, "Our ladies are coming in on the train. We're not sure when. Although we had a substantial lunch not long ago, I believe if your invitation extends to the dining room at our hotel, we accept. If the women show up, they'll find us there."

43

SHERIFF RORY AND DEPUTY IVAN

THE WHITE-JACKETED WAITER HAD NO SOONER TAKEN THE men's dinner orders when Ivan, facing the door, jumped to his feet. Oscar and Rory turned. Standing at the dining room entrance, looking exactly like what they were, two beautiful ranch girls come to town, stood Julia and Tempest. The fact that they were dressed more for riding than dining meant that they stood apart from the other ladies in the room. To these ranchers, business-men, and travelers, their appearance was more enticing than it would have been in expensive finery. Several heads turned their way as one man at a table would nudge his companion, commenting on the newcomers. Rory and Oscar stood, showing respect in the western way. Rory followed Ivan, winding through the tables toward the entrance while Oscar held his place at the table.

The girls' faces brightened as they saw the men approaching. Rory greeted Julia with a big hug rather than words. Ivan, more circumspect, stopped a foot away from Tempest and offered a handshake. Tempest shook her head in dismay and, with a grab at Ivan's shirt, pulled him into a more affectionate embrace than the handshake he had offered.

Rory was the first to speak. Ivan wasn't sure if he could get words out or not. At the very least, he needed a minute to compose himself.

"We're seated with the state man. Oscar Cator is his name. We were hoping you would arrive. Come. Meet Oscar. You'll be ready for dinner. The table was chosen to provide room for all of us."

The foursome wound their way back to the table, and the introductions were made. But before they took their seats, Tempest said, "I am definitely ready for dinner. But more than that, I'm ready for a bit of a cleanup. We're dusty from our ride to Cheyenne. The stifling heat in the rail car didn't help any either. The desk clerk said you already have rooms reserved. I'm in favor of having a quick clean-up while you men choose something from the menu for us. We'll be back before we're hardly even gone."

Without waiting for a response, Tempest turned and walked away. Julia followed, a couple of steps behind.

The men watched them weave their way through the tables, back to the door, and disappear into the busy lobby. Rory turned back to Ivan and said, "I know they told us to order for them, but my limited experience tells me to hold off on that. 'We'll be back before we're hardly even gone', holds a completely different meaning than what we might think. Oscar lightly slapped Rory on the shoulder and, through a wide grin, said, "You just might make it in this marriage business."

THE MEN HAD CLEANED up their plates, and the waiter had removed them, refilling their coffee cups on the same trip from the kitchen, when the women returned. This time, although they were still dressed as ranch girls, the dust was gone, their faces had been scrubbed to a fine polish, and somehow, they had balanced their wide-brimmed hats over the mass of sweeps and curls worked into their long hair. The riding britches created by the seamstress in Stevensville, out of men's pants, had been replaced with split riding skirts and colorful blouses. There was no possibility they could wind their way through the tables to join the men without causing a stir in the room. Several women, elegantly dressed, found themselves looking and then pressing their hands along the many folds of their long, cumbersome evening dresses, as if examining themselves by comparison. Although no one really noticed, their husbands were careful to cast only furtive glances before turning back to their wives and then, reluctantly, to the dinners sitting before them.

Tempest accepted Ivan's assistance in finding and taking her seat, saying as she sat, "I thought you men were going to order. Have you waited all this time for us? What gentlemen."

Oscar, the longer married and experienced man in the group, burst out in laughter. When the two women turned their searching eyes on him, he stopped laughing, pushed his chair back, and said, "I do believe we've talked over our business sufficiently, men. I'll be getting on my way. Good night, ladies. It's been a pleasure to meet you."

Rory stood and pulled Oscar's chair away from the table, stowing it along the wall. He then rearranged his own chair, with Julia sliding a bit to his direction, to balance the seating to more easily accommodate four instead of the planned five. Tempest picked up a menu and, glancing over the top of it at Ivan, asked, "What catches your fancy, deputy?"

The first words that entered Ivan's mind were, 'be careful'. As if she had never asked, Tempest spoke to Julia. "I never seem to tire of roast beef and hot gravy, Julia. What do you think?"

"I think these men went ahead and ate while we were away. Are you sensing a distinct disinterest in the discussion?"

Looking up as if the thought had never crossed her mind, Tempest started to laugh. She lay her menu down on the table and said, "And to think, I had hoped I would find a man whose eating habits somehow differed from what I grew up with, surrounded by three brothers, a father, and a bunch of ranch hands, none of whom would know the first thing about etiquette. My other hope was that I may catch someone who was still young enough to learn new things. It seems I'm going to have to revise my goals in life."

Ivan, throwing caution to the wind, said, "Well, at least this way, you get to order anything you wish."

Tempest cast him a weary look while Rory studied the grain of the mahogany wood the room's wainscotting was made from.

As the ladies were finishing their dinners, followed by a slice of apple pie for each of the four, the sun had slid behind the western peaks, leaving a pleasant glow and warning of the darkness to come on the streets of Denver. The waiters lit the dining room lamps. A hushed glow ascended on the room as if sunset marked the beginning of a whole new portion of the day. Couples seemed to lean a bit closer to each other in the dim light and speak more confidentially. A few couples were seen to hold hands across the white tablecloths, as if evening brought with it the undefined right to show affection.

Over the next half hour, one by one, the couples stood and moved into the foyer, often with the man holding his lady close, with an arm around her waist.

Julia broke the spell with, "I know I'm spoiling the evening for you all. It's so seldom we get to any sizable town it seems a shame not to go for at least a walk. And I'm sure there must be theaters offering live plays or musicals. If we can stay over another night or two, I'd love to explore the town a bit, but right now, I'm going to fall asleep at this table if I don't get some rest."

When she made motions to rise, Rory stood and pulled the chair back. Tempest said, "I'd love to go for a walk if you thought it was safe, Ivan."

With no comment on the safety involved, Ivan rose, and the four of them were soon in the foyer, with Rory and Julia offering their goodnights as they turned toward the stairs.

44

RORY COULDN'T SLEEP. HE TRIED TO LAY STILL SO AS NOT
to disturb his wife's rest. Julia was sleeping peacefully,
her gentle breathing not sounding anything like the
heavy breathing, almost snoring, Rory knew he was
occasionally guilty of. He found her breathing had a
calming effect on his thinking. Calming, but not neces-
sarily leading to a solution. He had things on his mind.
Or rather, he had one thing on his mind. All else could
and would be dealt with at the proper time.

He had been asleep. It wasn't the deep sleep typical of
those who would lie still till morning. It was, rather, the
sleep of one who has something on his mind that had to
be dealt with. And even in that short time of light sleep,
the voice had come to him. The voice in his head.

They had left the lamp lit, turned down to where the
flame came close to going out, casting a dim glow in the
room, fluttering a bit as a light breeze found its way
through the open window. The window had been left
open to allow a nice cooling breeze in, along with some
of the street noise. The curtains fluttered too close to the

lamp. Smiling inwardly, thinking of how much trouble he would be in if he lit the hotel on fire, Rory slid out of bed and moved the lamp to the top of the four-drawer chiffonier. He no sooner lay back down when he realized the reflection of the lamp in the small mirror atop the chiffonier was going to be a problem. He rose again and moved the lamp back to its original position, but this time tying the curtain in a loose knot so it hung less than halfway down the window.

Again, sliding into bed, determined to go to sleep, he wondered why he hadn't just blown the lamp out. He settled his head on the pillow and stretched out his arm, draping it just above Julia's head, trying to fit himself onto the narrow bed. As if his movements were an invitation, Julia, never breaking her rhythm of breathing, lifted her head and snuggled herself into the fold of his arm with her head lying on his bare chest.

They lay that way for a short while, with Rory convincing himself that all his movements in and out of bed hadn't disturbed his sleeping wife. But it wasn't long before her breathing rhythm broke. She lay still, clearly awake, but not saying anything until she rose on one elbow, opened her eyes, and said, "You're having trouble sleeping. I felt you moving around."

"It's nothing. Go back to sleep."

Julia, probably knowing her husband better than he knew himself, sat up and turned her head back and down until she could see him clearly in the dim lamplight.

"It's not nothing. I know you better than that, Mr. Jamison. Or is the problem directed toward Sheriff Jamison? Whatever it is, if we're to get any sleep this night, you'll either have to talk to me or go register for your own room."

Chuckling a bit, he pulled her back down into a hug, saying, "You'd for sure not sleep if I moved down the hall somewhere."

"So, talk to me."

How does a man tell his wife he's been hearing voices? Or is it really voices? Perhaps it's more simply thoughts. But even private thoughts must have an origin. Where did these thoughts come from?

Finding he couldn't say what needed saying while he was lying down, Rory struggled back into a sitting position, again propping the pillow behind his back.

"You'll think I'm crazy. Or perhaps I've breathed too much campfire smoke. I've been having thoughts. It's almost like a voice in my head. The voice comes with a message. Always the same message. The exact same few words. It's not a message I would have thought up myself. I had no leaning at all in the direction the words push me into."

"Alright, Mr., Sheriff, Jamison, or whoever the words are addressed to. What are these mysterious words?"

"Only two words, actually. Repeated from time to time. Usually, when I'm riding or searching or finding my prey. Or, like tonight, when I'm sleeping. The voice says, 'It's enough'."

"Enough? Enough what?"

At this point, Rory hesitated, taking so long to answer that Julia finally said, "Is it possible the Lord is speaking to you? Is that what concerns you. Is He leading you in another direction, and the thought scares you?"

"When it's laid right out like that, it sounds pretty otherworldly, but yes, that's what I have come to believe."

Julia rose, pulled on her robe, walked around the bed,

and sat in the chair beside the window. The young couple held their eyes glued together for a full minute. Rory finally swung his feet to the floor. From his sitting position on the edge of the mattress, just a couple of feet from his wife, he hesitated again and then said, "I'm way out of my depth here. You know that, don't you.

"I don't recall a time, even in my youngest years, that I didn't believe in God. My father and I spent hours talking of those things. He showed me words from that worn Bible I still carry with me. Often, when I feel safe enough, I'll huddle up to my campfire and open the book. On every page, there are challenging words. Comforting words. Words of warning about the eternity to follow this life. Warning words for the unbeliever and words of promise for those who believe."

Julia gently said, "And you believe. You've told me often enough that you do. You've talked about how you've been kept safe and somehow survived the many deadly chases and arrests you've made. And for the fact that you survived when your father was murdered, even if you took a nasty shot, leaving a groove in your skull that still shows through your hair. You have always credited the Lord for your safety and for your successes as a lawman. What would make you think that same Lord wouldn't speak to you if he has another path for you to follow?"

Rory stood and pulled the covers a bit straighter before he rolled back under the quilt. He held out his hand, saying, "Come. It's time for sleeping, not for figuring things out. You know as much as I do now. We'll face the details in the morning."

AT BREAKFAST THE FOLLOWING MORNING, Rory and Julia were the first to take a table. Tempest joined them after about a ten-minute wait. Ivan was nowhere to be seen. The three at the table ordered and were near to completing the morning meal when Ivan wandered in from the street.

Tempest greeted him with, "And here I thought you were just being lazy, enjoying the mattress time and comparing it to the hard ground you men so often find to take your rests on."

Ivan was clearly in no mood for bantering. Soberly, he responded, "I've been up for a couple of hours. Had coffee and went for a walk. A long walk. Not much happening in the city this time of day."

Rory, thinking he might understand what had dragged his friend from his bed, said, "Good time of day to sort things out. Face up to some truths. I've been doing that too. Me and Julia. Only we didn't go for a walk. We dressed and came down for coffee. We've been holding down that leather couch in the foyer for the last hour."

Tempest turned her head from one man to another and then settled on Julia. Her quizzical look said, "Someone better put some meat on those conversational bones."

Continuing his talk, Rory said, "Perhaps what Julia and I have to tell you will help you with your thinking, Ivan. And you too, Tempest. At least it will give you a glimpse into the future."

As Ivan and Tempest focused their eyes on this man who had earned their respect over several years and who had always seemed like the bedrock of law and order in the county, and beyond, they waited, any joking or teasing forgotten for the moment.

"I'm not going to attempt an explanation other than to say that I believe we are following the Lord's plan for our future. He has been some time getting through my thick head and my stubbornness. But after weeks of first saying 'no', then saying 'perhaps', then, finally, really listening to what He had to say to me, I had a pretty good idea what I had to do. But I needed private time with Julia to finalize it. This trip to the city has been our first opportunity to talk. You will have to admit that what happens with me will have a bit of an impact on Julia.

"So last evening we talked. And this morning, on that foyer couch, we made the decision. I'm going to walk down to the state office and pass my resignation letter to Oscar Cator. I'm through being county sheriff."

The silence around the table was profound. Ivan stared at his friend as if he couldn't believe the words spoken. Tempest wasn't sure what to think. Not disrupting the silence, they both waited for the details.

"You know, of course, that Colorado isn't really a state, although we talk as if it is. It soon will be, so that's good enough. I mention that because I'm not exactly sure what authority Oscar holds. Along with my resignation, I'm going to request that he appoint you, Ivan, as county sheriff. You have all the experience and the ability needed for the job. You would have to win the next election, of course, which is some months away. But if Oscar can appoint you, it would make things work more smoothly."

Ivan pushed his chair back a bit, crossed, and then uncrossed his legs with his eyes on the ceiling. Tempest gently laid her hand on Ivan's as it rested on the menu lying before him. The waiter approached and then backed away after a moment's study of the four table guests, sensing that they needed some privacy right at the moment.

Tempest was the first to speak.

"I have two brothers acting as town marshals, mostly at your request, Rory. And everyone, except Ivan, has figured out that he's special to me, and I'm hoping to be a part of his future. So, you might say your decision impacts me and the Wardle family. What brought you to this decision, and where are you going from here? Are you heading back into ranching? Or perhaps you've decided to take up the long-standing offer from the federal marshals."

"Neither of those Tempest. We're unsure ourselves if we're talking of the long term. But for this fall and winter, we're going to take the train to California. Los Angeles, to be more precise. Or perhaps to San Diego. We won't know until we get there and sort it all out, have a look around.

"I can't stay at the Fort. I'm figuring it would be difficult to have a new sheriff with me still hanging around. I prefer to leave cleanly, and the new man needs to have a clear path. It could be we'll be back in the spring."

Dropping the subject for the lack of words, Ivan turned to the menu.

A BIT LATER, taking his last cup of coffee to the foyer writing desk, Rory sat down and carefully worded his resignation letter to Oscar.

Ivan went for another walk.

The ladies left the hotel, walking arm in arm on the sidewalk, looking in store windows but with no words passing between them.

45

Oscar, glancing from one to another of the four sitting across from him, looking as if he was wondering how to deal with the news, and Rory's request, finally said, "Did the death of Anthony Clare have anything to do with your decision, Rory?"

"No, it didn't. Every man who takes on the badge knows the risks. No, I've had this on my mind for a couple of months. I fought off the thoughts at first. But finally, I knew it was the right thing to do and the correct time to do it. And Ivan is the right man to take up the position.

"It's also the right time for the state to put some money into the hiring of a larger force. Even in the few years I've been involved the population has grown substantially. And along with the population, the work of law enforcement has grown significantly. Ivan and I, we're hardly ever off the back of a horse, and we're seldom home. You need to put a lot more men in the field."

Again, there was silence. Each person there, men, and

women alike, were thinking of the days ahead and how the growing state would police itself. It was as if Rory had thrown down the gauntlet, and Oscar had yet to pick it up. Finally, Oscar stood. He walked around his desk and held out his hand to Rory.

"Mr. Jamison, and no longer Sheriff Jamison, you have done a fine job for the state and for the people who put their trust in you. If ever we get around to writing a manual for policing the state, I'll be calling on you to participate. Enjoy your new freedom and whatever lies ahead of you. I hope you won't forever be a stranger to us."

Glancing at Julia, he said, "Young lady, you take care of this man as I'm sure he will take care of you. Go on to California and know you take our best wishes with you."

Oscar then held out his hand to Ivan, who by this time had risen to his feet, prompting Rory and the women to rise, as well.

"You've been a credit to the team, Ivan. And now, as Sheriff Ivan Ivanov, I know you'll continue to do a great job in your northern county. You already know that this office door is always open to you. I wish you the greatest success and safety in your future work."

Grinning at the two couples, Oscar completed his speech-making with, "Ladies, it's been a bit of a custom for Rory and I to go for lunch after our meetings. I'm hoping we can continue that, starting right about now."

Tempest broke the formality and slight tension in the room when she coyly asked, "Does that mean you're paying?"

Through a broad smile, Oscar answered, "As long as no one tells my wife how I'm spending my money, that's a deal."

46

THE TRIP TO THE FEDERAL MARSHAL'S OFFICE TOOK EVEN less time. Donavan Gaines, sitting as Oscar had done just a couple of hours before, facing the two couples, said, "Sheriff, we will greatly miss you. I know Sheriff Ivanov will do a fine job, but somehow, Rory, you have driven your name and reputation into the unwritten annals of the marshals' service in a way no one else has. Of course, if that history is ever written, we'll have to leave out the part of how you claimed an entire herd of federal government cattle, selling them and depositing the funds toward peace-keeping in your own county. I mention it now, not to make you think we are re-addressing the matter, but to let you know that it was a smooth move and that I haven't forgotten. As disruptive as you have been from time-to-time Sheriff, we will miss you. I know the marshals in Washington will say the same thing.

"Now, down to business for just a brief minute. And for that, we need Deputy Marshal Block Handley."

Donavan Gaines left the room for a moment and

returned with Deputy Handley. Not allowing time for greetings or introduction of the ladies, Gaines said, "Deputy, tell these men what you've been able to put together."

"I'm happy to. But first, I have to know who these ladies are. Have you recruited female deputies, Rory?"

The two friends grinned at each other. There had been a lot of water running under the bridge while these two men were working together on several cases. Rory's response was, "No, but sometimes it might be nice to have a female deputy, if for no other reason than to have a decent cook along on the trail. But that will now be left for another day and another lawman.

"Block, I'd like you to say hello to my wife, Julia, and to Tempest, who has some connection with Ivan that no one, including themselves, has figured out yet.

"Ladies, Block and I go back a ways. We've ridden a lot of miles together and ducked a bit of lead. Block is a great example of what the marshals' service was meant to be."

Allowing time for quick handshakes and nodded greetings, Rory said, "I'm supposing you've been working on that last mess we brought down to you?"

"Yes. And when you call it a mess, you're saying nothing but the truth. But it's amazing what can be accomplished when the marshals and the state lawyers, men with the authority to make deals and promises, can accomplish. I know you were concerned that the legal case would require your attendance and that of My Way, Dancer, and Ivan's, of course, but you'll be happy to know that we have confessions in place and a straight path ahead of us on the way to the courts. You men are free to go about your business. You won't be needed in court."

"That's a good thing, Block. Especially good because we have no intention of being here."

In response to Block's questioning look, Rory explained the situation.

The handshakes in parting were long and sincere. The foursome managed to catch the evening train. Rory and Ivan loaded their horses on a cattle car, and they were soon headed north. North, and then where? What did California have to offer? It was all a mystery, but one that Rory and Julia were looking forward to.

Julia broke the reflective mood only once. "Can we bring the dog on the train?"

IF YOU LIKE THIS, YOU MAY ALSO ENJOY JUST JOHN: THE COMPLETE JOURNEY

ONE SLAVE'S COURAGEOUS JOURNEY DELIVERED IN THE FORM OF A HEART-STOPPING AND ACTION-PACKED WESTERN TALE BASED ON TRUE EVENTS.

In *Just John*, John Ware is tasked with the job of delivering a valuable stallion to a horse farm in Tennessee—in return for his freedom. Upon successfully completing his task, he embarks on a road to Fort Worth, Texas where his expertise with horses opens doors for him that he never thought possible.

Northward to Home follows John as a well-known, highly loved, and acclaimed black cowboy who arrives in Alberta at the beginning of an extraordinary ranching story in the grasslands. Participating in the building of some of the greatest ranches, John realizes that he's put off his dreams of owning his own ranch and growing a family of his own for too long.

Don't miss out on this exciting and historical duology! John Ware's story is infamous, but—having never learned to read or write—he left no record of his wondrous background.

AVAILABLE NOW

ABOUT THE AUTHOR

Reg Quist's pioneer heritage includes sod shacks, prairie fires, home births, and children's graves under the prairie sod, all working together in the lives of people creating their own space in a new land.

Out of that early generation came farmers, ranchers, business men and women, builders, military graves in faraway lands, Sunday Schools that grew to become churches, plus story tellers, musicians, and much more.

Hard work and self-reliance were the hallmark of those previous great generations, attributes that were absorbed by the following generation.

Quist's career choice took him into the construction world. From heavy industrial work, to construction camps in the remote northern bush, the author emulated his grandfathers, who were both builders, as well as pioneer farmers and ranchers.

It is with deep thankfulness that Quist says, "I am a part of the first generation to truly enjoy the benefits of the labors of the pioneers. My parents and their parents worked incredibly hard, and it is well for us to remember".